Entities Part 2
Entities Divided

By Barry S. Brunswick

ISBN- 978-0-6452266-5-2

Editing by N.T Anderson
Cover Design by 100covers.com
Published by Barry S. Brunswick

Acknowledgements

I'd like to once again thank N.T Anderson for her editing work, mentorship, cool Christmas presents, but mostly her friendship. You completely rock though you can be a little troublesome!

I'd also like to thank Sarah and Karoline (Sparky) for Beta reading, giving me encouragement and feedback, and for joining me on the journey. Your light makes the world a brighter place!

Finally, for the newest member of the team, Nora, my heart felt appreciation and thanks for her awesome promotional work and being a wonderful friend. Keep shining, Little Star!

"The winds of change blow in the cosmos. Darkness falls in this galaxy, ushering in a new dawn. A tornado approaches, and there is no stopping it. If only they knew what is to come.

Between the stars, a vast expanse of emptiness stretches out like twisted fingers, yearning to swallow the matter it holds apart. The matter to wrap in shadows, the matter to consume.

These whispers of evil echo through the nothingness, infecting souls as they go.

A tsunami rages, frothing, longing to bleed the life from all things in its relentless path then, in turn, in its deadly wake.

Dreams flash through minds of the weak, the countless unknown. Their numbers will dwindle, their foolish hopes extinguished, followed by their lives."

Guilty

As the casket disappeared through the curtains, the music started. It did little to drown out the sobbing.

The family gathered together, holding each other tightly, bringing each other comfort, while Penny sat alone at the back of the crematorium. Her eyes were streaming, her heart broken. She wallowed in helpless devastation, alone, doing all she could not to wail. Her only real friend, her best friend, was gone, and she would never be the same again.

She hadn't known his family and had awkwardly introduced herself to his mother and sister. They had virtually scowled at her. She knew they blamed her. He was fine when he left, and now he was gone.

Only she knew how much she loved Liam and that she had been there for him through it all. Only she could know how great and true a friend she was to him. That didn't matter to the family. To them, Penny had corrupted him.

So, there she was, both devastated and in need of some comfort, yet hated by all the mourners. His family wouldn't even allow the other students to come. They wanted to be alone as a family with only his closest friends from childhood. They hadn't wanted to invite her, but they knew she was his best friend. Whatever they wanted, today was about Liam.

Penny had done what she came to do, which was say her final goodbye. She couldn't bring herself to go to the wake where she'd only be unwelcome. She slipped away unnoticed to make the long train journey home.

Two changes and three trains later, she was on the final stretch. The whole time a cloud of depression hung over her. She wallowed in the deepest sadness that she'd ever felt. It was like a part of her soul had been ripped out and, frankly, it had. The only thing that stopped Penny from crying the whole way home was the other passengers on the train. She only cried sometimes.

She just couldn't forget the last time she'd spoken to him. He seemed kind of spaced out even though he said he was okay. He promised to meet her for coffee the next morning and uttered the final words between them before he hung up the phone.

"Everything's connected, Penny, in a way you could never understand. Things will be better now. I love you, Tiger."

How she scolded herself over and over that she hadn't been right there with him when he needed her most. The phone call had freaked her out enough that she went over to his apartment. His phone with the smashed screen was there, but he was not. She cursed herself. Why didn't she get there in time? She'd let him down, and it broke her. She was splintered like shards of glass from a cold, cracked mirror.

She had headed out to the places she knew he went—the coffee shop, the library, and even asked around in the bars, although he wasn't a big drinker and never had enough money to go out.

Then she got *that* call. Liam, living so far from home, had listed her as his emergency contact at university. It seemed an obvious thing to do at the time, but the moment she received the call, the enormity of the responsibility fell upon her.

They said they found him in the river. They said he'd jumped off the bridge.

To Penny, it was the terrible dissociation one gets whenever tragic news is thrust upon them. The moment when they just can't believe it or accept it; those words can't possibly be true. Yet, very soon, with the wave of shock and pain, they become the truest words ever said, and just like that, your life is changed forever.

She froze over like a pond in the dead of winter and zombied through the following days, hardly leaving her apartment, barely eating, not even getting dressed. All she did was hurt and cry. She was lost.

She'd spoken with Liam's mother about the funeral and could tell by how abrupt she was that she wasn't happy with her, and Penny felt like she deserved it. She had let him down. If she'd been there, it would never have happened, and every time the thought came back, it shattered her already broken heart until it had almost crumbled to dust.

She was left with questions of confusion and anger. Why did he do this? How could he be so selfish? Then the pain came again.

For him to do what he had done, he must have had no hope. He must have felt like nobody in the world loved him. But Penny did love him. She had always showed him and told him that she did, so how he could feel so unloved? She simply couldn't understand.

Of course, her mind twisted it back on herself. Maybe she hadn't showed him or told him *enough*. A beautiful soul, someone who brought her joy and companionship, the person she leaned on and could trust with anything was extinguished from existence.

The day she met Liam, she knew they would be friends for life; she just never had any inclination that life would be so short. She felt separated, like half of her had been cut adrift and no matter how hard she swam, it was too late to reach the other half. It was gone with the current.

Weary and worn out from crying, tired from the endless pain that surrounded her, wallowing in guilt and the bitterest grief, finally, she made it home. She shut the door and locked it, put her pyjamas on, and just as she had done every night for the past two weeks, Penny cried herself to sleep.

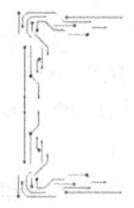

Them

"There's a call for you, sir."

He turned his gaze from the young couple to whom he was talking. "I'm busy, Thompkins. Can't it wait?"

The kafuffle of the party carried on around him. Sounds of laughter and ambient music filled the house. The murmur of a hundred voices fighting to be heard continued.

"No, sir. It's *them*," Thompkins said through gritted teeth.

His charming façade dropped in an instant, and tension filled him. He was visibly anxious and flustered. *They* were his biggest fear. He couldn't run or hide; there was nowhere to go. He simply had to face them.

Regaining his composure, graciously he bowed his head to his companions. "If you'll excuse me for one moment. I have to take an urgent call. Thompkins, get the Dillmore's more champagne, and old Jimmy's looking rather parched here, too."

"Right away, sir."

Behind his confident smirk, a flurry of thoughts rushed through his mind. His heart fluttered, and his stomach was in knots. He looked cool, but within, there was a rush of panic.

He took a deep breath, adjusted his tie, and strolled through the room, nodding welcomely towards any of the guests that met his eye. He headed down the long hall to the back of the house, down some stairs, and through a wooden door. Checking no one saw him, he closed it firmly behind himself and turned the key in the lock.

He walked through the room to the back wall where there was an electronic keypad. The keys beeped as he typed in the number, and with a whir, the wall slid across to reveal a hidden metal door.

From the keypad, a red light burst into life and entered his eye.

"*Retina scan verified,*" the computer said as the door slid open with a whoosh.

"Right, let's do this." He tried to convince himself he was prepared. Then, with his footsteps echoing off the walls, he entered the large, bright room. It was empty apart from a metal chair with a rubbery seat. The arms were strangely shaped with what looked like a metal bowl attached to each of the ends.

He drew a breath one more time, jangling with nervous energy. This was the one and only situation where he felt he didn't have any control. As the CEO of an oil company, he normally called the shots.

Sitting in the seat, he adjusted himself and placed his forearms on the arms of the chair with his fingers settled in the bowls. Energy started whirring through the chair, gently vibrating it. Slowly, within the bowls, a green glow built up, and like a jolt of lightning, he was flashed from where he was to another place.

He jumped as the tall figure stared down upon him. Its cold eyes fixed on the cowering human, with its tongue flicking in and out of its mouth. The creature's eyes were like yellow marbles with a slit-like pupil. Its breath hissed in and out of its nose as drips fell down. Scaley skin shimmered in the light in hues of brown and green and gold. A long snout protruded from its face, and there were rolls of leathery skin on its neck. Its long tail flicked menacingly and agitated from side to side. It stared, intimidating and primal, then the Reptilian spoke.

"You have missed your deadline, William. For this, you will be punished. We have a strict timeline."

"I... I... I've been doing my best, master. I'm sorry. Do you know how hard it is to work with these incompetent people?"

"Humans are weak, complex, and foolish, but they are necessary to us."

"Look, it's under control, I swear. A few things just didn't go to plan. The government came sniffing around, and a couple of people dropped the ball. I'll weed out the weak ones, and we'll work harder. I'll get it done. Just, please, don't hurt me."

The Reptilian reached out a scaly hand and gripped him around the throat. It hissed with intimidating eyes staring right through him.

William choked and struggled to free himself from the iron grasp. He had no chance.

"Don't fail us again! We don't need you to succeed. There are countless others. And hurt you? Pain will be the least of your problems. When your death comes, you will wish for it. It will be a relief from what we'll do to you, human."

"I won't," he rasped as tears rolled down his reddened cheeks. "I swear, I won't."

The Reptilian released him from its grasp, and his chest heaved in and out as he sucked in huge lungfuls of air. "We are watching you, William. We are always watching you."

William's teeth clenched, and he swallowed his rage. That was his reaction to being humiliated and frightened, a feeling that in his position of wealth and power he never knew.

"You are dismissed, human. Don't make me come for you again."

The Temple

Tall, slender, and pale-blue skinned, wearing magnificent robes of purple and gold, it stood with its long arms aloft. Words were chirping yet aggressive, like seagulls fighting over some bread spewed out of its mouth. Words of hate for their enemies brought spiteful hisses, but words of praise for their supreme being incited rapturous squawks of approval from the baying crowd. They were being whisked up into a frenzy. Everything they'd waited for was here. The ancient prophecy would soon be fulfilled.

The temple was grand, created from huge stone blocks many millennia ago, built masterfully by the ones that came before them. It was stolen grandeur from a bygone time, claimed by them. Now it was used to signify their own prowess, twisted by time and lies to pervert its original purpose. Originally created to celebrate the magic of life, it now stood simply as a symbol of hate.

The Sect, cultish and brainwashed, were fuelled by hatred of their enemies, and their enemies were everything that wasn't them. They were selfish and cruel, stealing children and indoctrinating them, turning them into zombies, controlled by ignorance and fear.

The High Priest stood on the stage in the centre of the chamber with the crowd in banks towering high above. The platform on which it stood was one huge block of stone that was carved painstakingly with intricate ancient scripture and pictures of strange, long-extinct creatures. In front of it was a twisted metal structure. Three silver prongs, smooth and shimmering, swooped round in a great circle then spiralled upwards, twisting together. It finished, jagged, like the claws of a monster with its fingers cupped as if to hold water.

The crowd hung on to the High Priest's every word. The hateful and angry rhetoric that it spewed stirred them into a wild frenzy. Their howls echoed off the walls and around the chamber.

The strange priest, with its luxurious clothing, was well fed and strong, yet its followers were in rags, frail and resentful of the cosmos that shunned their kind. They knew the truth, the fictitious truth made up by an evil being. One that searched for a means of control and yearned for power. The being they worshipped was the creator of all things with a name that cannot be spoken by the human tongue. Those within The Sect loved it. They made their sacrifices and chants to be sure their supreme being would grant them favour. Their deeds were in its name and its name only. In The Sect, the individual mattered not; they were servants to the High Priest, and in turn, their god.

The Spy watched on, copying the actions of the others. He didn't speak their language, nor could he make the sounds they used, but his host understood every word. Somehow, he chanted with the others, like he had known the language his entire life.

The host didn't find it difficult to mimic the actions of the mindless cult. He knew he waited for his moment to come. The Spy was one-minded. All he cared about was the mission. He twitched, waiting for the time, but he needed to remain patient. He needed to blend in with the others. If there was any clue at all he wasn't who he seemed, it would surely result in his death. Many others before him had tried to infiltrate The Sect, but each of them had been tortured and killed in an horrific manner. The members were almost impossible to imitate because they were so far detached from the rest of the universe.

Everything within The Sect, stayed in The Sect, and everything outside, stayed out. With any deviation from their ways, they would rip the infiltrator to shreds and feast on his flesh to show the supreme being how they would protect its teachings. They were savage, like animals at times, not always presenting themselves as the evolved beings that they actually were.

The Spy listened to the High Priest's words that were divisive and scathing.

"The unenlightened want to take your lands and your freedoms. They hate us with everything they are. All are heathens or worship false gods. The destruction of our way of life with blood and violence is the goal. Not only do they not follow the path set forward by the supreme being, our enemies defy its will. They take the teachings with scorn and corrupt them.

"But tonight, we fight back. Tonight, we will unite. The prophecy will come true, and the unenlightened will learn that our way of life is the only true way of life!"

It thrust its hands into the air again, and the crowd went wild, howling and baying for blood like rabid wolves.

"Now all we need is our weapons. At last, after a thousand years, now it is time to open the gate!"

Smoke started to swirl within the claws of the metal structure and spread out across the temple.

"Do not fear it, children. Breathe it in. This is your destiny." The High Priest vanished on a platform that lowered and took it below the stage.

The smoke continued to pour out. It had no smell, no taste, and no feel. All the pale blue-skinned creatures of The Sect vanished within the wisp.

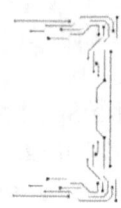

Hazy Memories

Within her eyelids, she saw strange colours. She was there, an entity floating in the bizarre reflection world. For a while she felt lost, like a stranger looking for a friendly face, but then she felt *him*. His hand reached for hers and Penny's greedily swallowed it in. She cried. It brought her comfort and warmth backed by waves of pain. The nagging and longing, the wishing it was real ate away at her.

A memory that had faded returned. They had been here together before. She felt that journey still, daily in her soul, but the memories were always hazy and blurred. It was like it happened centuries ago. It was as if a fuzz clouded over them. Here and now, those images surged back.

She looked around in wonder, then she saw the strange form that was her friend. Not Liam, something very different, but within it, she could feel his essence. She knew it was he who reached out to her. Not this weird being she saw, but *him*.

The creature spoke, but she did not understand the words. Her heart broke again for the millionth time. How she longed to know what he said. She was desperate to understand. She needed to understand. His hand held hers tighter still, telling her more than words ever could. Then the strange colour soup swirled like water circling the drain.

Penny held on. She gripped him tighter and fought the relentless flow with all her might. She struggled to hold on to him, but these forces, far greater than her, ripped them apart. She screamed out. She called his name as he was sucked out of sight. Penny slipped into abject lonesome darkness, into the despair-filled nothing that hurt her soul. She lingered there, hating it and hating herself. She seethed at her own failure, her weakness for not holding onto him, for not understanding his words. She had found him somehow and now cursed herself for letting him go.

Slowly, tiny balls of light ignited one after the other until the entire backdrop was full of them. She sat above the great cosmos, looking down. It made her giddy. It was almost too much for a human to bear. As if to spare her teetering sanity, she slipped back into darkness and then into nothing, and finally there came light.

"The Fleck!" Out of nowhere she screamed the words as she opened her eyes.

Now all that remained of the dream was grief. She curled into a ball and wept.

By lunchtime, Penny had at least taken a shower and eaten some toast for once. She didn't bother getting dressed. She slunk around the apartment in her pyjamas and dressing gown. She had no intention of going anywhere. She felt empty, like her soul had been cried out. It was like her hope and joy had been erased and a heavy black curtain draped over her. The world just wasn't as beautiful as it had been before.

She could only conclude that she would never be happy again. Her life had less meaning now that her friend was gone. She knew all the things people say, the cliches—that in time you'll feel better, that everyone handles grief in their own way. She didn't want to handle grief; she wanted her friend back.

She couldn't stop her mind from searching through imaginary slideshows of what she and Liam would have done together had he lived. They would have graduated and had amazing adventures, like they'd so often talked about. They were wonderful dreams, but now they could never come true, and that hurt her more.

She jumped as the phone rang. Reality ripped her from her internal dwelling. She was stolen from her wallowing darkness. She huffed towards it on the kitchen counter with disdain. She didn't want to talk to anyone. "Oh, go away!" The phone stopped. Three minutes later, it rang again. She put her hands over her ears, frustrated, irrationally annoyed. It stopped. It rang again.

"Oh, my God! Go away!" This time she jumped up with every intention of switching her phone off. She looked at the screen. It was her dad. She knew she'd better answer it or he'd be over in an hour banging on the door.

"Hey, Dad." She croaked the words. It was obvious she'd been crying.

"Hey, Pen Pen." He'd called her that since she was a baby. "How are you?"

There was no point in trying to convince him she was fine, so she told the truth. "I'm awful, Dad, just awful. I hate this. It hurts so much." She started to cry again.

"It totally sucks, sweet pea." He used another of his numerous pet names for her. "I can't say anything that'll make you feel better, but I'm here for you. You're not alone."

"Thanks. That means a lot to me."

"Your mother is away working this weekend, so I'm gonna come over."

"I appreciate it, Dad, I really do, but I just wanna be alone, okay?"

"Look, I promise I'll hide behind the curtain and not even speak. It'll be like I'm not even there at all."

She let out a snotty laugh. He always made her laugh. "All right," she whispered.

"What was that? I didn't quite catch it."

"All right," she said louder.

"Yeah, that's what I thought you said."

She laughed again.

"Righteo, buckeroo. I'll be there in an hour."

She shook her head with a half smirk on her face as she hung up. Maybe some company and love would do her good. Her dad always spoiled her, after all. By the time he arrived, she'd let herself get used to the idea.

When she heard his unmistakable knock, she opened the door and smiled. Her dad was standing there with bags bursting, full of things.

"Oh, Dad. What are you like?"

"Some say I'm a bloody great guy."

"You are that." She kissed him on the cheek he offered her as he made his way through the door sideways and past her. He put the bags on the kitchen counter, grunting, pretending it was a really heavy load. "Ohh, that was a close one." He clutched his eye. "I lifted so hard my eyeball nearly came plipping out."

Penny tutted and rolled her eyes, but she was glad for the lift of energy. "What is all that stuff?"

"Survival kit, of course."

"Weird. It doesn't look like one."

"Well, that's because you're just a wee whipper snapper, showing your greenness in survival techniques. When I was in the SAS, we learned how to survive."

"You were never in the SAS, ya clown."

"I was, ya know. I wasn't allowed to tell you, ya see. The Official Secrets Act. There's some stuff, if I told ya, they'd whack me or put me in prison for a hundred years."

"You are so full of it. Anyway, I'll ask again. What is this stuff?"

"It's a survival kit, I swear it. Look, there's this teddy bear." He rummaged around in the bag. "Some fluffy socks and a blankie for warmness. Ice cream and chips and dips so we can eat some crap. Oh, and your fave chocys. This bottle of wine, if you wanna get a little squiffy, and a couple of movies I stole from your mother."

"You're so old. Nobody has DVDs anymore. I haven't even got a DVD player. Half the guys at uni don't even know what a DVD is."

"Erm, okay, forget them." He threw them back in the bag. "If they're your mother's, they'll suck anyway. Books, eh," he nodded. "I got you three books."

She stopped him there, smiling, and hugged him. He drew her in, and her pain fell out. She wept into his chest as he rubbed her back. "I know how much it hurts now, but I promise, in time, you'll be okay, love." He whispered it gently. "I know now it looks like a black tunnel with no light at the end, but one day, you'll see that glimmer again. I swear it."

"It just hurts so much."

"I know, my little Pen Pen. I know."

After an age, their embrace ended, and stroking her hair affectionately, he said, "I'll need to inform you that I will be staying all weekend, and you can't stop me."

"I'm not going to try and stop you, silly."

"I brought some clothes. They're still in the car. They would have tipped me over the edge if I'd tried to carry them up the stairs as well." He reached round as if he'd hurt his back.

"Oh, you!" She rolled her eyes and smiled again.

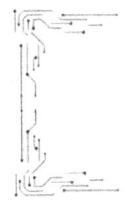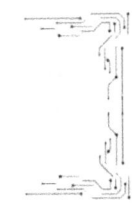

The Ice Cliff

The temperature dropped in an instant as the Spy appeared high on an icy cliff. He looked around, hugging his tatty robes closer to him, but it did little to stop the cutting breeze. High up over the landscape they stood, the Spy and the members of The Sect, each with a ball of wisp rolling around their heads. If not for that, in this atmosphere, they would have been dead in an instant. All around was a baron tundra. Dunes of ice, jagged and glistening, shaped by the savage wind sparkled in the strange planet's starlight. Their edges were like blades. The sky was deep blue, and even though it was daytime, the stars twinkled above.

The members went to their knees and began to chant. The Spy, almost without thought, hurriedly did the same. They blew steam as the warmth from their lungs met the freezing air. Breathing started to burn like ice cutting glass within.

The frozen surface burned the host's skin as it knelt, but the others seemed not to care. They *had* to suffer for the supreme being. In its name, they would happily suffer the pain. The supreme being would arrive on the ice cliff so they could be taken to become its warriors. They felt excited, high over the inhospitable landscape. It was a vision they had seen so many times in their dreams, and now it was real. They had no fear of the unknown or the cold because they were certain that before long the supreme being would come. They had the truth on their side, they had the prophecy, and they *knew* that they were the chosen ones.

The Spy watched on as the chanting grew ever more frantic. They called their god to them. The steam was now leaving their bodies in clouds. He sneakily looked around with the others, lost in the buzz of excitement within their religious trance.

What could live in such a place? It seemed the planet was little more than a snowball. Only then did fear hit him. How long could this host possibly last out there? The cold cut bitingly into the host's extremities. Its long blue fingers blackened as the very blood in the creature's veins began to freeze. It screamed, but the others kept chanting. The pain burned more by the minute as now its face started to solidify.

The wind increased, ripping at the Spy's skin, cutting through the robes. He clung tightly to them and wrapped his arms around his body. He was no longer worried about his mission, just his own survival. If the host died, then his important duty would be left unperformed, and the ramifications of such a failing were too real to even contemplate. This supreme being needed to arrive quickly or all hope would be lost. The snow started, tiny flakes to begin with, then larger ones whipping like icy missiles upon the wind.

The Spy stood up as a feeling of warmth filled him. The Sect members had stopped chanting and were stiff on their knees, eyes glazed over and glassy, frozen solid. He removed his robes and smiled. The host stood naked for a moment before sitting down cross legged. It opened its arms wide to the heavens and accepted its fate.

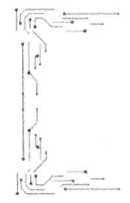

Terraforming

The mountain range spread far and wide, miles from any civilisation. Deep beneath the rocky terrain, networks of tunnels were cut, hidden carefully out of view. These tubes were not cut with drills that are loud and vibrate but with probes that burned extremely hot, making the rock in front of it molten. It set solid as it cooled behind the probe, leaving long tubes that had no need for supports or reinforcement. This intricate network was crafted by technology as yet unbeknownst to Earth humans. All that could be seen from the outside was the rugged inhospitable beauty of the range surrounded by the burning desert. There were shrubs and brush dotted around, but life was scarce.

Within the mountains and out of sight was a secret world that was a hive of activity. How long the tunnels had been there, it was impossible to tell. They were connected to different round rooms, each with temperature controls and UV radiation. The Reptilians had made it their home for thousands of years, brooding, gradually terraforming planet Earth.

These scornful creatures, fuelled by envy, could not yet live freely on the planet's surface. The climate was far too cold for them. Those homeless aliens needed the temperature to rise and oxygen to decrease to suit their biology. They cared not for the plants they killed or the animal species that died out. It was them who had been in control of the oil industry, slowly heating the planet. In short time, they would rule a world just as they once did. Never again would these powerful beings hide like rats in the dark in a world that would only fear them.

They bubbled and fumed that such a fate had befallen their kind. They mourned endlessly for their lost homeland. They were amongst the last of the Reptilians. A terrible fate had befallen their own world. The miniature blackhole came, silent and invisible, bringing death with it. It hit their planet, tearing a hole right through it, knocking it from its orbit. They never saw it coming to act; all they could do was survive.

They hissed, resentful that all that remained from their mighty species' grand history was their technology. They waited, silent in the tunnels, longing for the time when on this strange alien planet, they could reign supreme.

Their home planet slipped out of orbit, destined to become an ice ball. The surviving Reptilians had no choice but to flee. Earth was the only planet they could reach that could even possibly sustain them. They had lesser technology than some other species, but theirs far out-matched Earth's human inventions.

With the humans who understood the Reptilians could bring them power and riches, a treaty was made. The Reptilians controlled the industrial revolution—the oil, gas, and coal industries—pouring chemicals into the atmosphere. Earth's own inhabitants believed that they were killing the planet when it was the Reptilians that drove the changing climate. Though the scaley creatures didn't want to kill the planet at all, they wanted to own it.

"Humans go about their pathetic lives so unaware," the lizard creature hissed in a menacing tone, spitting a weird alien dialect, tongue flicking in and out of its mouth. "To reach our target, we need to push harder, but humans are starting to realise."

"Their greed drives them," the Reptilian leader replied. "The few control the many, and we control the few. Their greed drives and blinds them. Their power corrupts them. These fools will become masters of their own destruction, mark my words."

"Of course, but we grow impatient. We need to get out of these tunnels, my lord."

"The air must be deoxygenated, and the temperature needs to rise further. If we push hard, in a hundred years, we should be nearly there."

The Reptilian soldiers were down there in their thousands. There were more of their kind further out in the solar system. They lingered where they could not be detected. They hid behind the moons of Neptune, nearby but out of sight. They toyed with the humans, poised to take the planet the moment it was safe for them to walk the surface. They would spread out in numbers that would overwhelm the humans. Their technology was far superior; any resistance in the end would be futile.

They would not attack until conditions on Earth's surface were favourable to them and stifling for their enemy. They would purge the rightful sons and daughters of the planet and have it for themselves. The whole species, in their hundreds of thousands, awaited, like a finger twitching on a trigger, baying for its moment to unleash its fury. They awaited their chance to rain their deadly wrath upon a world that was not prepared.

The Exodus

Earth: The end of the last ice age...

The water trickled in, slowly at first, running through the caves. Then the wind howled wildly, pushing the flow ever higher. The angry waves dashed against the cliffside, exploding in frothy fury. Where once only the highest tides trickled in, now they were cut off completely.

The long-headed beings huddled silently. The fear was palpable. Having already breached the cave, if the water got any higher, they were surely done for. The stiff breeze whistled through the natural tunnels and thunder crashed, booming through their very souls.

The first wave sloshed into the cavern, bringing screams of abject fear and resignation. It rushed through the narrow rocky entrance and poured and swirled around their feet. Panic filled the cavern, and they climbed all over each other to escape the deadly flow. The Crypto-Terrestrials were trapped with no way to escape. It was already clear their fate was sealed. What was once their hiding place, their precious sanctuary from the solar flares, would become their tomb.

The water surged in again and every thirty seconds thereafter. It raged like a river's flow, now up to the waist, sucking out breath with the cold-water shock, leaving them gasping half lungfuls of air as their muscles locked, shuddering and tight. Those beings, humanlike but taller, with their signature elongated heads, were soon up to their necks in the freezing water, helpless and doomed.

The ocean was muddy, like coffee from the weeks of wild weather. The warming temperatures had melted the creeping ice flow quickly, causing the sea to rise suddenly, flooding huge swaths of the land. It was changing the very shape of the planet forever. These, the once custodians of Earth, the before people, would be all but wiped out.

They struggled and swam and held their children above the water in the hope of some miracle, but the ocean would provide no such mercy. It cared not if they lived or died; it was a raging animal, an undefeatable monster, relentless, and unfeeling. It was there for their souls, and their souls it would have.

The final wave flowed in, now completely swamping the caves. The screams stopped as the cavern flooded and the Crypto-Terrestrials inside were lost.

On the higher grounds, the Crypto-Terrestrials had eked out an existence. They, too, had had to go below ground due to the deadly solar winds. Those that remained on the surface were ripped apart by radiation. Cancers attacked their altered DNA. It killed them fast or killed them slow, but it killed them all the same.

The polar auroras could be seen right to the equator from the mass coronal ejections. They had little warning of the impending doom. All they could do was get beneath the ground. For many, it was too late. The ones that survived, even now that they could come out of hiding, had unusable technology from the floods and their very existence threatened.

Food was scarce and no longer nearly enough to sustain the population. With their intelligence, grandeur, and civilisation, they had no clue how to hunt or forage. Some went feral, joining tribes of human hunter gatherers, sharing their knowledge, upgrading their weapons with their crafting skills. In return, they were taught how to survive.

For many centuries, the Crypto-Terrestrials had been in communication with those from beyond Earth. They knew that they were children of the stars, and that one day, to the stars they would return. This was foretold in the ancient tales. By us, they are known as tombs or monuments, but to the Crypto-Terrestrials, pyramids were so much more.

Spanning every continent, some could heal using sound waves or negative ionisation, others generated electro-magnetic power, and some could even communicate beyond this planet. They beamed messages to other civilisations by generating torsion fields that shot out across the vast expanse of the galaxy, moving quicker even than the speed of light.

"They've responded to the beacon, Leader." The words were spoken in a long-forgotten dialect. "It will not be long before they will be here to take us."

"This is the final exodus. No time remains. We need to get off-planet before it's too late. Gather the chosen now. The rest must remain."

It brought enormous pain to his heart, to flee and abandon his people in their time of need, but the survival of their species was at stake. His thoughts were with the souls lost in the solar storms or the floods. It brought him close to tears, but here and now, they needed his leadership more than ever. To remain on the planet would be suicide, and even if it was not, he still could do nothing to help them. He had to escape to ensure his people survived.

Many thousands he had rescued in the two exoduses, but for each life he saved, hundreds of thousands were lost.

"Come, Dilad, we must get to the platform now. Are the guards in place?"

"Yes, Leader. When the craft comes into sight, the citizens will try and rush the platform."

"Give the order. We will use deadly force if we must. Nothing can stand in our way."

They emerged from below the ground and trotted to the platform. There was a waiting crowd. The final elites—the engineers, the doctors, the historians—all of the society's most useful and prominent members. They were representatives of their species, their culture, and their history. They were all that would survive.

The platform was encircled by guards. There was a nervous murmur amongst the people. There they awaited the star people, their parent species, to finally come and take them home.

Silently, the huge silver craft gently passed above the crowd. The round shadow loomed large, completely engulfing the Crypto-Terrestrials below. Just as there had been the two times previously, there was the desperate rush and stampede for the platform. It was their last chance to survive. For a moment, carnage ensued, but the guards quickly opened fire, sending the crowds scattering and leaving lifeless bodies on the steep stairway.

The craft hovered then shot down a beam of bright white light. Little more than a second had passed, and the platform was empty. With the final exodus, the chosen Crypto-Terrestrials would become extra-terrestrials.

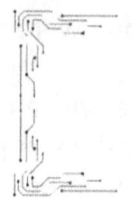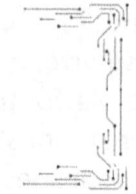

Coincidences

Her phone rang. Penny immediately took her eyes from the bad movie her dad had chosen and stared towards it.

"Leave it, Pen Pen. Just watch the movie."

She agreed. She had hardly answered the phone at all for weeks, that's if it was even switched on, but something drew her towards this call. No matter how much she wanted to ignore it, something about it summoned her senses. She jumped up and answered. "Hello, this is Penny."

"Hello. Erm, you're Penny Dowler?"

"Yes, I am. Can I help you with something?"

"I don't know. I don't even know where to begin. I'm looking for some answers." The woman sounded distressed.

"Huh? Well, just tell me what's going on, and I'll see if I can help."

"It's my daughter. She passed away three weeks ago."

"Oh, I'm terribly sorry. That's awful!"

"They said she jumped off a cliff. But I know my Isha; she would never do that."

"I'm really sorry to hear about her, but I don't understand what it has to do with me?"

"Your friend... he jumped, too, right?"

Penny went cold. Suddenly she no longer felt comfortable with the conversation. "Look—"

"I'm not explaining myself well. Let me try again. My daughter and your friend Liam. They died in the same way on the same day at roughly the same time."

"What?"

"He just went for a walk, didn't he?"

"Erm, well, yes."

"Isha did, too. On the same day. Please, can we meet somewhere? We need to talk."

Isha's mother was there, looking nervous and wearing her long overcoat when Penny and her dad arrived.

"Hi, I'm Penny, and this is my dad, Danny."

The woman stood and shook their hands. "Sangeeta. Nice to meet you."

Danny ordered them all coffee, and they huddled in the corner of the cafe. Sangeeta looked terrible, like she hadn't slept for days. A deep furrow crossed her brow. Her eyes were darting around the room. She was clearly anxious.

"Sangeeta," Penny reached across the table and took her trembling hand, "it's okay. Just say what needs to be said. We're listening, okay?" Penny ducked her head a little to catch Sangeeta's eye and gently shook her hand. "Okay?"

"Okay." She half smiled. "It's just that I'm not used to talking so openly."

"I understand. This is a safe space. We won't judge you. Just take your time."

She sipped her coffee, took a deep breath, and began. "Isha disappeared one night. She just up and left without saying a word. It didn't take long for them to find her... in the water." She stopped for a moment as she fought back tears. Penny squeezed her hand again. "She was so full of life. She would never... She was odd recently. Sleeping in. Being short and snappy. I mean, more than usual." She did a snotty half laugh. "Teenage girls." She semi smiled and stared out to space for a moment as the painful memories flashed again, just as they had every moment of every day since her daughter was found. "After a few days, I started searching online to try and understand what would drive someone to do, well, what she did. That was when I came across Liam's story. It was so similar, on the same day. I don't know. Maybe it's a coincidence, but maybe—I know it sounds crazy— maybe they were connected. Of course, these are probably the words of a desperate woman looking for answers where none exist."

"No, no, I don't think it's crazy at all. I mean, I doubt it, but if it's even a faint possibility, it's worth looking into. What do you think, Dad?"

Danny dropped his chin into his hand with his elbow on the table and was thoughtful for a moment. "Look, I'm not sure how healthy it is. Like, admittedly it is weird, but it's most likely just that. They didn't know each other, did they?"

"I seriously doubt it. She was only fourteen," Sangeeta said.

"Did she leave a note or any clues?"

"Not a note, but I did find one of her notebooks on her desk. I don't know if it means anything, probably not, but she just wrote 'everything's connected' on the last page."

Penny froze, her heart skipping a beat in shock. She had thought that surely it was just a strange coincidence, but this, this was *too* much of a coincidence.

"What?" she asked.

"Everything's connected."

"I don't believe this! Liam, on the phone, the last time I spoke to him, he said, 'Everything's connected in ways you could never understand.' This really is incredible."

"What?! What does any of this mean?"

"I don't know, Sangeeta, but I think we should try and find out."

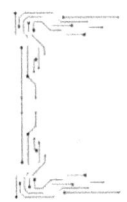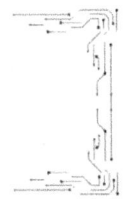

The Army

From the depths of shadowy darkness, the Spy emerged, confused, discombobulated, unsure of what had happened. His head felt like it was filled with pressure. His hearing was like he was underwater. His eyes were teary and blurry like they had never seen the light. He tried to move, but he was fixed in place. Trapped. He struggled to free his arms, but they were seemingly shackled to something. He kicked his legs, and while they were free, they dangled helplessly below him. He was suspended high above the ground, hardly breathing. Panicking, he looked around. Other forms surrounded him, all suspending and flailing.

He wanted to scream out as he fought to free himself but could not. The heart in his chest thundered through him. It seemed only a moment ago he was freezing to death and now, helplessly imprisoned.

His eyes grew accustomed to the light, and his vision finally cleared. He frantically turned his head from side to side. It seemed he was inside a mountain surrounded by blank-faced beings with milky, translucent skin. He squirmed. They were all suspended from above by flexible pipes. They appeared identical in every way. Each was naked, tall, and muscular.

With a whir, inch by inch they were moved along by a mechanism above them. There was a loud hiss as if gas was being released. One at a time, the beings were freed from their bonds and tubes and lowered onto a conveyer belt that took them through a door. None of them tried to escape; they were totally compliant. It was almost as if they had been hypnotised. The being next to the Spy was lowered down, and next it would be his turn.

The gas hissed, and the pressure in his head lifted. His hearing became clear. There was a *clunk*, and suddenly the Spy was on unsteady legs being moved along by the conveyor belt. He passed through the door and into a white tubular room. There, he was crammed, hardly able to move, with the countless others of his kind. They were silent and still. The floor beneath his feet moved. One at a time the beings were taken out of the room and out of sight.

The Spy awaited his turn anxiously. It was half fear, half nervous anticipation. He dared not do anything that would make him stand out in the crowd.

He was taken along into another tighter tube, where, for a few seconds, he was alone. There was whir, then a mighty pop followed by a flash of light. From nowhere, the Spy felt weight in his hands and clothing covering his naked body and head. He looked down. He was wearing thick body armour, a helmet, and had a heavy weapon in his hands. For the first time since he'd become aware, he breathed. The floor of the tube dropped like an elevator. The Spy went down through darkness and back into light before the platform beneath him slowed and then stopped.

Packed shoulder to shoulder, the beings in their thousands stood in a huge room. Each wore the same clothing and held the same weapons. It was clear that the Spy was now part of an army. They were far more in number than only the members of The Sect. Were these things sparked into life only by the death of another being? They stood in tight rows, in formation, facing forward, unmoving. Apart from the collective breath, they didn't make a sound.

There was an air of anticipation that the Spy could feel. He could tell they were expectant. In the silence, the Spy sensed a buzz of excitement. These blank-faced beings around it were awaiting something. The Spy could feel it but had no idea what it was. It was like the other beings collectively whispered secrets to each other, words that he couldn't quite hear. It felt as though they were all in on it, and the Spy alone was out of the loop.

Time ticked by while the rest of the room was being filled; at least, that was what the Spy assumed. He couldn't risk looking around while the other beings stared expressionlessly ahead. He could little afford to do anything out of step with the others. If he was noticed, there would be no chance in a fight.

He hated the fact he was scared, despite the training he had done, despite the warnings. The truth was nothing could truly prepare him for what was happening around him. Those that had trained him couldn't possibly know themselves. The Spy was so confident when the mission began, but every step had been a shock. It made him question his own sanity over and over. So far, he'd handled everything, but what was happening around him was far bigger than he could have ever expected. He drowned in isolation, knowing that alone, he couldn't accomplish anything while stuck with the mindless army. All he could do was blend in and try and go unnoticed.

His craft, skill, and training, his cunning and intelligence were all wasted in this situation. If he did anything to get himself noticed, he knew that he would be torn apart in seconds. He stood, bored with staring forward and irritated by the waste of time. He waited for what must have been hours.

A platform rose at the front of the room, emerging from below the ground. Standing there was a figure, hooded and cloaked, rising up into the light. The figure was small, seemingly no more than a child. The Spy felt a tingle of power flowing off this being that stood before him. The child ripped their hood back and thrust their arms aloft.

For the first time, the crowd broke their silence and vacant staring. They roared as one, a deafening cry that echoed around the room. The Spy joined the chorus, though a split second after the others. The sound died down, and again, there was complete silence. A moment passed and the child spoke, only not with their mouth but with their mind.

"Children, welcome. You have been granted the honour of becoming my army. My soldiers, war is upon us, and we must answer the call."

As with every other figure in the room, the words sounded clear in the Spy's mind. This child was powerful, and the Spy knew that made them very dangerous.

"Each of you have this body. Each of you must do battle. Your body is modified to suit the conditions in which you must fight. You, my instruments of death, will not feel fear or pain or fatigue. Each of you has weapons—rifle and blade—and body armour.

"There is one more thing that will make you, my soldiers, unstoppable. Look up and embrace the power of the mighty halithstord!"

The Spy looked up as a clear ball was slowly lowered down on a pipe, right towards him. The sphere opened, leaving a hole. It lowered around him and clicked into place. He was sealed inside.

"Remove your helmet," the child telepathically demanded.

The Spy did.

The pipe at the top opened, and strange swirling gas rushed in. Then came the writhing snake-like symbiote, the halithstord. It was greedy for its bond, rushing towards its new host.

The Spy wanted to run or scream, but he was trapped in place. He wanted out and out now. He fought back against his flight response. That would surely get him killed. The child had told them in this form they would hardly feel any fear. That certainly wasn't true for him. The symbiote would not wait.

Immediately, it burrowed its way violently into its new host's skull. There was savage, painful gnashing as it tore through the flesh. White blood like milk filled the dome around his head. The Spy braced himself for his final painful moment. There was a horrendous crunching and then a loud pop that echoed inside him. Instantly, the Spy felt great strength surge through his new body. Power bubbled inside like he had always had it, only now it was unleashed. He roared a mighty war cry skywards.

The Tall Whites

Earth: Approximately 780,000 years ago...

Another explosion boomed out, vibrating the floor. The tall white beings were sent scattering, knocked off their feet. The alarm blared shrill and loud.

"Get them to the escape ship. Now. We don't have long!" The spindly being's words were in a strange language, like the whistle and tweets of birds.

With a lingering goodbye that was interrupted by yet another rumbling explosion, the father stayed where he was while the other three ran. Again, a bang echoed through the corridors, closer this time. They were sent stumbling down to the floor. With not even another second to lose, they rushed back to their feet and took flight.

The mother ushered the two children through the crammed corridors of the mothership. A panic had taken hold upon the decks. Smoke was starting to fill the halls as a frantic surge of white beings desperately made their way towards the escape ships. Anxious looks greeted their glowing eyes as they passed by others in the corridors. The birdlike whistles became squawks of fear until they morphed into an intermingled cacophony of noise.

The mother surged forward, barging past all that got in her way. She only stopped for a second when each explosion boomed around the ship, shaking it in its orbit. She charged through the crowd with her children's hands in hers. Children were the most precious of all to the Tall Whites, so the guards protecting the escape pods held the crowd back and let them through. There was hardly any room, but the two of them squeezed inside.

The mother said her goodbyes to her beloved offspring, turned her back, and walked away. She couldn't bear to see them ripped from her. She took silent comfort in the fact that, although her fate was sealed, her beloved children would be safe.

The small craft lifted off the pad and shot out through the bay doors, heading the short distance to Earth. Above, the mothership rattled and shook. More and more explosions lit up space, and the enormous craft began to tilt. Huge chunks of metal broke away, and bodies of the Tall Whites, who were dead in an instant, drifted out into space.

The meteor bombardment continued, each smashing huge holes through the craft, coming in at the speed of a bullet. With one hit too many, finally, the ship exploded, sending out a mighty shockwave. Debris from the craft rained through the atmosphere, becoming molten metal, balling up as it fell. The Tall Whites' mother craft that had been locked in orbit around Earth for many centuries was now little more than space junk.

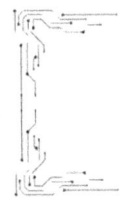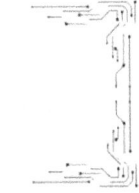

The Note

"You'll have to excuse the mess," Sangeeta said as she let Penny and Danny into her house.

It was dark and musty within. They could tell she'd been dwelling in there alone for quite some time. Her days were spent in the dark, consumed by her grief, crying until she slept. Penny's heart broke for her. To lose a friend was tragic enough; to lose a daughter must have been too much to bear.

Penny and her dad both felt uneasy, though it wasn't because of the house itself or because of Sangeeta. It was that they didn't really know what they were doing there or what they hoped to accomplish. Was Penny just being a fool and looking for a connection to something that had none? Was it even healthy for either her or Sangeeta to explore the subject? The grieving pair searched for light in darkness, clinging to hope where hope may not exist. It was as though a candle had sparked into life. A flame that could show them the way or flicker out and die, leaving only blackness.

Sangeeta made some tea then led them upstairs to Isha's room and opened the door. "I haven't touched anything since... well. Feel free to take a look around, but please, be careful and put everything back where you found it."

"Don't worry. We'll be really careful." Penny looked around, her eyes meeting each object in the room. Her gaze settled upon the photograph in the frame on the bedside. "Is that her?"

"Yes, that's us together. It was her thirteenth birthday." A tear left Sangeeta's eye.

"Oh, she's so beautiful." Penny smiled.

"I... I can't be in here. I just can't. Look around. Be careful. I... I'll be downstairs." She left the room in a hurry before rushing down the stairs.

Penny and her dad empathically hurt for her as the audible sobs came from below.

"Do you think I should go downstairs and check on her?" Danny asked, looking awkward at the thought.

Penny shrugged. "I dunno. Maybe."

"Yeah, I think I should." He let out a nervous laugh. "She can always tell me to go away, right?"

"I guess."

"This room's pretty small anyway. I'll leave you to it, yeah?"

Penny stood alone in the room, looking around for anything that may give her a clue. For reasons she couldn't know, her eyes were drawn towards the notebook on Isha's desk. Something about it called to her. She sat in the chair and started to read.

She felt like she was doing something which she shouldn't. It was like she was invading someone's privacy as well as disrespecting the dead. Her nature screamed at her not to, but something beyond her told her to keep going.

For some reason, each page made sense to her, like she had known Isha herself. She felt connected to her for reasons she could never explain.

She flipped the pages, not reading every word, but taking in things that caught her eye until she reached the last one that had writing on it. Amongst the half-scribbled dream Isha had attempted to write down, Penny's eyes were drawn to something. Her heart nearly stopped. This surely couldn't be a coincidence. She looked again to be sure.

Faintly written in the bottom corner of the page were the words "Fleck-Flick." She read it over and over again, always expecting it to change, but despite her disbelief, it remained there on the page. The initial gut-dropping shock was too much for her. She glazed over. She felt numb. There was a wild mix of confusion and disbelief.

She remembered back to when Liam had told her of The Fleck. She had even heard its voice once, within the reflection world. Memories came flooding back to her and with them came emotion. The longing for her friend took over. The pain for her loss, the guilt that always accompanied such thoughts dominated.

Maybe she could never make sense of it, any of it. This thing felt bigger than she would ever be. It felt like a code that needed to be deciphered when she couldn't even see the symbols.

She thought deeply, looking for answers, but the more she fought for them, the further away those answers felt. She was uncomfortable. She couldn't sit still. Whether it was the dark cloud of death that hung over the house or not knowing how she could ever explain this to anyone without sounding crazy, she didn't know.

She stood up, compelled to move. She needed to get out of that room. Quickly snapping a picture of the page with her phone, she thudded down the stairs.

Penny poked her head around the door of the living room, where Sangeeta and her dad were sat in intense conversation.

"I'm gonna wait outside, Dad. Take as long as you need. I need a moment." She turned to walk away, but Sangeeta called out.

"Penny, did you find anything? Anything at all?"

"No, sorry, nothing." She was accidently abrupt. She headed out the door and onto the street. The late London winter was bitterly cold. She could taste the traffic as she blew steam and walked briskly up and down the street. She couldn't sit or stand still, so this seemed her best option. She spoke to herself firmly, trying to calm herself, trying to slow the thoughts and emotions that flowed within.

The car pulled out of the parking space and painfully crawled through the traffic towards Penny's apartment. She silently stared out the window, holding her hands in fists up her sleeves to warm them.

"Are you gonna tell me then?" Danny asked.

"Tell you what?"

"What you found that freaked you out so much."

"Oh, I can never hide anything from you." She said it half-jokingly.

"Well, no. I'm psychic, ya see."

Penny rolled her eyes. "You're about as psychic as a ham sandwich."

"A mighty ham sandwich, though. The all-seeing ham sandwich. The knower of all hammy and sandwichy things."

Penny giggled. "Look, I did find something, but I'm not quite sure how to articulate it. Let me think about it for a bit. When I tell you, I want to say it right. But don't worry, I will tell you. It's just... It's just a bit confusing and weird."

"Ah, I see. Confusing and weird. Story of my life, that."

Penny giggled again.

Danny took a more serious tone. "You can tell me whatever you want, whenever you want, or even not at all. All you need to know is I'm here for you."

"I know, Dad. Thanks." She squeezed his arm and offered him a smile. A few moments passed in contemplative silence. "I felt bad about leaving like that. What about Sangeeta? Is she okay?"

"Frankly, no, she's not."

"It's so sad."

"Yep. I gave her my number. I think she could use a friend."

"I think she could, too, you know. That was good of you. Isha was so beautiful. I can't even imagine."

"That she was, Pen Pen. That she was."

Drifting

"What was that?" He thought he heard a voice. The sound of a haunted whisper somewhere in his dreamy state. There was no answer, but then, surely this wasn't even real.

Silence filled the backdrop. Unearthly silence. The traffic's hiss, the car horns, the people shouting all faded away. The music booming that normally emanated from upstairs had stopped. He didn't know if he was awake or asleep. It seemed, indeed, he was somewhere in between.

His sleep had been weird and unsettled recently. Dreams, vivid, yet random and strange, left him exhausted in his waking hours. It was like he'd been running marathons when he did sleep. The rest of the time, insomnia left him lonesome and haunted. It was as if he was afraid of what would happen to him if he dared drift off.

Now he was anxious and snappy, his rest stolen from him. It took his disposition and demeanour and left a mere stranger in their place. Alex was a shadow of his former self.

At that time, he floated in nowhere or, at least, in between places. He was lost in thought, almost meditating, almost dreaming, flittering in and out of his body. Maybe at times he'd even slipped out of existence completely. Where many would be awash with confusion, paranoia, and fear, he remained calm.

Alex wore false bravery like a badge. False bravery not because he faced his fears, but because he felt a numbness to them. He simply didn't care what happened to him. What is there to fear really? Pain, suffering, or death? When you have experienced enough of the first two, the latter doesn't seem to matter as much.

Alex had experienced a lifetime of both. He had suffered abandonment and abuse, loneliness and depression forever. So much for so long that his reality told him the only person that he could rely on was himself.

He stumbled into situations and dealt with them accordingly through instinct, not with thought. He had done so his whole life. Now that he was nineteen, he'd had enough of fear. He was done with it, or so he thought. He told himself he would be scared no more. He fooled himself into believing it, when the truth was it controlled everything he did. Not terror, but fear that nags, hidden away like a secret box in the soul. There it silently dictated his actions, while he carried on with his life, hardly even aware of its existence.

He wore his beard and tattoos like armour. They made him look older and tougher. Scars from countless street fights adorned his face, but the deeper scars of trauma were hidden within.

He lay in his bedsit, freezing. It was a single room with only a fridge, a kettle, and a microwave as his kitchen. The bathrooms were shared with the other residents. Some of them were clean, many of them were not.

This was the place where the lost souls gathered. The people without families or homes. Those shunned by society, the addicts, the criminals, the crazies, and, unfortunately for him, Alex. He wrapped himself tight in the blanket to block out the cold, and knowing he'd have to be onsite and working by seven am, he tried to sleep.

For a moment, he dared to sleep deeply, glad of the rare silence around him, but as always, those strange visions came. They rushed into his mind, flowing like a river, leaving him twitching in his slumber. Before long, Alex was on a journey, dreamlike and cosmic. He floated amongst the stars, like his body was no longer a prison that weighed him down.

Artistic and beautiful sights drifted by, and his being fluttered with exhilaration. He smiled inside as he was overcome by joy and a feeling he hadn't known in forever—childlike wonder.

Everything was so certain in his waking hours. He knew the truth. At least, *his* truth. People couldn't be trusted, life was an endless web of problems to stumble into, that pain was his destiny—of all these things he was certain. But in this journey, he wasn't sure. It was like nothing he'd ever known.

This didn't scare or threaten him like everything in his life had. Just for a lingering moment, Alex was free. The vast and mysterious cosmos stretched out before him. Every second seemed an age, leaving him awestruck. He laughed joyously in what seemed the first time in forever.

Tunnels of light gathered round him and guided him further away from the bitter reality he knew. Vibrant colours swirled, and he swooped, weightless and free. The planets and stars blurred as he rushed by them at amazing speeds.

Alex asked himself again if he was in a dream. He had no way to tell; he didn't even care. It was like he was as one with himself and the universe beyond and a part of the cosmic map before him. He was connected. Onwards, he drifted, maybe lost in a moment or even lost in forever. Here, in this place, those questions didn't matter. He didn't dream of the past or the future; he was simply present.

Alex zipped past the cosmos' artistic wonder. The lights and colours streaked by until he reached a great expanse of nothingness. The blackness of the universe stretched out, seemingly endlessly. No longer were stars or planets in view. Then, like a shadow had entered his soul, a deep loneliness filled him. From his joy, now he felt stranded, like he was cut adrift from everything and anything that ever existed.

The journey slowed, but this was not of his choosing. Alex would have done anything to avoid that depressing emptiness. If he had questioned it before, now he was certainly controlled by a force. It was something unrestrained, mystical, mysterious, yet relentlessly powerful. The stars reappeared, like they had been there the whole time. It was as if a black curtain had been lifted to reveal them in their magnificence.

Huge rocks, almost black, appeared, and he slowed further, almost to a crawl. These ancient asteroids, in their hundreds, schooled together in their orbit. He hovered, lingering over one of the bigger ones, staring downwards. Its surface was jagged, mountainous, and foreboding.

It was then Alex stopped for a lingering moment in silence and then fell, dropping like a stone and zooming out of the cosmos' wonderous beauty and towards a certain death. He headed for the rocky ground while panic filled him. He awaited the crushing impact, wishing he could close his eyes. For an instant, everything went dark, then Alex saw again, but this time through the eyes of another.

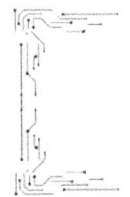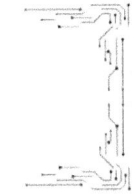

The Cabal

Earth: After the floods.

Katcha ran for his life, stumbling down the mountain. Naked and freezing, the Crypto-Terrestrial tore onwards. The jagged rocks ripped his feet to shreds. The pain surged, but he had no choice, he had to keep going. He heard the thunderous footsteps behind him getting louder all the time. The grunts and rumbles of breath coming from the onrushing beast, frothing and wild.

Katcha was tiring and slowing, the bear was not. He blew steam, and his lungs burned in the cold air. Now he could feel the thudding vibrations of the steps. He waited. At any moment he would feel the blow that would send him crashing down, then it would quickly be over.

A flash swooped through his peripheral vision, and then several more. The bear stopped, the spears hitting their target. Its wounds were mortal. It staggered only for a moment, then it crashed down onto the rocks, dead.

Katcha was still running when he heard the cry of a different type of animal coming from behind him. He stopped. He turned. The tribe of hunter gatherers were already setting to work on the corpse with their flint blades. The chief stared on with his spear outstretched, pointing it menacingly in the direction of the strange being in their midst.

It was clear he wasn't out of danger yet. He knew humans could be brutal; they wouldn't think twice to bash in his elongated skull if he was perceived as a threat. The options flashed quickly through Katcha's mind. He had no knowledge of their ancient tribal language, a language that was long since dead to the world.

He towered high over the chief—over any human, in fact—so he crouched down low. He knew that even the most basic animals would understand such a submissive gesture. Luckily for him, the humans did.

The chief offered him furs to warm himself. Katcha gladly took them. Always before he had feared the violence of humans. He was taught from a very young age to stay out of this, the most dangerous of animal's way. However, this showed him a very different side of them—kindness and empathy. The group of strangers, fourteen men amongst them, let Katcha sit by the fire, and like he was one of their own, they fed and clothed him.

"Nola, come, quickly. I have food and clothing for you. We must leave now." In his native language, Katcha spoke to his other.

"Where have you been?" she asked, hugging him tightly. "Where did you get these furs? I was so worried."

"That doesn't matter now. We've got a chance to survive, but we have to leave right away. You're going to have to trust me. Come on."

He wrapped her in animal skins to warm her and led her out of the cave to the awaiting human tribe.

Nola jumped in her skin and instantly started to tremble. She, too, was taught to be wary of humans. They stood with their weapons, encircling the pair, their savage eyes gazing upon them.

Katcha took her by the hand and went towards the men. "Come on, Nola. It's safe. They will not hurt you."

The human tribe welcomed her warmly in their strange language. The greeting put her at ease, and all at once, she felt safe. She was filled with relief. The winter was getting harsher, and without help, the two young Crypto-Terrestrials would surely perish.

They had no choice but to go with the human tribe. They were virtually helpless in the wilderness alone. They didn't have the skills to survive, and now, like so many of their kind, they wandered the wilds trying to find food. They had lived off the stored food in the city until it started to run out. That was when the violence began.

There were countless desperate beings on the verge of starvation, fighting for every scrap. Their grand and civilised society collapsed quickly, and somehow, they needed to learn how to be wild animals once again. They quickly forgot the luxury of knowing where their next meal would come from. They couldn't fight, so the pair had to leave. It truly was their only hope of survival.

They'd hidden in the cave for days. Katcha had to leave to find food. Not only had he failed to secure a meal, but he was on the verge of becoming the meal himself. But now, as strays, they had been taken in by the tribe of human hunter gatherers. The Crypto-Terrestrial's way of life and culture surely couldn't survive, but Katcha and Nola perhaps would.

Katcha and Nola lived with the humans as one of them. They used their superior tool-making and scientific skills to improve the lives of the tribe. Firstly, by creating more effective spear tips and better functioning tools, but eventually, they taught them how to settle and farm en masse, just as their forebears had generations before. Unbeknownst to them, these two Crypto-Terrestrials changed human history forever.

From that one small farm, tended by the tribe, to settling and building, and then from civilisation and cities to war and power. Thousands of years passed, and Katcha and Nola's legacy rolled on long after their deaths. This triggered the rise of the humans and changed their very nature. However, this had not gone unnoticed by far more powerful forces.

The fortress in the mountains was a haven for the few chosen Crypto-Terrestrials that remained. They were well aware of how others of their kind had mixed with the humans. Katcha and Nola were two of many. Survivors had readily joined human tribes, teaching them science and how to build. This influence certainly hadn't gone unnoticed by the leaders. These actions were a desperate attempt to save themselves but had set humanity on a dangerous path, one that would take thousands of years to play out.

"They're here now, Leader."

"Let them in," the Leader said.

They stayed hidden away, and for good reason. They didn't want humanity to know that they existed. These, the Crypto-Terrestrials that remained, for so long had hung on and merely eked out an existence, but now they were ready to take control.

For time long gone, these magnificent and peaceful beings had been the custodians of the planet. Without the cruelty and the bloodshed of the humans, they were harmonious.

Now with the coming craft to replenish their numbers, they would be powerful again. It was time to take what was rightfully theirs—Earth. These ancient and noble beings were wily. They wouldn't take the planet by force; they would take control silently, puppet masters pulling the strings from the shadows.

The Tall Whites strode in, gangly and thin. There were nine in their group. They gathered before the Leader. The Crypto-Terrestrials greeted them in their customary manner.

Moments later, the Reptilians joined them in the chamber. There were twelve of them in total, and all parties were introduced to each other.

They gathered round a huge circular table with a device that would translate each of the languages.

There at that table, the leaders of the three species destined to be upon the Earth plotted a future. A future behind closed doors, like the whispered secrets of gods, unbeknownst to humanity. They would set the path of humankind without so much as seeking their consent.

For months they plotted. The Crypto-Terrestrials, the Tall Whites, and the Reptilians became The Cabal.

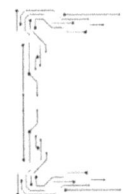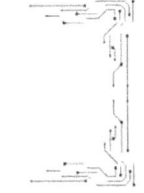

The Ambush

Alex looked around for the first time with his strange new eyes. He simply flashed into being. He was quickly greeted by a wave of confusion. The world, with its colours and the light, looked odd. This body was taller than Alex's, so his eyes were too high up. It made him feel dizzy, like he was stumbling around on stilts.

"What the—" He cut himself off from the question as his emotions swirled. They were his words but spoken in weird tones in an alien language.

Surprised he was, but somehow, Alex was not afraid. He accepted his dream for what it was, even though this was no dream. It was his shield, his defence mechanism hard at work. His own way of dealing with this and all things in his life. He, as always, would accept the situation and react to it.

He looked around through those alien eyes. He was standing alone in a metal room. There was an open sliding door which led out to a corridor. Only now did he look down. His body was long and gangly. A tight hugging black suit covered him. On his feet were huge splayed-out boots, which indicated weird flat feet within. His hands, salmon pink, had extended, seemingly delicate fingers with no fingernails.

He bounced slightly on his new legs then swung his thin arms back and forth. He swirled them round in windmills. Reaching up as high as he could, he stretched his fingers toward the ceiling of the room. Then he stood on one leg, letting out a little giggle. He hopped up and down on the spot, then he crouched low and leapt. Never before had he jumped so powerfully and high. Now his smile was huge. He proceeded to jump around the room again and again, laughing.

"Sollen, what the hell are you doing?"

The words were strange and alien, yet he understood them perfectly through a communicator in his ear. Alex stopped and turned. At the entrance of the room was a short, squat, pale yellow-skinned being wrapped in thick body armour.

"Erm... Nothing? Exercising." The words came out before he had even thought about it.

"Well, good to see you enjoying your exercise, son. I thought you were going crazy for a second."

Alex shrugged. "I might be. You never know." He laughed.

The other being didn't find it quite as funny as he did. "Time's ticking. Get ready. Stop fooling around."

"Oh, sure, yeah. Sorry."

"I don't want to hear your sorrys. Get your game face on. We have less than an hour."

"Right, got ya."

As the being walked away, Alex stood pondering, shaking his head. He had no idea what it was he was supposed to be doing in an hour. He had no clue what was going on. He stared into space in quiet contemplation.

As if from nowhere, something told him, not in words but in images. He could see what he must do. It was almost like it was a memory but one that was yet to happen. The images flashed in his mind's eye, compelling him to stroll across the room.

He waved his hand over a metal panel. It slid upwards. Alex's eyes lit up. They may not have been quite like others he'd seen, but he knew immediately that inside the wall, there were weapons. He didn't know what to do next, but his host body surely did. Reaching out and grabbing the huge weapon, Alex placed the strap on his shoulder, then the two side arms were strapped to his waist, and finally, his blade in a sheath on his back.

He stood smirking. "I'm such a badass!" he laughed to himself.

He put on the helmet, which locked around his neck. He looked at himself in the shiny metal wall, admiring his new form, doing a few practice draws of his side arms and swooshing his sword around like he'd seen in kung fu movies but without the speed or coordination.

After a while, the commotion started. A buzzer sounded, then there was a flurry of activity. Boots were clumping up the corridor as heavily armed beings of all shapes and sizes ran past Alex's room. That was the first time he felt apprehension. This dream was starting to feel a little too real for his liking. Having cool new weapons and body armour was one thing but using them was quite another.

With that, the reality clanked in on him. A battle was coming. He joined the crowd streaming up the corridor. These were beings of all sorts of different species, but they were clearly all one army. They rushed together all the way into a large hangar. There, the soldiers, at least one hundred strong, boarded an awaiting craft. Each of them was armed to the teeth with scowls upon their faces. Alex followed them into the craft, and imitating them, he strapped himself into his seat. Once all the seats were taken, the craft lifted off the platform.

It seemed an age that Alex was buckled in the seat. All the time he felt the tension building. The soldiers were quiet; their banter had subsided. As is the warrior's way, each of them had to accept this day could be their last. It was the unmistakable feeling, awaiting battle, the calm before the coming storm. Alex jiggled his leg nervously thinking over what was to come.

"We're landing on the asteroid soon. This thing's really moving. Expect a bumpy ride." The voice came from within Alex's helmet. The clever system both translated the words and carried them into his ears.

Only now did the nerves make way for fear. Only now did the reality of it all make him tremble. He was still waiting to wake up, but it appeared that he would indeed be heading into battle. He didn't even know what their goal was, but he was on this wild ride wherever it was headed. It was all he could do to keep breathing. He silently spoke to himself, trying to remain calm as the craft started vibrating.

"Woo hoo! This is my favourite part," a skinny blue creature screamed out almost joyously. It brought laughter from some of the others.

This *certainly* wasn't Alex's favourite bit. He clenched his jaw and clutched his thighs. The craft started shaking and rumbling, then violently swaying, leaving them bouncing around in their seats. It felt as though the craft was at times falling through empty air like a rock. Then, with a crunch, the craft would jerk violently, catching the turbulence again.

Alex's head was thrown from side to side from the violent movement. The vibration got worse as they swooped in for the landing. Were it not for being strapped in their seats, they would have been thrown all around the craft. Alex gripped at his knees with his hands, terrified. He just needed to keep breathing.

The craft hit the asteroid surface and bounced up again, jarring the bodies of everyone aboard. The second time, it crashed down and slid along to the sound of the grinding metal. The passengers were jerked violently in their seats. The craft twisted, rumbling, still moving, and rolled onto its side, crushing the metal walls. When it finally stopped, it was filled with smoke.

There were screams of pain and groaning sounds. Alex was lucky he was on the upwards facing side of the craft. That row had survived the impact. He shook his head and tried to gather his senses. He sat stunned, looking down at his dead shipmates, ripped apart in the crash. Others were maimed, destined to die slowly and in pain.

"Unbuckle the belts and get out of here. Move. Move!" the commander shouted as small fires broke out and the electronics sparked.

Alex fumbled for the button, pushed it, and fell forward onto the dead bodies below. They worked their way out of the carnage and onto the asteroid's surface.

"Sir, how will we get off this rock now?" one of the soldiers asked the commander as they gathered, panting and whiplashed, outside the wreckage of the craft.

"Son, we're here to capture the core. If we die here, we die here. But we will capture that core. Just do your job, and maybe we'll get out of here alive."

They took time to treat the injured. Those that were capable moved on, those that were not were pumped full of pain killers to make their final moments more comfortable.

"These are the coordinates of the dropship. Take cover. You and you and you, up there." The Commander pointed to each of the soldiers and then to some rocks up high. "Salif, take your crew down to the ridge. The rest of you, come with me."

The soldiers scattered. Alex followed the Commander. They took cover in a rocky outcrop. They crouched low, weapons ready, and waited.

They sat in wait for hours with Alex growing ever more twitchy by the moment. They didn't speak much. Each knew that it wouldn't be long before they would be fighting for their lives. The more his nerves jangled, the less he wanted this battle to happen, yet the more he wanted it to begin. The looming shadow of the fight awaited them. Each was silent in their contemplation.

Finally, a craft was spotted coming in from above. Now they ducked low and silent, not even daring to move a muscle. The craft, just as theirs had before it, shook and trembled and rocked coming in to land. This craft landed safely, but only just.

"When the door opens, unload on them," the Commander gave his orders over the coms.

The side of the craft opened, and a ramp came down. A figure stepped forward and started to descend the ramp. From all around, fire rained upon the form while Alex stayed tucked tightly against his rocky hiding place. For a moment, time stood still. The ramp was smoking and glowing with heat, but the figure upon it was still standing there. That could only mean that it was a hologram.

"Get down!" the Commander yelled out as suddenly a swarm of small creatures scurried out of the craft. They came, weapons blazing, returning fire, spraying the rocks, firing it all directions. This onslaught was swift and not haphazard. It was targeted.

The soldiers ducked low. Alex had yet to move. He sat huddled, shaking while rock and sparks rained down around him. The human-looking being beside him poked their head up with a grenade in hand. Before they could launch it, their hand was blown off their wrist, and the grenade dropped to the rocky surface.

As if his instinct drove him, for the first time since the battle had begun, he moved. He moved like lightning. He ran and dove headlong, hit the rocks, and rolled over. The grenade exploded in a mighty flash, instantly incinerating many of the men surrounding Alex.

"Sollen... Sollen."

"Huh?" Alex was rattled, out of focus.

"Sollen..."

Oh, Sollen, that's me. "Yeah?"

"Cover me."

"What?"

"Cover me!"

He was confused, lost for a moment, unsure of what the Commander wanted him to do. The host body knew what to do. He raised the biggest weapon over the rocks and unleashed an endless stream of plasma hail down upon the creatures below.

Now the Commander popped up and launched a grenade of his own. He was down again before the inevitable return fire that followed.

The grenade exploded, this time amongst their enemies. The remaining men, upon the order, streamed down the rocks towards the craft. They were ready to lay waste to anything else that was inside it. The cargo was onboard.

Alex followed the others, his heart racing, his hands trembling, bounding over the jagged rocks. Slipping and sliding as he went, he struggled to keep up with the soldiers.

As they approached the craft from all sides, defensive fire came from the side openings. Two were taken down while the rest of the soldiers quickly took cover where they could and returned fire.

Alex popped his head up and unloaded on their enemies. His weapon fired rapidly, spitting plasma blasts. He roared with wild fury as he unloaded upon the craft. Coming out from his cover, he marched forward with his finger locked on the trigger. The Commander called him back, but he didn't hear. He released the trigger and rolled like he'd seen in the movies, ending up parallel to the ramp.

The beings inside never expected it. Such a brazen and foolish attack was so suicidal, it worked. He opened fire again, blowing limbs off bodies or heads off necks. All that remained in the craft were dead bodies. Alex stood laughing, acting like he'd just won a video game.

If Alex, or indeed Sollen, was expecting a pat on the back for his display of heroism, he couldn't have been more wrong.

The Commander marched towards him yelling. "What the hell are you doing? What is wrong with you?"

Alex said nothing.

"You could have damaged the cargo, and if that thing had blown, we'd all be dead. Not only did you endanger yourself, you endangered every single one of us. Have you forgotten your training?"

"Erm..."

"Look at the damage on the craft. How the hell are we gonna get off this rock if this thing doesn't fly anymore?"

"I'm sorry." He looked around the group for support. They were shaking their heads. He'd let them all down. Internally, he castigated himself as he so often did. *I tried to do a good thing and*

I got it wrong, again. No matter what I try and do, I always make things worse.

"Look, just help the engineers look over the craft. If this thing won't fly, I dread to think what they'll do to you." He pointed around the disappointed faces amongst them.

"I'm sorry," was the only pathetic offering he had.

 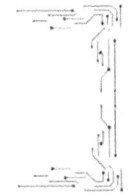

Point of View

Penny sat for hours researching whatever The Fleck was. She found no reference to it, and so, no answers. It was just getting more mysterious all the time. Her dad had gone, and she was free to stay in her pyjamas all day once again. A privilege she was more than happy to abuse. He'd stocked her up with food before he'd headed home, so she was set.

It was like the answers were never getting any closer, but it took her mind off her grief, even if only for brief moments. She felt like a dying flower that once again had been invigorated by the rain, if only to dry out again, over and over. She was frustrated by her lack of results but pleased for the distraction.

Now, however, she was at a loss. She thought it through and decided the time had come to try and tell her father what had happened. She texted him to come over that weekend.

"How ya doing, princess?" He always made sure he used his full pet name repertoire.

"I'm doing okayish. Well, you know. I did manage to go into college on Thursday and Friday. It's just so awkward. Like, no one knows what to say to me. They're avoiding me like the plague."

"Oh, I hear ya. It's just a human thing that most of us get wrong. They don't know what to say to you, so they avoid you. The truth is, though, you don't really need words of wisdom. They're all cliches anyway. You just want them to be normal."

"Yes, that's exactly it. I mean, no one really hung out with me much anyway, except Liam."

"Of course, but you never liked hanging out with too many people anyway."

"Nah, I still don't. People, they're just so… peopley."

Danny laughed. "I'll just leave then, shall I?"

Penny giggled. "No, no. Present company accepted."

He did a dramatic brow wiping gesture. "Phew, that was a close one. Hey, I'll cook some dinner and you can tell me what's going on. I'm an elephant's head."

"What?"

"I'm all ears."

"Oh, please. Groan."

"So, in the last few weeks with Liam, he was acting really strange."

"How so?"

"I'm getting to that, please just let me speak... I'll take questions afterwards." She smiled cheekily, slightly softening the blow of the rebuttal of his question.

"Okay." He nodded and his eyes smiled as they always did.

"Right. Erm... He started missing college and stuff, and when he did show up, he was all distant. Like, dreamy. He said he hadn't been sleeping, and I mean, he looked terrible. He explained that he'd been having these weird dreams, like he was living other lives. I know it sounds mental, but honestly, that's what he was saying.

"He said some scary stuff about having to kill a child and all this—our lives, your life, his life—didn't matter. All he had to do was what needed to be done at the time.

"He was clearly wired tight, so I took him to the doc's, and there wasn't really anything wrong with him. He talked about a voice that communicated with him. Something that lived inside him. I don't know if it was telling him what to do or working with him or just speaking."

Danny couldn't help but interrupt. "That could be some kind of serious mental illness. Like, schizophrenia or something."

"Yeah, you'd think so, wouldn't you? That's what I thought. Until one day I went back to his place, and he was huddled in the corner. A total mess. I panicked a bit. Wanted to call an ambulance, but he wouldn't let me. This strange dust just appeared and started drifting down all around the room. It was weird, like all chemically. I don't even know how to say this bit, so I'll just say it. Please don't have me committed," she semi-joked, again trying to soften the blow of those unbelievable words.

Her dad's face was already showing shock and worry even though he was fighting to keep it neutral. "It's okay, love. Just keep going. You'll get no judgement here. You know that."

"Yeah, I know... Okay... Here goes... Then I went with him. Like, skipped somewhere else. He was this weird being in this weird world, and I was, too. I can't even remember it well now. Like it's fuzzy. I couldn't describe the place to you if I tried; I just know I was there."

"Well, you couldn't have had the same hallucination." Danny couldn't help the outburst, but this one encouraged her.

"Exactly! And then you know what else? I heard the voice myself."

"What?"

"Yeah. I swear it."

"It's okay. I believe you."

"You do?"

"Of course. Why would you lie?"

"Well, it gets even weirder from here, so buckle up. He told me about the voice and said it was called The Fleck. I couldn't forget the name. He said it was like a force inside him. Then inside Isha's notebook, she had scribbled two words: Flick and Fleck!"

"Wow!"

"Yeah, that could be a total coincidence, but the coincidences are becoming too many. You don't think she could have had The Fleck voice in her, too, do you?"

"I have no idea, but I think it needs investigating further."

"I did research, but I can't find anything online at all, and I'm good at researching. It's kinda my thing."

It was an hour later when they finally sat down for a late dinner. Penny was happy, though, mainly because she felt like a weight had been lifted off her shoulders by sharing her experiences. Most of all because, unlike her, her dad was a great cook.

They chatted about other things while they ate, but then Danny stopped and chewed thoughtfully. He stared into the mid-distance even though the wall was only a few feet away. "This may sound like a weird one," he finally expressed what he had been thinking about for the last five minutes. "Have you maybe considered going to see, erm, a psychic, perhaps?" He couldn't have sounded more awkward. "Look," he started to justify himself immediately. "Your mother is right into it, as you know, and I dunno, maybe if science won't help…"

"It's not as stupid as it sounds."

"Well, that's a relief," he chuckled.

"I think at this point, I'm willing to try anything."

The Treaty

Earth: Early 15th Century...

The Cabal gathered, still within the mountain fortress, hidden away out of sight.

"The humans are spreading. We foretold their violence and their greed, but now they're like a disease infecting each part of the globe. It will not be long until they have covered it all." The translator repeated the Crypto-Terrestrial leader's words in both the Reptilian and the Tall White's language.

"Yes, they are colonizers," the Reptilian hissed. "They are on course to become an interplanetary species. They will infect all the planets in time. By the time the sun makes the Earth uninhabitable, they will have filled this solar system, destroying as they go, then they will stretch out beyond. It is inevitable."

The Tall White was animated. "They are the destroyers, warlike, greedy, angry and blinded by their own grandeur. Look how they torture and enslave all that oppose them. Violence is their way."

The elongated-headed leader responded. "It has not gone unnoticed, by us or by others beyond this planet." He turned to face the door. "Send them in."

In swooped three Mantises standing ten feet tall. Their robes were vibrant and flowing out behind them. The other beings felt their immense power as they entered. They each rose respectfully to welcome them. These were the ancient ones with massively extended lifetimes. They were considered the most evolved species in the alliance. They were masters of space travel and experts in DNA and genealogy. They didn't travel unless they saw no other choice. Normally they would send their minions, the Grays, a type of advanced biological artificial intelligence, to do their dirty work, but they needed to address the issue of humanity now, before it got too far out of control.

First, the leader of the Mantises addressed the Tall Whites angrily. "You spliced their DNA too fast. They are evolving too quickly because of you."

Every eye in the room turned to the gangly white beings with looks of disgust.

"You lie!"

"No, I do not." The words were slow and menacing. "There is an obvious splice in genome at around 780,000 years ago. You increased their intelligence when your kind arrived on this planet. After the asteroid bombardment, there were only basic hominins here. You used them as your slaves. You came to them as gods. You needed a bigger brain capacity so you could keep downloading your consciousness into them when you were on the verge of death. You bought your species time from the very brink of extinction. They were not ready. What should have taken millions of years happened too fast. They needed to leave their animal instincts behind. Now they think their minds control them, when it is still their instincts. Seeding is against the code, as is hybridisation!"

The Tall Whites couldn't respond. The Mantis knew everything.

"Your kind." It pointed to the Crypto-Terrestrials. "You are not blameless. Your kind gave them technology and scientific knowledge. Now they make weapons to not kill for food but to kill each other, to take and then maintain dominance. It created a hatred between them once they had land to defend. Before they would fight, yes. They killed each other, but only in chance encounters and only if there was no choice at all. Now they kill to rule over others."

This was indisputable. None of the beings could argue against the intimidating insectoid.

Finally, it pointed to the Reptilians. "We know you're feeding them technology. You want to pump CO_2 into the atmosphere so you can rule the planet's surface. Even if it wipes out all life here.

You're going to use fossil fuels so this planet will be uninhabitable for the humans earlier. They will have no choice but to leave. We have seen this before. You plan to make them utilise the fossil fuels by feeding them snippets of technology. This work has already begun. Terraforming is against the code!"

The Reptilian moved menacingly towards the Mantis. "We Reptilians are not part of The Alliance. We are not bound by your rules!"

"If you don't stand with us, you oppose us, and I think you already know what we are capable of. You can squabble over this planet as long as you want, all of you, but the one thing we can never allow is humans to leave this solar system. It's gone too far. If they've done this much damage since they were upgraded, imagine how much they will do in a million or a hundred million years from now. It is their nature to explore, it is their nature to colonize, and it is in their nature to destroy, dominate, or displace those in their new lands. The same will be true of each planet in the galaxy. They will never stop."

"Then guide us. What shall we do?" the Tall White leader asked.

"You must make a treaty with The Alliance to stop them spreading further than this solar system. The humans are a danger to all space-faring and interplanetary beings. If you do not, The Alliance will eject you. You will never survive. You know our power and our goals, and you risk it all for selfish gains. This we cannot accept.

"Reptilians, you may not be bound by our rules, but you shall be by the treaty. Tall Whites, cease altering DNA and changing the native animals of this planet. You must create your new mothercraft and leave this place."

"But that'll take centuries before the humans can make the materials."

"You can download your consciousness into them. I know your numbers are few, but breed. Your species lives long."

"And you." This time it addressed the Crypto-Terrestrials. "The custodians of this planet. Although your ancestors long since left, you must ensure that the humans never leave this solar system. This is your one and only task.

"We will be watching your every move. Defy us if you dare."

They sat around the table for a year to make a draft of the treaty between them. There were many disagreements and fights as each species fought for the maximum benefit for their own kind. Each of their roles was defined, each boundary negotiated and met. All the time, the planet Earth kept spinning, and the humans went on, oblivious to the alien presence that watched over them and controlled them.

The Admiral

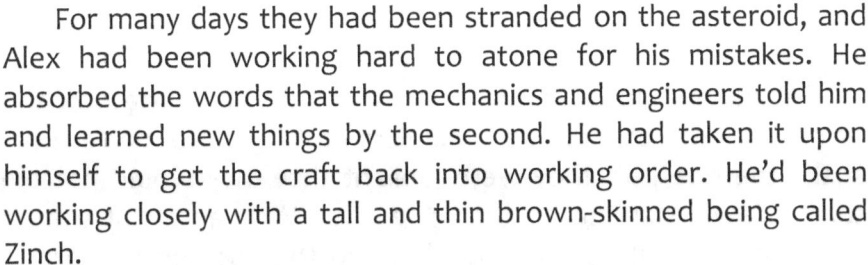

For many days they had been stranded on the asteroid, and Alex had been working hard to atone for his mistakes. He absorbed the words that the mechanics and engineers told him and learned new things by the second. He had taken it upon himself to get the craft back into working order. He'd been working closely with a tall and thin brown-skinned being called Zinch.

"You know eventually they'll come back and try and retake the core. We haven't got long," Zinch told Alex.

"How long before we can take off?"

"Maybe another day or so. You somehow managed not to fry *every* circuit on this thing."

"Dude, I tried my hardest." They chuckled for a moment. "Lucky the other craft had some spares on it."

"It was indeed, Sollen, my friend. It was indeed. Now hold this thing here for me while I just tighten her up."

"Sure thing, boss."

Alex had lost count of how many times he'd travelled to and from the crashed shuttle carrying back spares. It was a long, hard trek, but he would happily do it a million times if he needed to. During those hours alone, so many times he had contemplated when this dream would end. He was in a weird place mentally. Really, he knew deep down it was not a dream, but that was his only way of rationalising it.

The fear or confusion melted away over time, and for the first time ever, he felt a true sense of purpose. Here amongst these rugged warriors was where he belonged. He was a part of something bigger than himself. That was something that, sadly, he had never felt in his life. It was like an awakening. He had left his cold world behind for a vacation, however he had arrived and however it would end. Even though he had messed up and most of the group were still angry at him, Zinch seemed to like him, and that was one more friend than he normally had.

At times, Alex contemplated how Sollen had grown up and ended up doing what he did. He had control over Sollen's actions and intentions and access to his instincts but knew nothing of his memories. All of them were his own.

Finally, and not a moment too soon, the craft lifted off the asteroid to the cheers of the soldiers on board. No matter how shaky the ride got, they were jubilant that they would not die there, slowly starving on that cold rock. With an air of elation onboard the shuttle, they flew back to the base on the larger, more stable asteroid.

All the way, Alex was lost in thought. Well, at least while he wasn't being teased by the others who seemed to enjoy nothing more at the time.

Certain aspects of the mission didn't make any sense. They needed to secure the core and take out the guards, but why did they take such a chance of the risky landing on a baron asteroid? Who were they delivering it to?

Zinch had told him that the core was an interstellar engine and a powerful generator. He also pointed out that such technology was very hard to manufacture and was worth a fortune. Being in his lowly position, Alex wasn't sure that he'd ever find out what was going on.

Gladly, when they reached their destination, the landing this time was nowhere near as hair-raising.

"Sollen, the Admiral wants to see you."

"Yes, Commander. Where is he?"

"Where do you think he is? His office."

"Oh, okay." He headed off.

"Sollen?"

"Yes, Commander?"

"It's that way." He pointed in the correct direction.

"Yeah, right, I knew that."

The Commander watched on, shaking his head as the gangly alien disappeared down the corridor.

It was then Alex started to worry. The Admiral was sure to castigate him for his actions on the asteroid, and he wasn't looking forward to it. He'd had enough of that for days now.

After asking directions twice, finally he arrived at the office. The door was open, and the foreboding figure of the Admiral was sitting at his desk.

The Admiral looked up. His piercing blue eyes met Sollen's. They were wise eyes that scanned him like a computer, taking in details and making mental notes that lesser beings wouldn't even notice. He was a chiselled man that looked almost human. A scar ran right down his cheek, eye to mouth. His chin was bearded, dark but with grey mixed in. His hair was short but surprisingly untidy. Alex stood by the door, looking in like a dog that was waiting to be let inside.

"Come in, son." His voice was gruff and commanding.

Alex nervously stepped into the office and stood to attention.

"At ease. Take a seat, Sollen." He smiled a welcoming smile.

Alex sat down in front of him.

"How are you?" the Admiral asked.

It took Alex by surprise. Here he was ready to be yelled at and the Admiral was asking about his wellbeing. "Erm, yeah, I'm okay."

"You're feeling well in general?"

"Yes. I feel fine..." Alex was going to stop there, but something made him say more. "I mean, I had a bit of a brain fade back there, but I'm okay."

"A 'brain fade' and not a death wish. That's good to know." He paused thoughtfully, never taking his eyes off Sollen's. "What were you thinking out there, son?"

"I... I don't really know. I just thought I could take them all and was trying not to risk any more lives. I know, I did completely the wrong thing. I'm sorry."

"You don't need to apologise, Sollen. Look, one thing I've learned about us emotional beings is we make mistakes or have 'brain fades' as you'd call them. That means that we cannot judge one's actions so much as the intentions of said actions."

"What does that mean?"

"It means that mistakes we learn from. Bad intentions, we do not."

"So, I'm not in trouble?"

"Well, that depends how you define trouble, really." The Admiral smirked, which was both devilish and ominous.

"Wait, what does that even mean?"

"I have some special duties for you, Sollen. I think you'll enjoy them greatly." He laughed out the words. "I like you, so it's extra special."

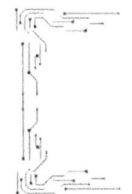 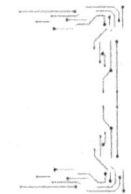

The Psychic

"You've got to be kidding me. What is this place?" Penny eyeballed the over-elaborate A-frame sign on the main street. "Mystic Maggie's: All your psychic needs." Then an arrow pointing down one of the cobbled alleyways. The sign was the only indication the place even existed.

There was a vintage record shop, a haberdashery place, and finally, Mystic Maggie's. The most horrendously glaring golds and yellows you've ever seen made up the hand-painted sign above the smallest shop.

"Your mother swears by her. She says she's a little eccentric, but what do you expect from a psychic?" He laughed a little uncomfortably. They were both sceptical to say the least.

"Oh, please tell me it's not gonna be all misty and she'll have a crystal ball. Cos I'm out if she does." Now it was Penny's turn for a nervous laugh.

They opened the door, and a bell rang. The smell of burning incense hit them as they went through the beaded string curtain.

It was dark inside and lit mainly by the candles burning.

"Hello, how can I help?" a woman's voice croaked out. "Oh, wait, you must be Penny."

"What? How did you know that?"

"Oh, it's not as miraculous as it seems. I met your father once before, and your mother told me you were coming." She cackled for a few seconds.

Penny smiled awkwardly. Danny gently nudged her with his elbow.

"You lost someone recently?"
Penny nodded.
"I'll see if I can contact him."

"Okaaay." She lingered on the word for a little too long, accidently showing her scepticism.

The woman went silent and stared ahead. "Yes, I have him." She sounded confident.

Penny just watched on.

"His name is Liam?"

"Yes, it is!"

"He tells me he has a message for you."

"What is it?"

"He wants to speak through me. Let me channel him directly. He'll tell you himself." Her voice dropped a couple of octaves. "Hello, Penny. It's me, Liam. I have a message for you."

Penny didn't hesitate. "Hi, nice to speak to you. What was your favourite nickname for me again?" Then she addressed the psychic. "What was his favourite nickname for me?"

There was a slight pause. "Penny.... Erm... Farthing."

"Oh, for crying out loud. Tiger. It was Tiger, you bloody fraud! You've just been talking to my mum about me. I'm gonna give her such an earful! I would strike your palm with silver, but you already stole my tenner, ya bitch!"

"Erm, I..."

"Oh, shut up, you old hag, before I slap ya!"

Danny heard his daughter yelling and rushed to the back of the shop. He gently put his hands on her shoulders. She shook them off aggressively. "Listen, come on. Let's go. Come on, Pen Pen. It ain't worth it. Let's just go... Okay?"

She huffed in anger and turned to leave. Her dad followed her. She turned her head on the way out. "I don't know how you sleep at night. I hope the money is worth your soul." The words were as cold as ice.

The woman said nothing. Cowardly cheats that prey on the vulnerable never do.

Penny ran further down the alleyway to where there were no people. She was surrounded by the huge skip bins from the shops. She stopped, turned quickly to her left even though there was nowhere to go, and then back to her right. She stood still for a second and burst into tears.

"Penny... Penny."

"Leave me alone, Dad. I just need a minute."

He stopped and turned and walked back towards the shops. He lingered just out of sight, but nearby. Danny knew it was best to wait, even though he was concerned to say the least. He'd never seen her so angry, and certainly never threatening violence before.

Penny didn't know what to do with her emotions. She was angry and sad and grieving. She felt cheated, then she felt guilty because she got so angry, then she felt worse because she'd snapped at her dad. She stomped her feet a bit and let out a frustrated roar. She grabbed her phone from her pocket and texted her father.

The phone blared its ridiculous message tone, one that goes on forever. Penny heard it coming from just round the corner. She smiled and shook her head.

Danny looked at the message: *"I've had my minute."* With a smile emoji.

It took him all of ten seconds to get there. He approached a little timidly, not altogether sure what he was going to find. She rushed towards him and hugged him and cried into his chest.

"You know why it got me so much?"

"No, love. I wasn't in there."

"Because just for a second, I believed."

"She's just a fraud. I can't believe your mum hasn't seen through that."

"She probably tells *her* everything first." Penny let out a snotty laugh. "You wait 'til I see her."

"Now don't you go crazy on her like you did on old Maggie's ass."

"Was I scary?"

"Guuurl, she was petrified." He ruffled her hair like she was an eight-year-old boy. "That's my girl," he teased. "Maybe you can stop the PhD and do MMA instead."

"You mess up my hair again and I'll MMA you." She threw a couple of imaginary punches.

"Oh, yeah? You're gonna give me a knuckle sandwich and a bunch of fives too, hey? Don't forget I was a Navy Seal."

"Yeah, it was the SAS last week."

"Well, what can I say? I get around, see. A long and varied existence.

"*Long* would be right."

"Woah, there! White flag. Truce. Now you're just being mean." He put his hands up, giggling. "Come on, you. Let's go have a cheeky beer. I reckon a chat in the pub is way better than one in a stinky alleyway. What do you say?"

"So, she was just saying stuff your mum told her?" Danny sipped his beer.

"Yeah. Like I wouldn't notice. It's such a scam, and it hurt me. I had... Well, it was just a glimmer—just for a moment—when maybe it could be true. If only." She sighed.

"Well, there's plenty more psychics we can try."

"Nah, I don't wanna be ripped off anymore, thanks. I'm never going to see one again."

"What are you going to do next then?"

"That right there is the problem, Father dearest. I haven't got a clue."

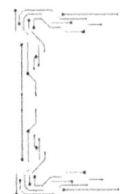 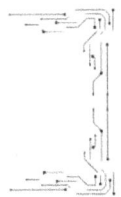

Observers

Earth - Alamogordo Bombing Range, New Mexico: 1945

Inside the Tall Whites' silver disk-shaped craft, they observed from above. These were the escape craft that came from the mothership that had exploded all those millennia ago. They were cloaked, unseen, and had remained so for quite some time. The humans were oblivious to their presence.

Far below, ripped into the earth, was an enormous crater. This was a site of devastation and destruction. The scars in the landscape told the harrowing story that The Alliance had long since feared. A terrible new weapon had been unleashed upon humanity—the atom bomb.

For the first time in centuries, the Mantises entered the chamber. As always, each being stood up as a mark of respect for their intimidating and uninvited guests.

"Matters have been brought to our attention that need an urgent response. This war of their world has yielded a terrible and powerful weapon. This weapon will probably be their destruction, but it could be the destruction of many things beyond this planet. They only create such a force to wield it."

"What would you have us do?" the Crypto-Terrestrial leader asked.

"Monitor their weapons. We must know their capabilities inside and out. This power will put an end to this war, but I fear for the future. These creatures are dangerous."

The Mantises had a deal with the most prominent human world leaders through their biological AIs, the Grays. The deal was they would not wield their power against humanity if they could take a certain amount of humans for experimentation each year. Experiences that for these beings were traumatic. The Grays may have had methods to haze the memories, but that trauma always remained.

The Grays were now tasked to not just monitor the humans, but also observe what the Tall Whites, Reptilians, and Crypto-Terrestrials were doing.

A bright light buzzed the squadron again as it had on their whole journey. The Airforce pilots were anxious. Awash with the fear, it could be an enemy technology that they couldn't comprehend.

Amongst the most modern aircraft of the military, these lights flittered around them with impunity. The drones would appear by the wingtip then, in a flash, be above them. They couldn't know where they would appear next. They had toyed with so many planes that now the order was to not engage.

That wasn't because they didn't see them as a threat in those, the most sensitive times, but because they were impotent against such technological marvels. Whatever technology the humans possessed, the drones that skimmed by them were far more advanced. They could seemingly travel at incredible speeds, change direction in an instant, and even vanish completely.

So far, they had been benign, but at any time that could change, and the humans could do little about it. They were told to stop shooting at them because, one of these days, they may start shooting back. These drones, the Tall Whites' craft, were seen so often they were given a name— foo fighters. They were the observers, endlessly watching every move the reckless human species made.

They observed a hurting planet, straining under the pressures of war. Death and pain were everywhere. It was a constant reminder of the duality of humans. From the outside, a species that loves to kill and conquer, but up close, the stories of love and heroism that were their strength. From the terrible to the beautiful, the horrendous to the wonderful. The very worst side of humanity, however, was yet to come.

In a flash, a single instant, things changed. The lost souls crumbled to fire from the sky. Buildings were blown to rubble, countless lives snuffed out. A bell that never should have been rung now could never be unrung. August 6, 1945 was the day the world changed forever. The atom bomb, named Little Boy, was dropped on Hiroshima, Japan. By the end of the year, it had killed one hundred and forty thousand people. The second bomb came three days later. That one, named Fat Man, killed seventy-four thousand in Nagasaki. Countless died in the subsequent years from radiation, and a part of humanity died with them.

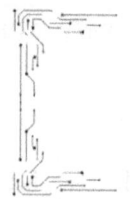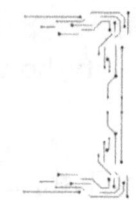

The Lindoona

Alex sat looking out the window as the strange vehicle trundled across the asteroid's surface. To him, the amazing scenes could never grow old. Every glance was met with a child-like wonder long since forgotten to him, that is if it had ever existed at all.

In the craft with him were the Elders, the Admiral, and seven others that seemed to be higher ups or officers and his friends. The way they interacted made that clear, and it left Alex feeling uncomfortable in their presence.

Around him, each was an experienced and mighty warrior and certainly not the kind of company he wished to make a fool of himself amongst. They sat making banter. They were bold and brash and laughing. Each of them had strange weapons, while Sollen sat silent with his. He was the only one who had no clue what was happening, and the Elders were most certainly enjoying that.

A well-spoken, milk white-skinned alien with a long wispy beard addressed him. "Hey, kid, I'm Jas. You see, son, there's methane lakes in a valley up ahead, and in them is a type of bacteria. In turn, there are small animals that feed off that, and then other ones that feed off them, and finally, we get the lindoona."

"The what?"

"The lindoona. Are you not listening, kid?"

"Yeah, I just don't know what it is."

The Admiral piped up over the top of them. "Don't worry, son. You'll meet them soon."

They all roared with laughter, which only succeeded in making him even more nervous. A small purple being sitting across from him produced a flask from his bag and handed it around the group. Each took a sip until, finally, it came to Sollen. They all looked at him expectantly.

"Have a nip, lad," the Admiral urged. "It'll put fire into ya. You'll be needing that where we're going."

He knew he had no choice with the eyes of the Elders on him. He sipped, he recoiled, he coughed, he spluttered, bringing another roar of laughter from the group.

"You'll be all right, son." The Admiral chuckled.

"What are we doing?" Alex asked, hating the suspense.

"We're going for lunch," Jas told him, which again was greeted with much hilarity.

He knew then they were never going to tell him. They certainly would have by now if they had wanted him to know. He played it as cool as he could, but inside he was an anxious wreck. He felt dwarfed by their power, their poise, and their confidence. Simply put, he wanted to impress them and do the right thing this time. He knew that this was a punishment. While the others seemed to be having quite the time, he sat there scared and clueless.

Finally, the vehicle rumbled to a stop.

"Right, helmets on." The Admiral issued the order, but the others were already doing so. Alex quickly fumbled with his. It clicked into place.

The Elders sat poised to move, their weapons in hand. Alex started to ready his own. The Admiral reached over a hand and stopped him. "You won't need this." He grabbed Alex's big gun. "Or these." He took his side arms. "This, you can keep." He pointed to the blade on his back. "You need to be travelling light."

Alex's fear showed clearly in Sollen's face as he gulped hard. The others never took their eyes off him, each with weird smiles etched across their faces.

"Disembark, people." There was a rumble of movement followed by each of the beings leaving the vehicle. Alex followed and they gathered on the asteroid's seemingly inhospitable surface.

The Admiral came up beside him. "Sollen, look, you see the valley drops in levels. There's dozens of methane lakes on the different levels. The lindoona hang out at the top, preying on the dozers as they climb up to the other levels."

"Oh, wow! That's amazing." He looked on, awestruck. The jagged rocky landscape, the amazing blue lakes. He was fascinated yet still afraid. He knew all too well that the suit, his helmet, and gravity enhancing boots were the only things between him and a certain and instant death.

"So," the Admiral went on, "what we're here for is lunch. We hardly get any meat nowadays, so we're hunting lindoona."

"Oh, cool! You want me to stab them with this?" He reached over his shoulder and tapped the handle of his blade.

"No, don't be stupid. You're the bait."

"What?!"

"You know, the bait."

"What does that even mean?"

"Well, what you do is take your blade, and tap it on the entrance of those caves. That'll draw 'em out, then we'll take them down, quick and clean... Oh, yeah... I almost forgot to mention, they'll chase you a little bit. So, you'd better run. Like, quick."

"They won't hurt me, will they?" Now Alex did sound scared.

The Admiral smirked. "Nah, not at all... As long as they don't catch you, you'll be fine."

The Elders again laughed at his expense.

For the second time in moments, he exclaimed. "What?!"

"Don't worry, we've all done it, and we're still alive." He looked around and the group nodded in confirmation.

"Oh, okay." He was obviously petrified. "H...How many of those things are in there?"

"Oh, normally just a family, maybe ten to twenty individuals. They'll come from all three of those caves at once, so creep up and rattle the blade on the rocks and run back this way as fast as you can."

"Right."

The Admiral put his hand on Alex's shoulder. "Look at this group, lad." He paused for a second to give him a chance to do so. "These are your proper bloodthirsty rabble. Pure warriors. Killing machines. They've gathered from the corners of the galaxy to create this fearsome army. They're well and truly badass, trust me. No one messes with us. They've killed more beings than you've ever even seen in your life. You are in good hands. We won't let anything happen to you, okay?"

"Yeah, okay." Alex blew out an enormous breath. "Go now, yeah?"

"Wait until we're in position and switch off the lights. I'll give you the signal."

"Now!"

Alex gently crept up towards the caves with his blade ready. His breathing was heavy, his hands were shaking, his heart was racing. He took long strides, approaching quietly in the darkness. The anticipation built within him with each step. His breath quickened as he went. With only the light from the nearest star reflecting from the carbon ice mountains and the ancient black rock, it was almost hauntingly dark. The caves were small, which at least put him slightly at ease. Small caves meant small creatures.

He held his blade so tightly it hurt his hand with the tension. The moment was upon him; that moment he both never wanted to come, and he couldn't wait to get out the way.

He took one more step, reaching out a trembling arm. He half turned his body, ready to tear back towards the others. He couldn't believe what he was about to do it. That was his final thought the split second before he actually did it. He tapped the blade firmly on the rocks, got on his toes, and ran.

Only a second passed before alien labrador-sized creatures emerged from the hole. They were the deepest black and spindly limbed. Each had a jagged slashing claw at the front and eight legs like a lobster. A deadly crushing beak adorned the front of their eyeless heads. They moved fast and jerking, hardly touching the rocky surface with their scuttling legs. They clearly belonged on this rock. Alex did not.

He roared as he ran, straining each muscle, pushing the host body as fast as it could go. He surged with adrenalin. He outran them for a few seconds, but quickly they started gaining on him. He sprinted, arms and legs pumping, grunting with the effort. His heart was thundering inside his suit. Now the creature's growls were mere inches away from him, and they were about to lunge.

He screamed in fear. He wasn't quick enough to get away from them. The deadly alien creatures were snapping at his heels. The one at the front of the pack leapt at him. The lights came on. There was a flash, and then a mighty crack. The creature hit the ground, instantly dead.

The Elders emerged and swarmed, each with deadly fury. Quickly, the lindoona were taken out, such were their skills. They even did it so as not to spoil the meat. The last creature was dead, but Alex kept running.

The Admiral called him on the comms. "Yo, Sollen. You can stop now, buddy." He chuckled and the rest of the group howled with laughter once again. "Good job, though, son."

He returned to the group, panting. They cheered and applauded, slapping him on the back. Now he punched the air in celebration, egged on by his companions. He was rather pleased with himself. Of course, he wasn't about to tell his comrades that he'd been scared out of his mind. The truth was, however, they already knew. He was scared out of his wits just like they were when it had been their turn.

It took quite some time for them to bleed and load all the carcasses into the vehicle. Alex willingly did as much as he could to please his masters. He absorbed their encouragement. He loved them egging him on and showing him their approval. He felt great, like he was one of the Elders himself. He never wanted this dream to end.

"Those things are gross." Alex finally took his seat.

"Yeah, they don't taste so great either. The worst part is grilling them. They stink."

"I'm glad I don't have to..." He stopped himself when he noticed the smirks around him. The Elders, as one, doubled over laughing, once again at his expense. "I do have to. No way!" He put his head in in his hands before joining the laughter himself. He'd had one of the best days of his entire life.

"Dark forces emerge from the night. The taste of blood is nigh. Spirits yearn to swallow the lives of the faceless whole. These, the tiny, the insignificant, the no one. These who fall through life blinded by things that matter not.

They love, they live, and inevitably fall. They are fragile, even those who feel that they are strong, even those who are brave and fight. They fight for love or freedom with a hope that is hopeless. It is merely illusions as consciousness drifts and falls then is snubbed out. It leaves nothing but a shell, buried in the soil or floating through space. They bide their time, even though their time will surely run out. Like the sand, it falls steadily until the time is gone. Their own time. Their bodies will be broken, and their minds turned to dust.

The time that they forget, still it comes. For they, these creatures, their lifetimes are but a second in this cosmos. It creeps towards them. Little do they know, this is a battle that they can never win."

The Raid

The Spy sat locked inside his new body strapped in the seat of the craft. Around him there were nine identical soldiers. They were one of three shuttles that had left the ice planet. Each was flanked by two more manoeuvrable fighters. They guarded the precious cargo that was the fearsome soldiers within. He had no idea what his task was, but he was certain it would be a battle. He was a prisoner on a ride that it felt like he had been on forever. This army were given their orders not through communication technology but telepathically. Directly into the Spy's mind came the voice of the child.

"Recover the core from the asteroid. If it is no longer there, find it. Do not fail me."

It was many hours later when they finally hit the bumpy turbulence above the asteroid. It was that same asteroid that Sollen and his shipmates had been stranded upon only a matter of days before. The Spy fought to keep his body neutral like the others, but he was scared as the little craft vibrated and shook. At last, after a bumpy ride, they touched down safely. The other two shuttles were not far behind. The fighters now split and flew formations in orbit. The shuttle doors opened, and these super soldiers, thirty strong, poured out and onto the rocky surface.

There they searched, always with their weapons poised, ready for battle. Each symbiote within each soldier yearned for blood, but for that, they would have to wait. The asteroid was deserted. They scanned the tracks of the soldiers and debris. They marched across the surface, scouring every inch until eventually they reached the crashed craft and the dead bodies.

The Spy shuddered with the grotesque and harrowing sight before him. There was nothing to recover and no point spending even another minute on the barren rock. They marched back to the shuttle craft and took back into space. Their thirst for blood remained unquelled.

"The drones have spotted them. They are upon asteroid nine. There's a base there. Go there, kill them all, and recover the core. Bring it to me."

"There's incoming craft, Admiral."

"Send out the fighters."

"They have fighters of their own. They are a higher class than ours. They'll rip us to pieces."

"We lost too many fighters taking the cruiser. I knew that would cost us. Those who are left will just need to buy us some time."

This was when a leader was tested most. He had no choice but to send out a few fighters to slow down the invaders, knowing full well whomever he sent would have little chance of returning. The Admiral's priority was to get the core out of there. That had to be what they were coming for. He needed to evacuate the base, get his warriors out of there, and most importantly, retrieve the core.

"They're all lost, sir. Already." The voice came over the comms.

"They didn't even last a few minutes. What the hell?" The Admiral's face showed great determination, but inside his heart sank. Twelve lives, snuffed out in moments, and the precious fighters with them. He couldn't know that each cloned enemy pilot had the mighty and fearsome halithstord enhancing their abilities.

"Gather the Elders. I'll head down now. We'll have to hold them off while the troops and the core get the hell out of here. Lockdown defences. Ready the sentry guns. This is gonna get hot."

The Admiral ran out of the control room and down the corridor to the Elders' meeting point. That was where their weapons and armour were stowed.

Alex saw him along the way. "Admiral, what can I do to help?"

"Nothing. Get out of here, kid," was his sharp response. He didn't even look at the fully armed Sollen as he rushed past him.

Alex turned and followed the Admiral through the base. He was only a few steps behind him when he entered the meeting room. The Elders were already there, most of whom Alex knew from his hunting trip. They all turned to look at him in disbelief.

"What are you doing here, kid?" Jas the well-spoken bearded alien from the hunting trip asked.

"I just thought I could help."

The was a rumble of laughter from the foreboding group as they kitted up.

"Get out of here, son. Live to fight another day."

"I'm not going anywhere... Admiral, I'm staying. You can't make me leave."

"Oh, for crying out loud! You wanna get yourself killed, fine. We ain't holding your hand though, Sollen. We've got business to take care of. This is no game."

"I won't let you down, sir."

The Admiral shook his head. "Can you believe this guy?" he asked to head shakes from the group.

"Yeah, I can actually, Derk. He sounds like you when you were his age," Jas said. The laughter rolled out again.

Quickly, the eight Elders and the Admiral were ready. They stood growling, their war faces on, ready for the coming battle. There was Varget, big and muscley, his skin nearly jet black. He had a beard and a huge, rotating gun strapped across his shoulder.

Tall, pale-skinned, and covered in tattoos stood Nessa, a glowing battle axe in her hand. Her hair was in tight braids of dark blue.

The small purple being Alex had met on the hunting trip was Jarg. He only reached the hip height of the others. He wielded two arm cannons and a string of grenades across his body.

Then there was Jas holding a long, pole-like, tubular weapon.

Two large and gangly twins with long spindly bodies were covered in short and spikey hair. They both had small rotating cannons attached to either side of their helmets and a long blade down each leg.

Finally, the newest members of the Elders, two human looking women, one with a plasma sword and one with a whip attached to her wrist where her hand should have been. Jax and Nik, having recently joined with the Mercenaries, were ready for battle.

Sollen was dwarfed by his new comrades, maybe not in stature but certainly in presence. He was humbled to be in their number, but now he started to feel fear again. He knew a bloody battle was on the horizon.

The fearsome group headed out into the corridors as the first explosions of an arial bombardment began shaking the base like an earthquake.

"The base is nearly evacuated, sir. But we need more time to load the core," a young officer bleated as the Elders rushed by.

"Do what you need to do. Get it airborne, and get the hell outta here, son."

"Yes, sir!" The young officer ran back down the corridor.

"We need to buy them some time. I just hope the fighters don't rip them apart when they take off."

"No, it'll be okay. They won't risk damaging the core," Alex said from inside Sollen.

"And how could you know that, kid?"

"Erm, I dunno. I just do."

"Well, I hope you're right because if that thing blows, it'll take all of us with it."

For now, that was out of their control. They had a job to do. The Elders streamed up the corridor and to the doors. They spread out, encircling the landing pad. This was the only place where the three shuttle craft could safely land. The Admiral had chosen that location for their base for a very good reason.

Unlike his shipmates, the Spy was afraid. The fire from the sentry guns below grazed the shuttle constantly, rattling it and testing its structure. With no windows, he couldn't see anything outside the craft, but he could tell they were surrounded by heavy fire. All he could do was try and survive, and at that moment, helplessly strapped to a seat, it seemed his fate was not in his own hands. He could only hope he would get his feet on solid ground again soon.

"*We need to get away from here.*" Although it had remained silent for what seemed an age, The Fleck's voice finally spoke within the Spy.

"*Where have you been?*"

"*The Fleck has been here. The Fleck is always here. We must join up with the other.*"

"*The what? Why don't you ever make sense?*"

"*Maybe you are simply a fool, Asu. The Fleck does not have to explain anything to you.*"

"*Yeah, got it. You've told me a million times. Look, just tell me what I must do, okay?*"

"*The other is another entity hosting The Fleck. He is upon this asteroid. We can free ourselves from this army now. The Fleck knows where the ice planet is. The Fleck knows where the child is. We must return there with an army. We must destroy them.*"

At last, the Spy had a purpose. Up until then, he had merely been a passenger while everything happened around him. He clenched his jaw, clutched his weapon tightly, and readied himself for the battle that lay ahead, should they make it to the ground.

The Elders had taken up positions, under cover from the incoming fire from the shuttle craft and fighters skimming the base from above. The looming craft were now set for landing on the pad. The first started to descend and in seconds was blown apart by the defensive guns below. Molten hot debris rained down as the craft tilted onto its side and exploded in a blinding fireball on the base. Now the landing pad was far more treacherous. Jagged, skewed metal scattered around haphazardly, and mini fires were blazing all around.

"Those shuttles are not designed to carry many soldiers. They're mainly for cargo. I would guess only ten to twelve in each," Farg's voice came over the communication system.

The first shuttle certainly had no survivors. Nothing could have made it out of that fireball. That meant there were maybe twenty or so soldiers to take down. The Admiral smirked. With he and the mighty Elders facing so few foes, they could finish them quickly.

"Sollen, stay close," the Admiral told him.

Now Alex was trembling in fear, asking himself what he was thinking. The truth was he was compelled to stay, without thought or, it seemed, free will. He simply had to fight. He felt like he belonged there, as though there was an important reason he had to be.

The first shuttle rattled in and touched down on the landing pad. A few seconds went by, and the doors opened. The Elders opened fire, ripping into the clone soldiers, taking down the first two in a blinding volley of weaponry from every angle. The rest burst through, taking cover and returning fire as they did. The wreckage of the other shuttle provided plenty of places to hide. They were quick and almost impossible to shoot. The clone soldiers were momentarily pinned down by the Elders' fire.

Alex poked his head up, took aim, and fired from his side arm. The shot flashed and exploded into the nearest clone soldier's chest. It was sent flying backwards, leaving it blackened and dazed. What would have been a deadly shot against most foes hardly affected the clone. With the strength of the halithstord protecting it and feeding it, the soldier staggered back to its feet.

"What the hell?" Alex said.

Now the clones opened fire as one, pinning down the Elders while the second shuttle craft came in to land.

The Spy awaited his moment. The shuttle rumbled and vibrated all the way, but gladly it touched down on the landing pad. As the doors opened, the Spy positioned himself to be last out. That would give him the most chance to survive. One at a time the clone soldiers marched forward with their weapons blazing.

One of them was lit up with return fire, hitting the ground dead. The others spread out, ducking behind cover as they did. The Spy remained onboard the shuttle for a few moments longer.

That was when the child's voice leapt, uninvited, into his mind. *"Disembark now!"*

The Spy didn't move.

"You still have free will. How can this be?"

The child blocked the Spy's mind and issued orders to kill the traitor in their midst. He was completely oblivious to the communication. The Fleck within pushed him forward before the clone soldiers even faced him. He charged through the door, shooting his rifle rapidly and expertly, blazing fire, scorching the flesh of those that opposed him. The halithstord was pleased with its host. The Spy instantly killed three clones, cooking their flesh with plasma, then ran diving behind cover.

"Looks like we have a rogue, people," the Admiral addressed his army. "This could get interesting. Hold your fire on the rogue. Repeat, do not shoot the rogue."

"Wow, they're tough, man!" Sollen yelled to be heard above the noise.

"Just concentrate, son. Do your job. Don't let up for a second. And keep your head down."

The Spy started working his way round, keeping tight behind his cover, taking out any of the clones that came into his sights. His expert aim dropped the clones in an instant. Many had fallen to his might.

The Elders had little success in taking down their enemies. Each clone's strength was fuelled by the symbiote that bristled within, yearning for blood. Each one, a being designed to fight, was tough and deadly. They were void of fear, and they hardly noticed pain. There was an endless stream of plasma fire and grenades exploding, raining sparks around the Elders. It was all they could do to stay alive, let alone win the battle.

An explosion boomed. Borgas, the male twin, slumped to the ground, a huge chunk of his helmet gone. He was dead in an instant. His sister roared wildly with tears in her eyes, tearing towards her stricken brother. It was too late to save him. If the explosion hadn't killed him, the vacuum of space would have on that rock with no atmosphere.

Kell crouched beside him for a moment. "Borg." She grabbed his hand. "I'll avenge you, brother. I will kill them all. I will kill them all!"

Like a wild beast, she flew forward, weapons blazing, towards the clones. She came from behind her cover, drawing her blades and charging towards the crowd of enemies. Two of the soldiers saw her coming and rushed right at her. She slashed at them with her deadly weapons, roaring with wild fury as she did. She fought them blade upon blade, finally running one of her attackers through.

She fought bravely and well, but she had no chance against the powerful soldiers. A shot went off behind her followed by a hail of weapon fire. The deadly plasma lapped at her armour like waves, burning the flesh below as she screamed in pain. She fell to the ground.

The Elders reeled at the sight of their friends being slayed so mercilessly. The twins had been fighting by their side for many years, but now, those comrades in arms and friends were lost. The inseparable twins would have wanted to die together, which was the only comfort. The pain of one of them living without the other would be too much for either of them to bear.

There was no time to grieve their losses; this battle was far from over. The clone soldiers were unnaturally tough, fast, and deadly. They would never quit their assault until the very last one was dead or they had the core. They didn't care for their own lives, only for the prize they had come to claim.

While one of the clones was distracted in the midst of the fight, the Spy swooped silently and quickly towards it. The Admiral and Sollen poured plasma upon it, pinning it in place. The Spy waited, coiled like a spring, ready to explode. He launched himself, pouncing like a cat. He grabbed the soldier from behind, taking its head in his hands, and twisted his body. There was a fearsome *crack,* and the clone soldier fell limp to the ground.

The Spy rolled and ducked behind the shuttle craft as a volley of weapon fire lit the night. Metal turned molten with the heat, and the clone soldiers encircled the shuttle. They wanted the traitor's life even more than the Elders.

The Admiral issued his orders. "Close in while they're distracted."

Each warrior burst forward, coming out from behind their cover, closing in on the clones. They opened fire, working together, concentrating their plasma on a single target at a time. Slowly the clones were cut down.

Some turned their attention back to the Elders and rushed zigzagging towards them. Now only feet away, they ducked and dived to avoid the barrage coming their way.

Soon, one of them reached Jas. His tubular weapon shot jagged plasma spears from either end, but even that didn't stop the charge. The clone stood facing the warrior. Jas' weapon glowed and sparked as the clone drew a blade. Now Jas was in his element—hand-to-hand combat. He twirled his weapon menacingly around his body. Two fiery spikes burned at either end of the pole and glowed brightly.

They clashed, weapon against weapon. Jas flowed in beautiful symmetry, gracefully and quickly, yet his enemy blocked each of his blows easily. The soldier seemed to always to be one step ahead. It was like it knew what Jas would do before even he did. Never had he fought a being with the speed and strength of this enemy. The clone kicked out like a flash, knocking the warrior flying. Before he had even hit the ground, the clone was over him, blade flashing. The blade came down sharply with a woosh. Jas closed his eyes.

There was a flash and a spark followed by a mighty crack. Nik bounded towards Jas. The blade was forced flying from the clone's hand, as were its fingers. Then, with a fizz, Jax jumped through the air, swiping her blade, removing the clone's head from its body. It fell lifeless to the floor.

She offered her hand to help Jas back to his feet as he thanked them for their assistance.

The Spy with his blazing fire was taking down the clones with relative ease, unlike the Elders. He had all the strengths of the soldiers but not their inexperience. He was well-trained. He had fought countless battles in the past. Now that he was within this clone's powerful body, the others were no match for him. They were fuelled only by instinct and rage. He worked his way along, meeting each foe in battle and taking their lives. They were lives that these empty vessels wouldn't even miss.

The Admiral, with Sollen in tow, moved gradually forward. They covered each other as they went. There was a clone behind cover ahead. It poked out its head, unleashed from its weapon, and sent the onrushing mercenaries sprawling. The Admiral singled for Alex to go left, while he would go right to surround their foe.

Alex had managed to calm his trembling hands but could do little to slow his thundering heart. He was lost in the heat of battle. Nothing else mattered; he was as present as he had ever been.

He took one last breath and came out from his cover. Almost like it was telepathic, they moved at the same time. They rushed towards the clone, first firing and then drawing blades. The clone dropped to its knees as its flesh was cooked by the white-hot plasma. Alex reached it first and thrust his blade through the clone's chest. It roared as it sat bolt upright, clutching the blade. Alex placed a foot on the clone's chest and ripped the blade from its flesh. The soldier fell onto its back.

The Admiral reached Alex with a smirk on his face. "Well done, Sollen!"

A shot went off behind the Admiral, grazing his helmet. He spun around, weapon ready to take down his foe. Behind him, the stricken clone soldier reached out a trembling arm and pulled a grenade from its belt. With its life force fading fast, it didn't have the strength to throw it. It bounced and rolled gently towards the distracted Admiral.

Alex heard the metal hit the ground and looked down. Without thought, he sprinted towards it and launched himself forward. He flew through the air, opening out his body, and landed on top of the grenade. For a lingering second, he awaited his fate, then the explosion boomed out, ripping his host's body apart.

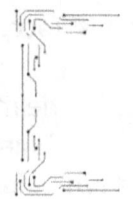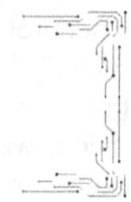

Dreaming

"Do you remember?"

"No, I can't remember. I can't remember your voice. I can't remember your face. They're gone. You're gone."

"I'm here. This *is* my voice. Open your eyes, and you'll see me again."

"I can't. It'll break me again. I just can't break any more."

"Open your eyes, Penny. It's me. I'm here."

"Oh, please don't do this to me. You're not real. You're not here."

"If you don't open your eyes, you'll never know if it's real or not."

"I'm afraid."

"Don't be afraid, Tiger. It's me."

Her heart skipped with the words. She gasped and opened her eyes. Her soul glowed as her gaze fell upon the face of her beloved friend. She touched his face, half expecting him to burst like a bubble and be gone. But he was there. She could feel his skin. She threw her arms around his neck. He squeezed her back. That was when her soul melted from her eyes. Tears fell— jumbled tears. They were tears of disbelief, tears of joy, and mostly, tears of grief.

"Shh," Liam whispered into her ear as he gently rubbed her back.

"It is you. It *is* you." She sniffed. "Are you here? It can't be."

"I'm here. You can feel me, can't you?"

"Yes, yes, I can. I still just can't believe."

"Don't waste this time with disbelief, Penny. Just accept it for the moment it is. I miss you so much."

Penny nodded, scrunching her face up like she was about to burst from emotion. More tears flowed freely from her eyes and rolled down her cheeks. "I miss you. I hate this world without you."

"No, no. You have so much more to do in this life. Your time is just beginning."

"How could you do this? How could you leave me? Was I so bad? Such a bad friend?"

"You're the best friend anyone could ever have. I love you. It wasn't like that. It wasn't me. I would never leave you." Now it was his turn to weep. He took her trembling hands in his. "I didn't take my own life, I swear. It was the thing inside me."

"The Fleck!"

He didn't respond. He didn't need to. They both knew the truth.

"Why have you come here?"

"I have a message. You will soon have an important task. One that you must complete."

"What task? What are you talking about?"

"You're asking questions that I don't have the answer to. I came to tell you that nothing that happens is a coincidence. Remember, everything is connected." His form started to fade from her vision.

"Wait, Liam... Wait. Don't leave." She reached out her hands to touch him again, but like smoke drifting away, he was gone.

Penny awoke, emotional and confused. She wasn't sure. Was it a dream? Was it real? Did it even matter? In part, her heart was just as broken as it was before, but in part, somewhere inside, she felt hope. It was like the truth was embedded deep in her soul. Liam's consciousness was still alive. What she didn't understand was if he was out in the cosmos or somewhere within her. Like her best friend had told her with his final words, "Everything's connected."

Awakenings Part III

He jerked awake, heart thudding, immediately putting his hands up to his sweat-soaked face. Alex took a moment to gather his thoughts. He peered at the ceiling through his fingers. He was in his room, in his bed, and he was human again. His heart sank at the realisation that it was only a dream. He was disappointed. For a time, he felt as though he had a purpose, and now here he was, back in his life. The worst thing of all was he was back under the cloud of depression that had become his home. He tried desperately to capture those memories, tried to hang onto them, but for the most part they had drifted away to nothing. It was like there was a haze in the distance.

He threw the blankets off almost angrily and staggered to the sink. He washed his face in the freezing water. He came over slightly dizzy, then he zoned out. He felt like someone was watching him. He tried to shake the feeling, but still it lingered, somewhere, like a shadow in the background. There were echoing whispers, swirling, coming in waves, somewhere in the recesses of his being. He washed his face again. It felt like he hadn't slept at all. He was exhausted.

He looked at the time. He had to go to work, but he decided to call in sick and climbed back into bed. It wasn't really an issue for him as he was self-employed, apart from the fact he would lose a day's wages. He'd just have to suck that up for another week.

In bed, he drifted. Not that he slept, but his mind went floating elsewhere. It zipped back through the misty flashes of the asteroid and the Elders, yet none of the memories were complete. He'd see the Admiral or the others, he saw their faces and heard their voices but never what they were saying. He remembered pointless things, things that had no significance to anything. Maybe a joke that was told, or mundane conversation, or seeing someone walking into the room he was in. His head movie could never quite reach the important things or the battles, although he knew they were there somewhere. He wanted to delve further and deeper but could only ever skirt the edges of them. He huffed with frustration.

"Alex."

The voice came from nowhere, within his mind. Never before had he heard it, but still, it felt so familiar. He didn't answer, just opened his eyes. There was no one there. There was no way anyone could get into his room, but how he hoped someone had. That would have been far better than a disembodied voice in his head.

He ignored it and refused to answer. He attempted talking himself silently down in his mind. *It's not a thing. I'm not crazy. Don't answer.*

"You can't ignore. The Fleck is still here."

Alex jumped out of bed and walked, thudding circles around his room. The whole time, The Fleck within made its presence known. Occasionally it would speak, but mostly it lingered.

Alex quickly got dressed and walked out the door. He rushed down the stairs and out onto the street. He had no idea where he was going; he just started moving. Through the crowded morning streets, he rushed and echoed down the stairs onto the tube station. He jumped on the train, with no reasoning behind his choices. He sat, people packed tightly around him, but still The Fleck always watched.

Did this thing compel his actions? He floated without thought, drifting down a stream to who knows where. Perhaps The Fleck drove him on. He didn't know where he was going, but Alex knew one thing for sure. This path would lead towards his fate.

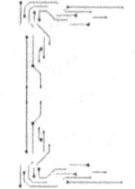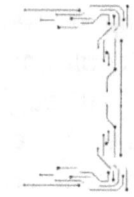

The "Prisoner"

"Man, he was just a kid. I never should have let him stay. Sollen's blood is on my hands." Despite how many times before the Admiral had lost soldiers—so many times he could hardly count—this one hit him harder than most. Each fallen warrior under his command had left an invisible scar upon his heart, but this one seemed to leave a gaping wound.

"He did what he chose to do with his own free will. It is not your fault." Jas was his oldest friend and by far the wisest of any of his warriors, with his species' extended lifespan. His friend offered his council. "He was brave and keen. He sacrificed his own life for yours. It wasn't your fault, Derk."

"Yeah, well, I keep telling myself that, but I'm not sure I'm convincing myself. That grenade had my name on it. It would have blown me apart. He saved my life out there, of that there is no doubt." He paused for a second as rage bubbled up inside him. "And I had to leave him on that rock! I couldn't even give him or the twins a proper burial. They deserved at least that."

"They fell, as many of our brothers and sisters did. Sometimes they die in the dirt like animals. We all know this our reality. It is the warrior's way. He was destined to sacrifice himself for you, that was his and your fate. That was the part he was meant to play in this tale."

"I'll be okay, just this one stings. The twins, Jas. I thought they could take on anyone, and that poor kid. That core has cost us much. We have to make sure they did not die in vain." He did his best to shake the thoughts out of his mind before he went on. "The core is safe. That's the main thing. Without that, we'd be out in the cold."

"Sure thing. They took some heavy losses out there, but the fleet is heading for the rendezvous."

"Very good, Jas, very good."

The Elders lingered uncomfortably. The loss of their comrades left the atmosphere strange, each of them in deep contemplation. It was a savage reminder of not only the challenges they faced but their own mortality. Any one of them could have been left on the asteroid.

The Admiral broke the momentary silence. "So, I think we need to chat, people. What the hell were those things? Thoughts?"

"They appeared to be clones. They were identical," Jas pointed out.

"Quick, strong, super hard to kill," Nik said.

"I dunno, that one's head seemed to come off pretty easy," Jax joked.

The Admiral gave a half-hearted laugh. "Their heads come off, which is good, but hard to kill is right. There's something more about these things. We need to be very careful. If it hadn't been for the prisoner, we probably wouldn't have made it off that rock either. Why do you think it went rogue?"

"I don't know. Something strange is going on," Jas offered.

"Well, we have him as a prisoner, so we must interrogate him."

"To be clear, Derk, he gave himself up. He's a victory or death kinda guy from first impressions."

"I know. Just bring him in here. And I want all the Elders here. If he tries anything, we'll need to take him down quick. He'll rip this ship apart."

"He won't do anything here and now. He could have killed us and taken the ship back on the asteroid if that was his intention. Somewhere there was cover and more weapons. Now he's unarmed and shackled. He will not strike now."

"You're assuming he's not insane, my friend, and there is logic to his actions."

"I have a feeling that isn't the case, Derk."

"Yeah, I know. That infinite cosmic wisdom of yours again."

"It's never let me down," Jas said.

"It's never let *me* down, either, as it happens."

The foreboding figure of the Spy flanked by Jax, Nik, Farg, Varget, and Nessa made his way to stand before the Admiral.

"I will ask questions. You will answer, or it's gonna hurt real bad. That's the way it is. Nod if you understand."

"Oh, awesome! I might get to torture him," Nik whispered to Jax, jabbing her with her elbow just loud enough for the prisoner to hear.

The Spy nodded his head.

"Who are you?"

The clone warrior tried to answer, but this creature could only make a series of mumbles. He tried again, straining, but only made incoherent sounds. The body he was within had clearly never spoken before. He couldn't be entirely sure if it even was capable of speaking.

"I don't really understand, if I'm honest." The Admiral lingered on it, like he thought the Spy was stupid.

Again, the Spy returned nothing but strained tones. He was frustrated. He was desperate to speak. He had a lot to say.

The group of Elders, weapons trained upon their captive, were blank-faced or shaking their heads with looks of confusion.

The Spy had to do something lest he be tortured by a worryingly eager Nik. So, he nodded his head towards the computer screen behind them.

Nearly all the Elders turned to see what he was signalling towards, apart from Nik. Her eyes never came off the Spy, and she had a cold smirk on her face.

"The computer?"

The Spy nodded enthusiastically.

"You want to write?"

He nodded again, even more enthusiastically than before.

"Right, let him use the keypad. Jax, undo his restraints. Nessa, stand behind him with your blade across his throat. If he moves, he'll kill himself." The Admiral looked at the prisoner, deadpan in his eyes, and rasped, "You can live, or you can die, it's up to you. You understand?"

He nodded once more, and with that, the Admiral gestured with his hand for his orders to be carried out.

"*I'm a spy. My name is Asu. I infiltrated The Sect, and then somehow ended up inside this clone. They put something inside me and the rest of the clones, hundreds of them. A symbiote. I need help. Please.*" He stopped typing.

There was a gasp from Jax. "Erm, this is bad. Really bad."

Nik looked at her, "Like Daze?"

"It sounds like it."

"Okay, now you wanna share it with the group or shall we leave the room so you can have some privacy?" the Admiral joked.

"Oh, yeah, sure," Jax said. "Well, I'll try. Our friend Daze, she had one of these symbiotes before she died. Man, it turned her into a badass. Like, she was fearsome. Before she was a warrior, after she was like a super soldier."

"Yeah, that *does* sound bad. That makes more sense. I thought the smugglers were coming to take the core back and these super soldiers showed up."

The sound of buttons tapping began again as the Spy had more to add. He sat sweating with the sharp axe blade pressed into his flesh. "*The army was controlled by a child. They get inside your mind and issue orders telepathically. The child wants the core. For what, I do not know.*"

"Well, kid ain't getting hands on my core. I have the buyer lined up already."

"Derk," Nik said, "we've met this child. They are powerful. Really powerful. We're in big trouble here."

"*The child has many resources. They will come again. They will never stop,*" the Spy added.

"Jas, do you think we can trust him?"

"I do, sir. I do."

"Nessa, take your blade away."

She pulled back her axe blade, twirled it around her finger, and slotted in tidily in the holster on the leg. She took a step back.

"Can't we sell the core to the kid?" Varget's voice boomed through his enormous chest.

The Spy shook his head. *"No, that child is dangerous! They can never get their hands on the core. We should hide it or destroy it!"*

"Not gonna happen, my friend. We'll be taking it to my buyer. No one can stop us. This thing has cost us lives."

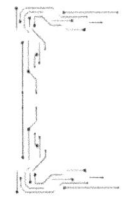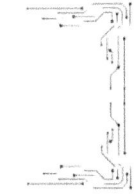

Chance Meeting?

Penny floated through the day, still trying to make sense of her dream. She went to university, but she was on autopilot for the most part. She hardly interacted with those around her. Silent, she stayed in the background for now. Life just whirred along around her. There was the buzz of humanity, but she didn't notice. It was like the whole world lived inside her head.

She finished her day not a moment too soon and headed out onto the cold streets. Shivering in her overcoat, she yawned, half asleep after her restless night.

The coffee shop looked warm and welcoming even though she didn't normally drink coffee that late in the evening. She went inside and grabbed a seat, intentionally avoiding the table where she and Liam normally sat. She ordered a coffee, and when it finally arrived, she sat hugging the cup in her hands. Penny half smiled. It was nice to be warm for a while. She held the cup up to her face and breathed the steam while closing her eyes.

"This seat taken?"

"Huh?" She opened her eyes.

"Is anyone sitting here?"

She looked up at the tall young man, then looked around the cafe. There were plenty of empty tables. "Well, no. But I'd rather be alone, thanks."

"Oh, I thought some company would be nice."

"Look, I'm married, okay? I'm not interested."

"What? No way, mate. You wish. You're way too old for me."

Penny laughed and did a half-offended huff. "Are you saying I'm old?"

"Nah, I'm not saying you're old. I'm saying you're too old for me is all."

She rolled her eyes. He had a certain boyish charm about him. "What do you want then?"

"Just a chit chat. Nothing else. What do ya say?"

"Oh, okay. God." She shook her head smiling. "You have to buy the coffee though, okay?"

"Deal."

He sat across from her and held out his hand to shake hers. She took it. He smiled as he gently shook it. "I'm Alex."

"Penny." She smiled back. "Well, Alex, if you're not trying to hit on my old ass, what do ya want?'

"Cappuccino, I think, and one of them sandwiches."

"That wasn't what I meant." She laughed.

"Do you want a sandwich or a muffin or something?"

"You're insufferable. You know what, yeah. I'll have a sandwich. They're good in here."

Alex took a huge bite of the sandwich he hadn't been able to resist and chewed. "Is it true then?"

"Is what true?"

"Are you married?"

"Erm, no." She glowed slightly. "I haven't even been on a date for a while." She didn't highlight the fact it had been two years.

"That's weird."

"Why?"

"You're pretty hot for an old lady."

"Oh, my God! You're the worst." She laughed again. "But thanks, I think."

"You're welcome." He smiled cheekily. "Wow! Those sandwiches *are* good."

"Erm..." Penny smirked and pointed to her chin. "You have some breadcrumbs in your beard."

"I do? Oh, yeah, I'm saving that bit for later," he said brushing it away.

She giggled again.

Alex and Penny chatted for an hour; all the time he had the nagging feeling he had things to tell her. He didn't know who she was, but he knew she was the one he needed to find. He couldn't very well start telling her all the things that had been happening to him and sound like he'd lost his last shred of sanity. He decided it would be best to befriend her and win her trust.

This was not some devious underlying plot to manipulate her. Far from it. He liked her and wanted to be friends with her. If anything, he felt like they were friends from the moment they had met. Their personalities clearly fitted well, and they made each other laugh.

"So, I gotta hit the road. This has been fun, though," Alex finally said. "Can I give you a lift somewhere?"

"Oh, it would beat the cold ass bus stop. Could you?"

"Yeah, sure, but first we have to walk to the cold ass bus stop."

"You're such a clown. I'll be fine, thanks. Anyway, hadn't you better get in on a school night, kiddo?" She pretended to look at her watch that didn't exist. "Oh, yep, it's past your nun nighs."

They both burst into laughter.

"Here, gimme your number. I wanna meet up again... I mean, if you do?" Alex was a little shyer about the question than he had been the rest of the time, fearing rejection.

"Sure. I like you, kid." She smirked pulling out her phone. "What's yours?"

He gave her the number, and she sent him a missed call so he could save hers. Then the new friends went their separate ways.

Humans Don't Work Like That

The Fleck bristled inside Alex. It was fiery, angry, and he could feel it. It didn't speak in words. It could communicate in many ways. He watched the stations come and go on his long journey home.

He was brooding. The negative energy built up inside him despite the joyous time he'd had that evening. It was The Fleck's rage, infecting his mind, his energy, and his very soul. He remembered the fun he'd had with Penny. He wanted to smile, but the smile wouldn't come out. It was like it was locked inside him.

His back finally hit the mattress. At last, he'd made it all the way to the bedsit, and he lay there in the dark. He closed his eyes, and he became aware of nothing but the presence that lurked in his being.

He had no idea why, but he blurted out, "What is wrong with you? Get out of my head!" The tone was sharp and filled with annoyance. So much of Alex hoped that the voice wouldn't answer, that his words were wasted on an illusion, but the voice did.

"What are you doing?" The Fleck snarled menacingly. "I told you to tell her. She was the one."

"I know! I don't know what you want from me."

"The Fleck wants nothing. The Fleck must do what must be done. You must do what must be done. That is all that matters."

"I know, okay? For some reason, I know."

"Then why did you not do what was required?"

"It wasn't the right time. It doesn't work that way."

"There is not much time. We need the human to help us. You should have spoken to her. Tell her you know of The Fleck. She will help you."

"Look, dude, I can't just go up to someone and blurt a load of crazy assed stuff to them when we've just met. She'd think I'm some kind of psycho or something and run a mile. Humans just don't work like that."

"*Time is limited. We cannot delay.*"

"Maybe not, but she would never have given me her number, and I would never see her again. It's that simple. Let me take care of the human stuff, yeah."

"*You have earned that from us. You have done well so far. But do not delay too long.*"

"All right. Give me a week."

"*A week we can afford. No longer than that. Do you understand?*"

"Yeah, I understand."

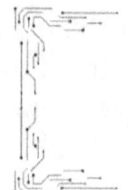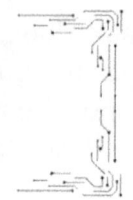

Out of Touch

"I think I made a new friend yesterday," Penny informed her dad after he'd once again given her the benefit of his amazing cooking.

"That's awesome."

"Yeah, he's—"

"'He,' woot woo."

"Oh, stop it. It's not like that. He's only young, like nineteen or something. I just met him in the café."

"That sounds cool."

"Yeah, I dunno. When I was with him, we laughed so much. I actually forgot my woes for a little while."

"Well, don't worry, your woes will always be there waiting for you."

Penny giggled. "Won't they just?"

Her dad looked at her inquisitively. "Just friends?"

"Yes, just friends, for crying out loud! He called me old."

Danny chuckled. "Oh, I always make friends with people that call me old on our first meeting, too."

"Nah, not like that. He's funny and nice. I enjoyed hanging with him. I could use some friends since…" She drifted off for a second, but before she even said the words, she stopped herself with a huge sigh.

"You're gonna hang out again then?"

"I hope so. I think so. We have each other's numbers. I'll wait for him to message me."

"Why don't you message him?"

"Don't be silly. You don't know how anything works these days, do you?"

"Right, got it. I'm out of touch."

"You never texted anyone when you were my age. You never even had mobile phones."

He feigned shock with an over exaggerated gasp. "How very dare you! We did have phones, I'll have you know. When I was about your age. They were as heavy as a brick, couldn't fit in your pocket, you could never get reception, and certainly no camera or fancy pants text messages like these newfangled gadgets you kids are so fond of."

"Yep, that's it. Confirmation. You really are out of touch, you crusty old geezer." She laughed a belly laugh.

"I am not crusty."

"So, you admit you're an old geezer then?"

"Yes, of course. Just not a crusty one." It was his turn to belly laugh for a moment. "I'm glad you made a friend, Pen Pen. That really is awesome. I'm pleased for ya. You deserve some good things."

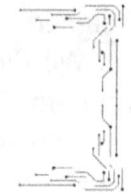

Finding a Voice

"I've done it!" Jax said excitedly as she rushed to the bridge.

"What have you done?"

"Nurilinked a voice program so it should be able to translate his thoughts into words. Now he can speak."

"Great work! Hook it up and bring him to me right away. I'm still not sure what he's up to. Something doesn't sit right. Be careful. Take Nik and Farg with you, and if he tries anything, well, you know the drill."

"It's a relief to finally be able to articulate my thoughts. Thank you." The Spy bowed his head humbly towards Jax.

She nodded back.

"Admiral, the child must not obtain the core. The clone army is fearsome and huge. We cannot stop them. It seems they have almost unlimited resources and power that we do not understand. *Ass!*"

Jax tittered with laughter.

"What did you say?" The Admiral's face scrunched with concern.

"I apologise. I don't really know what happened. *Big butts!*"

Jax and Nik giggled like schoolgirls.

"I don't know why, but... *Boobs! Poopy pants!*"

Now Jax and Nik doubled in two.

"Jax, what the hell is happening here?" the Admiral asked sternly.

"I'm sorry, Admiral. There must be some kind of glitch in the program. I'll take a look and get it fixed up right away."

"See that you do."

The Elders all started to laugh as one, and even the Admiral chuckled.

"You *so* did that on purpose," Nik whispered.

"Maybe." She flashed a devilish look towards her friend.

"Man, you're funny!"

"The glitch is fixed now, Admiral." Jax still had a glint in her eye.

He shook his head. "You certainly keep the spirits up around here."

"I do my best." She gave an exaggerated bow with a huge smirk on her face.

"He's not gonna say anything ridiculous now, is he?"

"Well, no guarantees on that, sir. He could be crazy. He can say crazy things, but it won't be because of the program."

"Bring him in."

The Spy was marched into the room, once again with the Elders either side of him. It was true that they had to keep their wits about them.

"So, tell me what is happening, soldier?"

"The child's army is coming for the core. We need to get it away from here, to hide it. You, you are mighty warriors, but you are nothing compared to this army."

"We dealt with them at the base," the Admiral argued.

"If it wasn't for me, you would all be dead."

"We had a few more tricks up our sleeve, my friend," the Admiral growled in defiance. "The core will go to my buyer. The plan will not and cannot change."

"Don't be a fool! You have no idea what you are doing. You won't even reach the buyer. We will all be dead, and then no one can stop them. We need to get to the ice planet. Now."

"This isn't our fight."

"With all due respect, it is now, Admiral."

"Why the ice planet? Didn't you tell us that's where his army is?"

"The army is there, that is true, but so are the symbiotes. Many, many of them. Our only chance is for your warriors to pair with them. We can sneak in quietly if there are only a few of us."

"No way. Those things are gross," Nik said.

"Asu, the buyer expects us. We cannot cancel the deal. Bigger things are at play here."

"Sir!" The Spy grew angry. "There will be no deal. There will be no payment. There will be no delivery. There will be nothing but death. Do you think the child will stop there? Do you think they've created an army of super soldiers for fun? The core will take them across the galaxy, conquering as they go. They will be unstoppable."

The Admiral rubbed his bearded chin with a look of concern. "Leave us, Asu. I need to speak to my warriors."

"How the hell did we end up in this situation?" The Admiral scoured the faces around him.

"I know, right?" Nessa joked. "You can't even steal powerful technology nowadays without someone getting upset."

"Well, it may be our fault." Nik indicated Jax next to her with her hand. "I mean, honestly, this is pretty typical of our lives. This stuff happens to us *all* the time."

There was a titter around the room. Laugher there may have been, but each warrior there was deeply concerned. They knew this was a bad situation and one in which now, for whatever reason, they were stuck.

Jas was next to speak in a more serious tone. "We should stash the core and head to the ice planet."

"What about the buyer?" the Admiral replied. "They've been waiting for delivery."

"The delivery will not arrive. I see darkness in the future. I see blood. I see death."

"It won't be long before we'll reach the fleet at the rendezvous. We can regroup there."

"No, Derk. The child can track the prisoner. They telepathically communicate. They know where we are. They are coming. We can only hope they don't know our intention."

"So, we turn and leave the fleet. The child doesn't know where the rendezvous is. There is an escape craft. Jas, Varget, take the craft, reach the fleet. Lead the infantry and the core to the buyer. I need someone I can trust. The buyer will be able to protect it better than we can. You know where to go?"

"Yes, sir," they said in unison.

"Say hello to old Tarvil for me. Good luck."

They wished them good luck and bade their comrades farewell and left the room.

"It would be better to cut Asu loose, but he is the only one who knows where we must go. We must find a way to block the telepathic connection to stand any chance at all. Farg, work with Jax. Make it happen."

The Admiral addressed his warriors. "We must go to the ice planet. I'm sorry. Normally I'd take volunteers for this kind of mission, but we're stuck here. Buckle up, crew. Things are about to get rough."

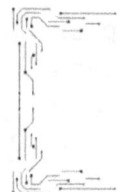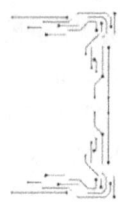

The Confession

"Hi, Penny, it's Alex. I don't know if you remember me... I was wondering if you wanna meet up this weekend for a drink or something?"

He typed, deleted, and retyped the message several times before finally hitting send. It wasn't until the next day Penny responded, by which time he was convinced she'd completely ghosted him. Being ghosted was bad enough in itself, never mind when Alex knew there was so much more to it than normal social issues. This time, there was a lot more at stake than his ego.

"Of course I remember you, silly! Sure, we can go out if you buy the drinks."

"Oh, cool. I thought you'd given it the Patrick Swayze.

"What???"

"Ghosted me! Anyway, why is this friendship becoming so expensive?" Alex added laugh emojis to make sure she knew he was joking.

"I'm high maintenance lol but mainly, I'm a student. I'm broke!!"

"OK... I'll meet you somewhere. That's not my part of town. Where do you wanna go?"

"I'll meet you at the tube station near the cafe, and we'll take it from there."

"OK. Can't wait." He cringed after pressing send. Perhaps he was a bit eager.

Alex saw Penny by the top of the stairs and smiled. She smiled back. Being undecided how to greet her, with a hug or a handshake, he awkwardly chose a fist bump. Little did he know that was always how Liam greeted her. It met her with a twinge of sadness yet, somehow, a comforting familiarity.

"Have you eaten? Do you wanna grab some food first?" he started.

"I could eat."

"So, let's eat. Where's good?"

They walked down the street, making small talk, before he followed her inside a big pub.

"Wow, this place is huge."

"Yep, it's pretty noisy down here, but upstairs there's a restaurant that's quieter. It'll get pretty packed later on."

They settled at a table in the corner and ordered their food and some drinks.

"So, I was wondering, what made you wanna meet up again?" an inquisitive Penny asked.

Alex took a moment to be clear of his answer. "To be honest, I don't really have many friends, and we seemed to get along well. I thought maybe we could be friends, really." Being one who struggled to open up, he was slightly embarrassed. Opening up never did him any good. It only ever made him vulnerable, and people always took advantage of it.

"Yeah, I think I'd like that as long as you don't turn out to be a total douche," she giggled.

"I'll try not to be, but I can't make no promises."

"Any."

"What?"

"I can't make *any* promises."

"Right, not sure I wanna be friends now." It was his turn to give a playful chuckle. "Nah, I'm a street kid, see. You wanna learn to speak proper English, like what I do."

"Oh, my God! You're so silly."

"Hey! I am not... Yeah, all right, I am, but that's the way I like it."

"Me too."

"That was good food. Great shout, Penny."

"Yeah, it's awesome here."

"So, what now? You wanna play some pool or something? I saw some tables downstairs."

"Erm, yeah, sure. I haven't played much, though."

"Well, we'll play for money then. I'm a proper shark."

"You suck at pool. Your pants are totally on fire."

"I said I was a shark, not I was good at pool. You should see me swim."

They laughed hard as they did so often in each other's company.

Penny's eyes lit up. "Oh, wow, look. It's karaoke night. The guy's setting up. Do you think we should?"

"Penny, I'm the worst singer in the world."

"Come on. We'll do a duet."

"I don't know any songs."

"It'll be fun."

She jumped up and grabbed the book. "Look, we can do the one from *Aladdin*, 'A Whole New World.'"

"I don't think…"

"Come on, live a little."

"Okay, they did used to play that movie in the home when I was a kid. I sort of know it."

"You actually *are* the worst singer in the world," Penny confirmed.

"I told ya. That bloke booing was a bit harsh, though."

Penny belly laughed.

"So, you're saying I ain't good at nothin'," he went on.

She laughed again. "No, don't be silly. You must be good at something."

"Guitar. I'm good on the guitar… and I guess I'm pretty good at fighting."

"Well, that's useful, I guess. Can't wait to hear you play."

"Probably won't happen. I'd be too shy. Mostly, I'm a proper survivor, you know?"

"You had it rough growing up?"

"Yeah. Let's just say it wasn't the best. I'm all right though, mate." He paused. "You're a pretty good singer."

"Thanks. I was quite the hairbrush diva when I was a kid. I have many hidden talents, you know."

"I'll bet you do."

"I had such a fun night. I really needed it with all that's been going on. Thanks," Penny said as they wandered the pavement towards the tube station.

"Tell her." The Fleck's voice echoed around Alex's mind.

"Me too. It was awesome. Have things been rough lately? Are you okay?"

"Oh." She paused. "My bestie passed away recently."

"Oh, that's just awful. I'm sorry, mate. I can't even imagine. I don't even know what to say to that."

"Nothing you can say."

"I guess not. You wanna talk about it?"

"I don't think so. I just want to enjoy myself for the first time in ages."

He put an arm round her shoulder and gave her little squeeze. "You don't have to talk about it if you don't wanna. You know you can, though, right?"

"Tell her."

"Sure, thanks. I appreciate it."

"Anytime, my friend."

"I'm busy next week, but we can meet up at the weekend if you want to?" Penny asked.

"Tell her!"

"Yeah, sure." Alex couldn't avoid the voice any longer. "Penny, can I talk to you about something?"

"Sure."

"Erm, I don't really know what to say."

"Come on, you can tell me."

"Well, here goes. You know when I met you in the café? That wasn't an accident. I *had* to find you. For reasons I don't know."

"What?" Penny's heart sank. It seemed he was some creep after all. Now she dreaded the words that would follow.

"I had to find you. It was important."

"You've been stalking me?" She started to feel unnerved, quickly morphing towards fear.

"No, no, nothing like that."

"That's what it sounds like to me!" She was firm and raised her voice. If he was going try anything, she'd make damn sure he had an audience.

"You don't understand. Lemme explain. We were meant to meet. We have to do something together. It's like, fate or something." He was flustered, only making everything worse, digging that hole ever deeper.

"You know what? I'm not doing anything with you. We're done, got it? I don't feel comfortable around you anymore." She was boiling inside, and now wary. She didn't feel safe. She needed to get out of there. "I'm going."

She turned to walk in the opposite direction.

"Stop her!"

Alex reached and grabbed her arm. "No, wait. It's not…"

Penny raised her voice. "Let go of me, or I swear to God, I'll scream!"

Alex looked around. People on the busy street were already starting to take notice of the altercation. She tugged her arm away from him. He retracted his, letting go as he did.

Penny started to walk fast at first, then broke into a run. Alex watched her vanish amongst the crowd with a look of desperation and anguish upon his face. He put his head in his hands and let out a frustrated roar. He thudded his palm onto his forehead several times, hard, rattling his brain. Turning with a huff, he stomped for the tube.

Self-Hatred

Alex took the endless trains once again across the city, brooding. He didn't look at his phone; he stared out the window. Occasionally he'd see his reflection in the glass and burn. The hatred he felt for himself, the utter distain. Once again, he'd got it wrong. Once again, he'd messed up another human connection. He swore to himself, as he had done a million times, that he was done with people. He only ever blew relationships apart. He was destined to be alone. This fool, sitting on the train, was hating and raging at his own stupidity, as well as his own reflection.

The whole time The Fleck bristled. It was angry, too. Alex could feel it. It was as though it took his emotions in its jagged black fingers and pulled, manipulating them.

Alex finally arrived home at around one in the morning. In a huff, he sat on the bed. He sat in silence listening to his breath, going over and over the things he'd said earlier that night. Now, in hindsight, he could have said it better, done a better job, and not come off like some stalker or weirdo. He regretted grabbing her. He could feel her hand tremble; he could tell she was scared. Someone he'd hate to ever upset or scare, and he'd managed both in about two minutes. He felt like a fool. He almost wanted to cry, but crying had always been a pointless endeavour for him. It never did him any good.

He was upset with himself, but mostly he was upset with The Fleck. It turned out, The Fleck wasn't so happy with him either.

"You failed, useless human."

"Yeah, sure, it's your fault. If you'd just let me handle it instead of banging on inside my head. You know what's worse? I like her. I've lost my new friend now."

"You must contact her again."

"Oh, right! Like she'll ever talk to me again. She thinks I'm a freak. She's probably blocked my phone number by now."

"Find out where she lives."

"Are you serious? She'll have me arrested if I do that. You haven't got a clue. Just leave me alone!"

"The Fleck cannot. We must do what needs to be done. We must find her. You must try and call her."

"Not gonna happen. Just shut up, would ya?"

The Fleck silently smirked. It had ways of persuading that were beyond talking. The Entity within wouldn't speak again.

Alex felt depression nagging at him. He'd had the best time on his adventure as Sollen, only to end up back in his life. Then he had found someone that he loved hanging out with. She was just the kind of friend he needed so badly in his life, only to have her stolen away from him by The Fleck. This was a curse he never asked for and one that he certainly didn't need.

He dwelled in his own darkness until about three AM before he finally drifted off to sleep. That was when a new journey began.

The Rescue

"What is going on?"

"Thanks for picking me up, Dad." Penny's voice was shaking, and she was still trembling from her ordeal.

He unclicked his seat belt so he could give her a hug, a hug which she so needed. She cried a little.

"It's okay, Pen Pen. You're safe now. I got ya."

It took her a while to pull herself together before Danny started to drive her home.

"What happened?"

"I'm sorry. I just got a little freaked."

"You have nothing to apologise for. What did he do? He better not have hurt you. I'll kill him!" This was an unnerving tone that Penny had never heard from her dad before.

"No, he didn't hurt me. He just scared me."

"Why? What happened?"

"We had a great night. Then when we were heading to the tube, he said our meeting in the café wasn't an accident. That he *had* to find me, that we had things to do together. Like he was stalking me or something."

"What the? What a filthy creep. Where can I find him?"

"No, leave it, Dad. I won't see him again."

"How can you know if he's a stalker weirdo?"

"He never really tried to stop me leaving. He grabbed my arm but let go when I told him to. He doesn't know where I live. I just have a feeling it'll be okay."

"Well, anyone ever grabs you again…"

"I know, kick him in the nuts."

"Nah, an angry guy could fight through that. Take your keys, hold them between your knuckles, and jab them in his eye. Hard."

"What?!"

"Yeah, he'll forget about you while he's worrying if he'll ever see again. 'Ahhh, my nuts hurt!' is nowhere near as bad as 'Ahhh, will I ever see again?' The self-preservation instinct takes over. You'll have a chance to get away."

"I guess."

"Trust me, Pen. Against a man, you'll always have a physical disadvantage. The way you even that up is by going full cold-blooded, psychotic savage. If he won't stop, stab him in the soft bits. Eyes, cheeks, neck. For everything he tries to do to you, you make him pay a price, and you make sure it's a harsh one."

"Woah, I didn't know you were such a lunatic."

"Only when it comes to you or your mum."

"Where did you learn this stuff."

"SAS, remember?"

She let out a snotty laugh.

Eventually the car pulled up outside her place and Penny opened the door.

"You gonna be okay alone?" her dad asked after they'd had another twisted car seat hug.

"Yeah, I'll be all right."

"I can stay if you want me to."

"Nah, I'm a big girl now, and it's super late. You have work tomorrow. Better get some sleep."

"Hey, you! Who's the parent here?"

They shared a giggle.

"I'll come by tomorrow, okay, Pen Pen?"

"Sure. Thanks again for rescuing me, Dad. I love you."

"I love you back."

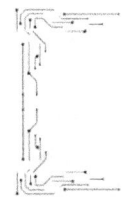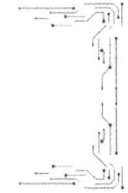

The Stones

Alex slipped away within the dream, out of his body and through dark and light. The tunnels of strange colours surrounded him, but quickly his journey came to an end. He zoomed like a spirit, roaming free in the cosmos, then he fell.

Like a light had come on in a dark room, suddenly, he was in body, but a body that was not his own. He was moving, running in fact, on long spindly limbs that took enormous bounds with each step. Then with a crack, gunfire went off behind him. Human guns.

He couldn't see well, but he was in the wilderness amongst the trees, running for his life. The shot boomed out once and again. Alex ran in zig zags, in between the trees as he went while bullets thudded into the wood. Dogs barked, baying for blood, chasing him down. His chest heaved in and out with the effort, blowing steam in the cold air. Ahead, something caught his eye. A white tree, haunted and alone. Its branches twisted skyward. The leaves long since gone, the wood decaying, life was escaping it, but still it held on.

For a moment, the shooting stopped. He was hidden from his pursuers by the thick trunks that surrounded him. He was drawn towards the white tree. Outside of his knowledge and without his will, his body yearned. Something inside dragged him along like an outgoing tide. All he could see was the tree. Every ounce of his being drew him closer. He didn't know why, but he felt that was where safety lay. The frail wood of the tree was too soft to stop the bullets, but still, that was his destination.

The gun boomed again as his tall host ducked its head and sprinted. With straining limbs and gasping for breath, he reached the pale trunk. He went round behind it and crouched low. The bullets flew and the dogs howled. He huddled there helplessly.

With no weapons and the snarling dogs looming, it seemed he was trapped.

The thud of boots drew ever closer. Alex frantically searched for something to use as a weapon. First a stick, uselessly thin, then a rock, then a handful of smaller rocks. So, it seemed it was him versus an unknown number of men with guns and dogs, and his only defence was throwing rocks. He semi-laughed at how pathetic it was, but Alex would fight to his last breath. He readied himself.

Like a flash, a green glow engulfed him and blinded him. It was warm for a second, then there was a crackling static and a mighty pop.

He roused to blackness, blinded and discombobulated. Gradually, in fuzz, his sight began to return. He was still in the crouched position. Alex stood as finally those blurs became form in his strange alien vision. He was not where he had been before. He was in a large tubular room that circled round him with sheer metallic walls that shot upwards. He was stood on a huge circular pad. White light poured down upon him. There appeared to be no way out. It seemed for the second time in not very long, he was trapped.

Although there was no sign of it before, a door hissed open in front of him. He stood contemplating for a moment, but there was only one course of action he could take. He stepped forward out into the bright hallway. It was illuminated in a way that he did not understand. There were no individual lights—the whole structure glowed. He had no idea what to expect, so he crept cautiously along.

In a metal panel, for the first time he saw his reflection. He jumped. He examined himself. He looked like an insect with a long and lanky humanoid body. He was a Mantis. Afraid, he jumped and took a step back.

Now he examined his hands and body and the flowing robes he wore. Through the alien eyes, his vision was not the same. He felt woozy. Standing ten feet tall, he felt disconnected from the body he was within. His feet shouldn't be so far from his head, and his eyes shouldn't see that way. His brain was scrambled briefly, but the memory of Sollen gave him at least some reference.

He talked to himself silently, trying to stay calm, trying to accept the situation. This was a time when, once again, his habit of just floating through life came to the fore. Although in many ways there were disadvantages to that, at times when things were bad, or in this case, just plain bizarre, it was a useful tool.

Whether it was the host or The Fleck, Alex couldn't know, but somehow, he knew the way. Once again, he had somewhere to be. It called. Through empty corridors he wandered, winding round, listening to the echoes of his own footsteps.

The doors opened one at a time from the walls on either side of him. More Mantises joined him in the hall. He fought to remain calm, to not do anything out of step with the others, though inside he was terrified. More of the insectoids joined them in what was quickly becoming a procession. The crowd of creatures were all headed to the same place.

Alex grew nervous, trying to guess what might happen. But how could he guess what would happen when, from his experiences so far, it could be literally anything? Not a word was uttered amongst the tall beings, which just made Alex even more nervous. The Mantises wandered silently and blindly, almost as though they were following the Pied Piper towards their destination.

Finally, the corridor came to an end, and the Mantises, now in their hundreds, poured into a chamber. Three strange glass tanks were stood in a triangle at the front of the room on a platform. Each of them was filled with a glowing mist that rolled around mysteriously.

Before them, the Leader approached across the stage. The mighty creature gave off an air of magnificence. It showed wisdom without speaking and grace in its movement as it swept into the room. Still the crowd stayed silent, standing in rows. Alex did the same; he dare not do anything out of the ordinary. The Leader stood still and spoke. It spoke in strange tones that were gobbledygook to Alex, but to his host, the words made sense.

"We have the volunteer. He will become the guardian of the base. Garard, come forward."

The creature was no Mantis; this was a Reptilian. It strode menacingly forward and joined the leader on the stage. Garard walked to the tank at the point of the triangle and positioned itself below it. A glass tube came up from the floor around the creature. It clinked into place in the bottom of the tank above.

"Insert the stone!" the Leader yelled, loud and shrill.

A grey panel appeared in the front of the tube. Garard held out its scaley hand holding a glowing pink stone.

Alex remembered everything he saw. He watched silently, more fascinated than afraid now.

The Reptilian clicked the stone into the panel, and with a whir, the bottom of the tank slid away, leaving a hole. The strange mist flowed into the tank, followed quickly by a writhing creature hidden within—the halithstord. The symbiote yearned for its bond and rushed towards Garard. It burrowed into its head violently while the Reptilian squirmed and rasped out blood curdling screams. It dropped to its knees, fighting the pain with all it had, trapped within the tube. With an audible pop, Garard rose and roared its mighty war cry.

Then words came in whispers to Alex's mind, but these whispers did not belong to The Fleck; they belonged to the Mantises around him. Statements of surprise and horror and fear broke out internally.

"What?" he asked silently.

"Still your mind. You shall give yourself away," The Fleck offered its warning.

"I can hear the Mantises speaking, can't I?"

"Yes. They do not speak with their voice amongst their own anymore. They only communicate telepathically. Do not ask questions. You need to get the stones. That is what we are here for. Keep your mind quiet or they will detect us."

Alex wanted to ask a million questions as is the human way, but he fought the urge. He was certain that, should they discover a spy in their midst, the consequences would be harsh. Now he had a problem. He didn't know where the stones were, let alone how to get hold of them and get out unharmed.

The tube hissed as it retracted, and now the Reptilian, oozing its newly found power, was free in the room. It stood twitching, the symbiote bristling inside it.

Alex felt a wave of fear amongst the crowd. It was in the air. He could feel it through his borrowed body.

Garard stared wildly at the crowd, drooling. The thirst for blood raged inside it.

The Leader spoke again, but now Alex knew it spoke only to an audience of one—Garard. The rest of those in the room were in the network of invisible energy. Alex could tune into it, but he sporadically flitted in and out. With the Leader's words, the Reptilian left the front of the room through a door. It dismissed the crowd silently but spoke directly to Alex. He heard the words echo inside him.

"Come with me."

At first, fear filled him. Had he been discovered? Then a feeling grew that his host was a friend of the Leader. One that it trusted and in which it confided. Alex was, in fact, the Leader's chief council and its most trusted advisor. Wanook, the Guide, Alex's host, was ancient and filled with wisdom. With the Mantises' immense telepathic ability, these beings did not make for easily controlled hosts. It appeared his task would be harder than he'd realised, and already to Alex, it seemed impossible.

He followed the Leader, always remaining a few steps behind as they moved gracefully, almost hovering above the floor. The Mantis went down some steps behind the stage, and as if from nowhere, a panel on a stand came up from the floor. The Mantis typed in a code, and a door that couldn't be seen before opened in the wall. It was a hidden room, perhaps a safe of some kind.

They went inside, and that was when he saw them—two stones, pink and glowing. They were just like the one the

Reptilian had. They were in a clear box and displayed upon a metal shelf that jutted out from the wall. There was nothing stopping him from grabbing the box.

The Fleck spoke for the first time in a while. *"Grab it now!"*

Alex didn't think, he simply reacted. He lurched forward and grabbed the box. It was solid and heavy. He swung it with a roar, and it crashed with a sickening thud against the Leader's head. The Mantis fell to the floor with white milky blood immediately pouring from the savage wound.

"Is it dead?" Alex asked silently, but The Fleck didn't answer.

Alex turned and ran out of the open door. The Leader lay lifeless behind him. That bought him some time to escape. Though, once again, he didn't know where to go, something guided him. Whether it was The Fleck, the host, or fate itself drawing him along didn't matter.

He tucked the box into his robes and made his way carefully through the corridors, doing his best to avoid any Mantises. He came across a few and walked casually past, going all but unnoticed. Had he rushed or panicked, he would have surely given himself away.

Finally, although he had no clue how he found it, he was back inside the weird tube room through which he had entered. He stood on the pad. A green glow surrounded him again, and in an instant, he was back behind the white tree in the woods. He looked around fearing the dogs and the guns. To his relief, it seemed they were long gone. That was hours ago; now it was dawn.

He kept his head low and sprinted out of sight, jagging in and out of the trees, his precious cargo—the stones—still safely tucked in his robes.

Behind Alex, a green glow fizzed by the white tree. It lit the inky dawn for an instant. Garard, the Reptilian, with its symbiote onboard and dressed in its environment suit, appeared by the tree. It hissed from its flaring nostrils. Its eyes flicked from side to side as it stood silent, taking in every sight and sound.

The Reptilian warrior had one mission—to retrieve the stones and destroy the traitor. He tore off following Alex's trail, much faster than a human could run, staying silent and out of sight behind trees. Light on its toes, it was almost silent even upon the dead leaves. It blended into the shadows like it was as dark as the night itself. Its long blade was sheathed, but this fearsome warrior had no intention of using it anyway. This Reptilian would rip its prey apart with its claws. Fuelled by rage, powerful muscles, and the symbiote, Garard was almost unstoppable.

Like it was instinct engrained in his being, Alex felt the energy change. It grew darker; he could read it. He could feel it. The danger warmed his blood.

"The host betrayed us. I felt it. It told the Mantises where we are."

"What now? What do I do?"

"Hide the stones. Hide them under a rock. Their scanners will not find them. They must remain secret. It is all that matters."

"What if the host gives that away, too?"

"We must stop it. Take over its mind completely. Our power combined can, but not for long."

"I don't have any power."

"Your power is far greater than you imagine. The Fleck shall guide you. Now, remain silent and run."

Alex followed a path that he didn't know, yet one that was set, mapped out before him. He tore blindly among the trees. Brambles with their thorns ripped into his thin flesh as he frantically searched for a place to hide his bounty.

At that moment, inside him, a battle for supremacy began.

Strange power surged through Alex; not through his host, not through his borrowed body but his own essence. It was drawn from the cosmos around him and filled him. He had visions of shadows and smoke in his consciousness, creating a dark swirl, clouding his host's mind. The Mantis' thoughts were gone, no longer jumbled in with his. The entities, for the time being, were divided.

Alex ran until his legs burned, until he found it, the place to hide the stones. Three trees in a triangle called to Alex. He stopped in the middle of them, searching around. He kicked at the leaves with his huge feet revealing a flat rock. He went to his knees and started to dig down into the soil beside and then beneath the rock. With his hands and a stick as his only tools, he struggled to dig deep enough to hide the box completely. He wouldn't quit. He dug until his hands were bleeding and sore, but finally, he made enough room for his prize. He wedged the box tightly under the rock and packed stones around it, then soil, and then he scattered dead leaves over the top. Now it was almost impossible to detect.

"Now, get away from here. The host will return soon. Time is short."

Alex's host body was tiring as he tore off as far from the stones as he could get. His legs burned as he escaped the tree line and ran out into open meadowland. He was gasping, his host's muscles trembling with exhaustion. He could run no more. He stopped. He heard a noise. Then something huge and powerful hit him in the back. He fell face first into the dirt. He struggled with all his might, but his might was useless against this foe. He felt long fingers wrap around his head. There was a jerk, there was a snap, there was an instant of searing pain, and then darkness.

Invasion Fleet

The clones poured from the bunker and into the hangar. In their hundreds, these super soldiers were armed to the teeth. Each was loaded with plasma weapons, grenades, and blades. They were twitching for battle, thirsting for blood, eager for the taste of death. So long had they awaited, silent and unmoving, for the order to be given, for them to go out and do what it was that they were created to do. So long had their hunger for battle built inside them. They had been coiled like springs, awaiting the test of their skills.

Each streamed up the ramps and into the awaiting shuttlecraft. They piled onboard, taking their seats and strapping themselves in. They sat, eyes staring forward, unmoving and unemotional. The shuttle lifted off the launchpad. They took first to air above the ice planet and then out into space.

They flew for hours through the inky blackness without a thought amongst them beyond the battle that was ahead. Outside they were patient and unenthused, but inside the symbiote told a completely different story. The mighty halithstord loved nothing more than the blood, the battle, and the carnage. That was its purpose, its only goal, its only reason for being.

Finally, they arrived at their destination. Two enormous spacecraft with room for thousands of beings inside hung there in space. They were the interstellar craft. They awaited, out far enough away from the ice planet to remain undetected, but close enough to be reached by the smaller shuttlecraft.

The shuttles headed towards only the nearest craft; the other would remain where it was, at least for now. The clones alighted, marching from their transport then thoughtlessly into rows in the enormous landing bay. Never was there dissent or difference amongst them. Now the fearsome army gathered in their thousands.

The interstellar craft burst into life, forming a hole in the fabric of the cosmos. The army, each a powerful warrior, each with a halithstord onboard, headed out to meet their sinister ends. They had only one purpose in their expendable lives, and that was war.

The sudden explosion of power from the interstellar craft created a gravitational wave that travelled quickly through space. It was lightyears away but was detectable to the Elders.

"What was that?" the Admiral asked.

"It's an interstellar craft, sir," Nessa said. "They're going somewhere in a real hurry."

"That is *not* what I wanted to hear. Damn. Where are they going?"

"You don't suppose they're after the core?"

"With a craft that size, it looks more like an invasion than an ambush."

"I'm worried."

"So am I, so am I."

They were close to their destination but feared they would have arrived too late. An invasion fleet, headed for somewhere, and the outcome was unlikely to be a good one. Urgency was the most important thing now. The clone army took its telepathic orders from the child, so taking them down should render the soldiers useless. It was their only chance to stop what was unfolding. Whatever it was, it was something big.

"We did it!" Jax announced.

"I know." The Admiral smirked. He never had any doubt they would. "It was just a question of when, not if."

"Why, thank you." Jax did her favourite dramatic bow. "It's one of these rings. It creates an electro-magnetic field around the head. That should stop the waves. At a relatively low power, it should repel them. If I were to make it stronger, it would probably turn him into jelly."

"Well, make sure he doesn't. He's a good warrior. We're gonna need all the help we can get."

"I've made them for all of us."

"Why?"

"Last time, the child's guards used telepathy as a weapon. It completely scrambled us. We can't afford for that to happen again."

"Okay, good thinking. We'll be there soon, and we have no idea what we're walking into."

"Ooh, that's the fun way!" Nik laughed. "Knowing what dangers are ahead is just sooo boring."

"Well," the Admiral said, "I'm probably not gonna enjoy it quite that much, but good for you, soldier.

"At least with you two around," he looked at Nik and then Jax, "marching to our death should at least be funny."

Mental Groundhog Day

Alex awoke in the strangest manner, like he'd fallen out of sleep. He was full of intense emotions as he was stolen from the blackness in which he'd found himself. He fought for memories that he knew were somewhere inside. They lingered there, yet they remained out of reach. He scoured the dark recesses of his racing mind. It was like dipping a toe in the ocean but not being able to fully submerse himself.

He was tired and confused, fuzzy-headed and grumpy. All he could see was that last moment, the final vision from the Mantis's eyes. But now, he couldn't remember the fact he was a Mantis at all. It was as though he drifted in and out of someone else's memories.

Nothing made sense. Jumbled, fantastical images from alien places flashed through his mind. He felt like he'd walked in another's shoes, one who was not of his world. He wished he could remember. If only he could make sense of all the crazy things that had been happening. He felt anxious, like a shadow loomed on the horizon. Something huge was coming, and he had important things to do.

He continued to accept and react, and that got him through. That was just what he did, but to the forces far more powerful than Alex, that was his biggest strength. He may have been accepting of the things that happened around him, but that did not mean he didn't have questions. This no longer felt dreamlike. It was real, and it was crazy. He had no idea why it was he who was wrapped up in this. He just had to survive and find a way out of it.

He lay somewhere between awake and asleep for a time, frustrating himself, trying to remember things that were lost, drifting out in the cosmos.

Alex sat up and a cloud hung over him. It was like a glimpse of the future, but this was a future of pain and darkness. Could that really be what was to come? The cloud became depression. There was something he must do that day, something he didn't want to do. Not like the crazy adventures he'd been on, behind another face, but something he, Alex, must do.

He worked on the building site, running wheelbarrows full of rubble all day. Luckily for him, this meant he could avoid the daily "banter," as they called it, only it seemed to mostly be at his expense being the youngest. Greenness on a building site is costly. His inventive workmates never seemed to run out of hilarious pranks to waste his time or energy. He had learned the worst thing he could do was get annoyed. Then they had you. They knew exactly how to push your buttons, and they would. The truth was, this was just the ritual of the site and most of them liked him. He worked hard and he was funny. Today he just kept his head down and his legs pumping.

At last, Alex finished work, and he could keep himself in food and rent for a little longer. He trudged home, past the argument in the hallway that no doubt would rage long into the night again.

He grabbed a beer out of his tiny bar fridge, which was the only thing that would fit in his bedsit. The ache in his shoulders, back, and calves, and the sore callouses on his hands told the nightly cost for his day's wage. He put on some music to drown out the shouting. He grumbled, swigged his beer, and sat down on his bed.

It was only now he realised what had been on his mind the most. Why he felt so terrible about himself—Penny. He couldn't believe how badly he'd misrepresented himself to her. He felt like a fool and a failure. He ran the moment he blurted out his revelation to her through his mind for the millionth time. Somehow, he'd thought she'd understand. He couldn't have been more wrong.

Now it was mental Groundhog Day, making up scenarios that never did or could happen. He was saying and doing things differently each time, trying to finally get it right. This was not only pointless and unhelpful, it was torturous. He longed to go back in time, to have a second chance, to not mess it up again.

He was driving himself crazy, so to take his mind off it, he played his guitar. That was the only thing that got him through the dark times. His guitar, scratched and dinked, was the only thing he'd always had. He closed his eyes as his fingers danced on the strings, and just for a moment there was nothing but the music. Despite the world around him and the pointless thoughts that wanted to invade his mind, he was calm.

The Message

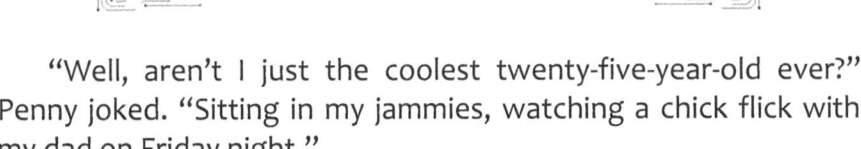

"Well, aren't I just the coolest twenty-five-year-old ever?" Penny joked. "Sitting in my jammies, watching a chick flick with my dad on Friday night."

"I quite like it myself, and I think you're cool."

"Hey, everyone, my dad thinks I'm cool. Yay!" She punched the air like she'd scored a goal. "No, I'm like a crazy cat lady already, and I haven't even got a cat. Most of the time I look like a bog witch."

"See, like I said, cool." Danny laughed. "Anyway, shouldn't a bog witch have a cat?"

"Nah, that's a different type of witch. We have a toad."

"Right, got it."

There was a beep from Penny's phone. Still smiling she reached to the arm of the sofa. She looked at the screen and saw Alex's name. She huffed slightly as her face dropped.

"What? Who is it?"

"It's him. The weirdo. I thought I'd blocked his number. I must have forgot."

"Well, do it now."

"That's exactly what I'm gonna do."

She looked at the screen again, ready to block the number, but something stopped her. She was curious despite her better instincts. I mean, it couldn't hurt, could it? She could see what he said and then block the number afterwards. She side-eyed her dad. He was watching the movie.

She opened the message. It simply read two words: *"The Fleck."*

Her heart felt like it stopped and then raced back into life. She tried to remain neutral so her father wouldn't notice the surprise on her face. "Right, he won't be able to text me anymore," she said, lying through her teeth. She had no idea why she lied to him; she never did, but a second later, she realised.

"Good! If he messes with you again…"

"It's okay. He's no one. Just forget it."

She sat acting as casually as possible, though inside, her mind was racing even faster than her heart. Was this the sign that Liam had told her of in her dream? Penny could think of no other explanation. She seemingly zoned out a little. She stopped being as much fun as she had been before the message. Danny noticed.

"You seem to be quiet, love. Is everything okay?"

"Well, things are never really okay nowadays. Sorry I zoned out. I just got a bit sleepy, and the movie is just awful."

"Not because of him, whatever his name is, is it?"

"No. He won't bother me again. I'm fine. I could just do with some sleep."

"Well, I'll find where he lives if he does. You're not to talk to him."

"Excuse me? I'll talk to whomever I please. I am not a child, and I don't appreciate that at all."

"All right, calm down. I'm only looking out for you. I'll go then, shall I?"

"Look, I know, but I can do what I want. I don't really need the strong-armed father at the moment. So, if you wouldn't mind. I would like to go to bed."

"Oh, right, getting kicked out."

"No, of course not. Don't be silly." She spoke firmly. He was deliberately putting a guilt trip on her, and at this moment, she really didn't appreciate it.

"Okay, no problem. I'll go then." He huffed and stood up.

She stood up with him and kissed him on the cheek. "I love you."

He smiled. "I love you too, Pen Pen." He walked out the door, internally castigating himself for upsetting her.

Penny was not nearly as upset as he thought she was. Firstly, she knew he was only human, and secondly, she had something important to do.

Now that she was alone, she sat staring at the phone screen. She didn't know what to say in her reply. She was scared to know the truth, and afraid of Alex, but she couldn't let it go. She'd searched high and low for an answer, and none had presented itself. Then this random stranger who had to find her, out of nowhere, says that word. After Liam in the dream and Isha's notebook, this simply couldn't be coincidence.

She tried a full range of messages that she typed and deleted. Everything from, "What do you want?!" to "Hi" to get him to start the conversation. She decided that was the cowardly thing to do, and she needed to control the situation. She was uncomfortable enough to not want to put the ball in his court. If she chose small talk, he'd just put on his charm. She didn't want chit chat; she wanted answers.

"What is The Fleck?" She typed the words, shut her eyes like she was about to leap from a cliff, and pressed send. Now it was late, and she could only hope a message would come back. She carried on watching movies and snoozing, then jerking awake and checking her phone before drifting back to sleep.

It was five AM when Penny awoke with a start to the beep of a message. She pushed away the hair that was stuck to her cheek and quickly looked at her phone.

"I don't know... We need to find out."

"We??? I don't want to talk to you. Just tell me."

"You're talking to me now lol. No, I don't know anything. I was hoping you can tell me."

"I don't understand."

"Neither do I... Pls, can we meet and talk?"

"I don't think I trust you."

"Look, I'm sorry I freaked you out and grabbed you. I've been in bits about the whole thing. I suck! I just needed to talk about this and was worrying I wouldn't see you again."

"Now you're freaking me out again! How did you know I knew anything?"

"I know I sound mental, but I just knew."

"Yes, you do! Please stop it."

"I don't know, Penny. I don't know what to say... I guess everything's connected."

With that, it was almost as if the blood in her veins froze. There were so many layers of emotion, she couldn't even process it. Her skin tingled, her hands and the sides of her head went numb. It was overload for her. She was astounded to the core, her mind swirling in such disbelief that she slipped into instant denial. It can't be real. It couldn't even be happening.

She threw the phone down onto the couch and rushed to her room slamming the door like she was an angry child. She covered her head with the sheets like she was a six-year-old trying to hide from monsters. These monsters, however, would not be fooled easily, for they lived inside her. She was cold and in shock. Had her whole world changed right then and there? She imagined every scenario, every possibility, searching for nefarious reasons he could know these things, but she found none.

She removed her head from the covers as they did little to stop the thoughts. She decided staring at the ceiling was better. The strange mix of fascination, shock, fear, and trauma churned through her body. There would be no sleep for Penny.

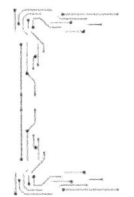

Life Lessons

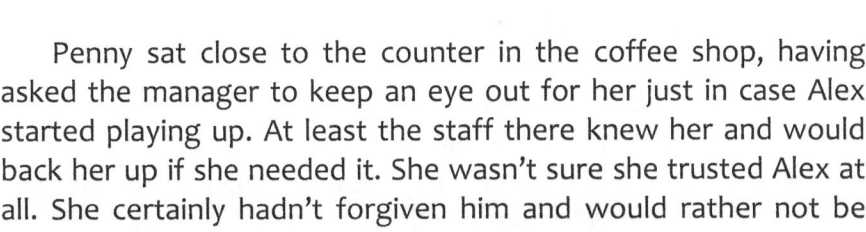

Penny sat close to the counter in the coffee shop, having asked the manager to keep an eye out for her just in case Alex started playing up. At least the staff there knew her and would back her up if she needed it. She wasn't sure she trusted Alex at all. She certainly hadn't forgiven him and would rather not be putting herself in such a situation.

She really had no choice in her mind; she simply had to find out what he had to say. Maybe she could finally make sense of it all. She had waited more than half an hour, which just ended up making her more anxious. She had almost convinced herself that he wasn't going to show up when he finally arrived. Penny became nervous when she saw him, not forgetting for one second how weird he'd been before.

He sloped over to her looking like a scalded child. He was too shy to make eye contact and unsure of what to say. In the end he sat down with an awkward, "Hi."

"Hi." Penny's tone was short and sharp.

"Look, first, I wanna apologise again. I was stupid. I just panicked. Not that that's an excuse... I'm just sorry."

"Yes, you *were* stupid. You can't just manhandle women. For any reason."

"I know. It was just a reaction."

"Well, your 'just a reaction' scared the hell out of me! I thought you were gonna assault me or murder me or something. You get that, right?"

"Oh." He paused, looking close to tears. Now, only for the first time, did he see it from her point of view. The guilt and disappointment at his own ignorance washed over him. The fact he had made her feel that way broke him a little. "I understand. Well, now I do. I'm so sorry, Penny."

She could see the pain on his face. "Right." Was all she said, even though it didn't really fit.

"Can you find it in your heart to forgive me?"

"Maybe, but if you try anything like that again, I'll use my dad's solution."

"Thanks for teaching me this lesson, too. I mean that."

"You're welcome."

"Wait, what is your dad's solution?"

"Stab you in the face and blind you."

"Right. I won't come anywhere near you again." He made an exaggerated wide-eyed fear look.

"You better not, buster."

The manager caught Penny's eye over Alex's shoulder with a thumbs up gesture. She nodded subtly to indicate she was okay.

"I guess the coffee and sandwiches are on me again?"

"Of course. That's how this works. You know that by now."

"What will it be then?" He laughed.

"So, from here on out, we're gonna have to be honest with each other. Don't leave anything out, okay?" This was Penny's way of remaining in control of the situation, especially if she made him speak first.

"Got it," he agreed.

"You start."

"Erm... This won't make sense, so I don't want you think I've lost it."

"Nothing's made sense for ages, and I *already* think you've lost it," she teased, which made him a little more comfortable.

"I had a dream and then a feeling. I didn't know where I was going, but I kept going. It was like I was being drawn." Alex certainly didn't want to mention The Fleck, that would be too much for her to swallow. "I was brought here, and when I saw you, I knew it was you I needed to find."

"Are you serious?"

"Yeah, I swear. I knew I needed to say the words, 'The Fleck,' though I didn't know what it meant. I fought the urge on our first meeting cos, well, insane and all that, and hung on through our night out. Then I messed it up. So, do you think I'm crazy or what?"

"I already said I think you're crazy. But if it happened like you said it did, it's super weird."

"What do you know about it?"

"I've heard it before. My friend, the one who died, said some stuff about it and then this other girl from the other side of the town. She's dead, too. Liam, my best friend that is... He said he had things to do, and I think it had something to do with this Fleck thing." She held back some of the details.

"Wow!"

"Yeah."

They both shared a few moments of deep thought and took a sip of coffee.

"What happens now?" Penny asked.

"There's something important coming. All I know is we need to do something together. What or when, I don't know."

"Well, that's useful." Penny giggled a little. She was now feeling a lot more comfortable. She didn't think he was lying to her and knew his apology was genuine. Why, she didn't know, but it was a feeling she had.

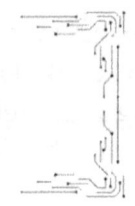

The Drop

"We're approaching now, Admiral. Nothing could live on the surface of this snowball," Farg's voice came over the comms.

"The base is underground," Asu told the Elders. "We need to land somewhere they won't be able to sense us."

"We'll land close," the Admiral addressed the entire crew. "We'll use the burn suits. They could maybe track a craft, but in the burn suits, we'll be on the planet's surface before they can scramble." Then he turned his attention to the pilot. "Farg, get ready to skim the atmosphere, then get out of range. You may have to come in and get us in a real hurry.

"The rest of you, suit up. Don't forget your light shields; we'll be needing them. Those of you that have never used a burn suit before, this is gonna be a wild ride!"

It wasn't long before the Admiral and Asu, Jax, Nik, and Nessa were suited up and ready for the drop. They climbed into the release tubes, and as the shuttle tickled the very edge of the ice planet's thin atmosphere, with a woosh they launched.

Their stomachs felt like they flipped upside down as they were shot forcefully out of the tubes. They plummeted at terrific speed towards the planet's surface. Some screamed in terror, some screamed in exhilaration, while others held their breath. White hot flames licked the sides of the burn suits, the only thing preventing what would be a certain and instant death. They hurtled down and down, smoking after they had passed right through the atmosphere. They were in a terrifying freefall, zooming right towards the giant ice ball below.

They neared the ground with their hearts racing wild. This was the moment of truth. The boosters fired, slowing them in an instant, saving them from what would have been a certain death. Filled with relief, they gently touched down. The blackened suits automatically sprung open and fell onto the ice. The warriors stepped out onto the planet's surface. There was no doubt that they would have been frozen solid in moments had it not been for the protective environment suits they wore.

"Asu, the light shield, you've never used it," the Admiral said. "I'll run you through it."

He touched the button on his wrist and the shield burst into instant life. It was rectangular, long, and tall, going from the ground to above his head. "That's standard defensive setting. This can stop plasma fire, but you still don't want to be too close to a grenade." Then he shrunk it to a smaller, round, dustbin lid size. "This is close combat setting." Then finally, he put it back to the original size, but now there was a slot in the side through which he could fire a weapon. "This is range combat setting. You got it?"

"I do."

"Well, then, lead the way."

The Spy didn't even know where they needed to go but within him, The Fleck guided him. He was overcome with an eerie feeling, a tingling of anticipation and fear of what may lay ahead. He simply didn't know what defences this clone army possessed, or the sensors and weaponry they had at their disposal. One thing that was clear was the best defence the army had was the location. No one had a reason to come to an uninhabitable ice planet so far out from its star. Well, almost no one.

The visibility was poor, and walking was difficult on the planet's slippery surface. They fought on and struggled across the tundra for hours. Safe inside their heavily armoured environment suits they were, but that didn't make them any less heavy and uncomfortable. They were fully armed, which weighed them down more. Noble warriors they were, robots they were not, and fatigue was starting to wear them down.

Over the howling wind, they heard a sound. It was like a skater carving through the ice. It was coming from close by. Very close. Their experience set them on full alert in an instant. They readied their weapons.

Glowing, worm-like machines burst from the ice. The plasma surrounding them melted right through it. They took to the air, swarms of them, shooting bolts of plasma down towards the warriors.

The Elders sprang into action, each ducking behind their shields. They repelled the initial attack before unleashing one of their own. Their weapons tore through the drones. Flashes of plasma boomed out, lighting the gloomy planet. Quickly the ice was littered with sparking metal and scorch marks.

"Weird, that was a lot easier than I thought it would be," the Admiral said when the last of their robotic enemies was little more than junk.

"If I may, sir," Nik offered her wisdom.

"Go ahead."

"My best guess is their main weapon is telepathy. We've dealt with something like this before. With these electromagnetic protectors, their most powerful weapons are useless."

"That's good news."

"That's far from our only problem, though. We dealt with all kinds of things. Crazy things. Stuff it's hard to even imagine."

"That's not even to mention an entire army of clone soldiers around here somewhere," Asu pointed out.

"We need to get below the surface and out of this weather," the Admiral said. "We can't fight in these conditions. We're sitting ducks out here."

From nowhere, Nik's arm cannon boomed, making the whole group jump. The fiery spark exploded into the ice, shaking the ground beneath their feet.

"What the hell are you doing?" the Admiral barked angrily.

As the smoke cleared, a hole was left in the ice. "Those things came from somewhere beneath the ice. There are so many holes in it, they've weakened it."

"Okay." The Admiral nodded in agreement. "You know what to do folks."

The warriors let loose on the ice, sending great glassy chunks flying. They leaned over the edge of what was now a huge hole.

Shining lights down, there was some structure below. There was some kind of tunnel under the ground.

The Elders fixed ropes. It was too far to jump.

"Asu, take the lead," the Admiral ordered. He wouldn't risk the soldiers and, more importantly, his friends if he didn't need to.

Asu was wise, he understood and respected that. He was the outsider in the group that had led them to what could be their doom. If any of them were to die, it seemed Asu would be first. Carefully, he lowered himself down into the darkness.

"It's clear," Asu's voice came through the comms.

"You heard him." The Admiral invited his soldiers to go first.

"Not this again." Nik rolled her eyes.

"Come on, it's character building," Jax joked.

"I think my character's built enough."

"You *are* pretty shredded."

"Why, thank you." Nik mocked Jax's dramatic bow. "And you're pretty hawt yourself."

"Naturally." She pretended to push her hair with her hand even though it was below her helmet.

Somehow, still they managed to laugh even though they were the only ones that truly knew the dangers the group faced. They were all too aware they had only just escaped with their lives last time. They only got away when the child was distracted by the symbiote. They had done what they never did and ran from the fight to spare their lives. Now that they were here with the Mercenaries and hunting the child, it seemed it was their destiny to escape that day. Not only to stop the dark forces there were now at work, but more importantly, vengeance for the death of their friend, Daze.

The sisters in arms wore the scars from the battles before. Nik had paid with her hand. She now could fit her whip there, or a robotic hand, or even a cannon, all of which she kept on her person.

Here she needed her robotic hand so she could climb. The soldier's lowered themselves down.

"Farg, come in." The Admiral reached out to their friend in the craft above them.

There was no answer.

"Farg, come in. Do you read me?" He waited again. "Damn!"

"Maybe he has a communication error, sir," Nessa's voice came over the comms from below.

"Nah, he's gone, I just know it. They must have sensed him." The Admiral said. Despite his sadness for his lost friend, his first thought was a practical one. Now they would need to find a ride off the planet, that's if they did survive. Their task was only getting harder all the time.

Finally, the Admiral descended the rope, and the Elders and the Spy were in a tunnel. It appeared like it had been melted right through the ice. There were no supports, struts, or reinforcements, just frozen shimmering walls.

Asu stopped and stood. He was silent and staring. He was standing in place just feeling, sensing, trying to find the way to go. He silently called upon The Fleck to guide him, and it eagerly did.

"You okay there, Asu?" the Admiral asked, it seemed to deaf ears.

Asu was frozen for a few more seconds before he shook his head as if to snap out of a trance or a dream. "We need to go this way."

"What makes you so sure?" the Admiral enquired suspiciously. "None of us know where we're going."

"I can sense it, sir. It calls to me. It's inside of me."

"Oh, I see. Am I supposed to follow your hunches or some crazy woo woo mysticism?"

"You'll simply have to trust me, Admiral. I have led you this far."

"That is true, but I still don't know if we're on the right path or not."

"Well, if I'm wrong, you can kill me yourself."

"I will do that, Asu. Do not lead us to our destruction."

"I have no guarantees, sir. We simply must do what we must."

"And only hope?"

"Hope is all the motivation we will need."

"Fine. Take point. We'll follow you."

"You mean, I die first?"

"If you wanna look at it that way, that is up to you. Look, we have your back. We will fight for you and beside you. If you're in our number, you are one of us. You've chosen to be here. You're taking point because you're the best soldier amongst us and you're our guide."

The Spy silently glowed. Such a compliment from this fine warrior meant far more than it would from most. With a humble tone he said, "Thank you, Admiral."

The warriors crept up the tunnel, Asu on point, Nessa covering the rear, and the rest spread out in between them. The flashlights on their rifles lit the dark as they went.

This was no natural formation. This tunnel was there for a reason. Between the icy walls, the Mercenaries were vulnerable. It would be so easy to ambush them at any time, and they would have nowhere to hide. There was no cover and only one direction to run. In that place, their only protection would be their skills, their weaponry, and their armour.

There was no chatter amongst them as sound would echo up the tunnel, giving away their position to any nearby ears. While this was no advantage, it did give them a chance of hearing their enemies approaching them, too. They were safe for now. The tunnel was long and straight and there was nowhere to set an ambush. Any movement from ahead or behind wouldn't go unnoticed. The mighty Elders, this fearsome group, walked softly, dulling their footsteps in the echoey surroundings. In such a harrowing place, stealth was their friend.

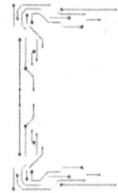

The Calling Part II

With it already grasped in her hand, Penny's phone beeped. Immediately, she opened the message. As she had hoped, it was from Alex.

"*It's on. Meet me at the station at 9. Dress warm and bring some food and water. I don't know how long it will take.*"

"*Ok. See U then,*" she replied.

Now the nerves started to grow. Anxiety made her twitchy. She questioned her sanity for the millionth time. She couldn't even explain to herself what she was doing. Logic had long since up and flown. Everything she was doing, she did based on feelings. The trouble was she had never trusted her instincts much. She felt like a child that had never left the house, or her parents' side, just to be thrust out of the door and told to discover the entire world. She doubted, and questioned everything, making her more and more uncertain which, in turn, drove her towards fear.

Here she was, blindly following Alex to some unknown place. Maybe she wouldn't have gone if she had listened to her mind, but at this point, her instincts were firmly in control. Somewhere deep down, though she was not aware of it, it was calling to her. Though the truth was, even her logic would have probably been persuaded to go the end. She simply couldn't *not* know the outcome of these, the most bizarre events she had ever known.

Penny made it to the station, somehow without completely losing her nerve. Alex smiled when he saw her, and Penny waved. As she approached, he handed her a takeout coffee, which warmed her heart at the gesture, bringing her a little comfort in the strange situation.

"So, I know it's weird as," Alex began, "but I'm just following the wind on this one. I have to go where it takes me. You sure you wanna come along for the ride?"

"No." She half giggled. "But guess I'm all in now. I'm here, aren't I?"

"Well, it looks like you," he joked. "But it really is up to you."

"I know. I've decided. I *need* answers. I don't know how else I will find them." She tittered slightly with laugher. "I mean, it's totally and completely nuts, but here we are."

"Yep, it's nuts, all right. Shall we?" He did a gentlemanly sweeping "after you" gesture towards the train.

They didn't speak too much as they took the train out of the city. Penny was reading a book. Alex stared out the window most of the time. Normally they were chatty together, but on this journey, often it seemed Alex was distracted and distant. It was almost as though he was quietly listening to a voice inside himself. Little could Penny know that he really was.

They went on the train for hours, through countless towns and then out into the country. The train hissed as it pulled into yet another small rural train station.

Alex grabbed his bag and jumped up. "Here."

"Here?"

"Yeah, here. Let the adventure begin."

They exited the train and watched as it rattled away. Penny looked around with her face scrunched up. "Do you reckon anyone's ever actually got off at this station? Like, we're in the middle of nowhere, dude. You sure about this?"

"Erm, no, of course not. Don't be silly." It was a half joke, but one with a point. "The woods. We need to go this way."

"I'm glad I brought my sensible shoes," Penny joked, even though she never wore anything but.

"You don't seem like the high heels type."

"Oh, no, you're on to me."

"Come on, you. Let's get cracking." Alex smiled.

They disappeared amongst the trees. The slippery ground was covered in fallen wet leaves. At times, the mud gathered in pools in their path. They had to jump over or zigzag between the tree trunks to navigate the worst of it and avoid getting wet feet.

It didn't take long in that fresh country air for Penny to start enjoying being away from the city for a change. She tried to remember the last time she had been hiking in the country. The memories were hazy, and several trips blended together in her mind. It had been many years. She deeply breathed in the earthy smell and the fresh clean air, watching the birds above flittering in the branches. The winter trees were bare and leafless, yet still they were beautiful beneath the steely grey sky.

Alex led the way, blowing steam in the cold with every breath, and Penny followed eagerly.

They went for hours. All the time, Alex was drawn along by the force within. He couldn't understand it, but somehow, he trusted it. Here he was in the middle of the woods, a place that he had never been in his life, yet somehow it felt familiar to him.

As the sun was setting, Penny began to grow tired. It wouldn't be long before the woods would be dark, then they would be stuck there in the cold for the night.

"I brought a torch so we could keep going," Alex said. "I feel like we could be close. We ain't got camping gear, so it's either sleep on the wet ground, or keep pushing on. Stupid northern hemisphere winters."

Penny wasn't looking forward to walking around the woods all night, but she didn't much fancy sleeping on the wet ground either. A spare jumper she had…a tent and a sleeping bag she did not.

They continued, but now painfully slowly. Penny certainly didn't like it out there at night. She was a little afraid. Even with her best reasoning, the unknown woods in the darkness were still a little scary to her. Of course, she would never show it and certainly she'd never say anything, but she was walking a lot closer to Alex than she had been in the daylight.

They traipsed along, but eventually they were really starting to tire.

"Is this ever gonna end?" Penny asked. "We've been walking for hours. I'm exhausted. What's the time?"

"It's one AM. We'll find somewhere to rest. Sorry, it's my fault. I felt sure we were close."

"It's okay. Don't say sorry. It's been kind of fun, for the most part."

"Oh, good. Don't worry, I'm a proper Jungle Jim. We'll have a little scout around and see if we can find somewhere dry to crash out."

"That's a great idea. I'm bloody freezing. I think my fingers are gonna drop off in a minute."

"Well, trust, it's lucky there's no wind. That would be super bad. The wind is what gets ya, especially if you're..." he drifted off.

"If you're?"

He stared ahead, shining his light, examining trees and the ground. "...Wet Come on. Here, just ahead."

They followed the light to a triangle of trees. Beneath the trees there was a large flat rock. It had lichen and moss growing on it, but it was a solid surface. A much better option than the wet muddy ground all around them.

Alex laid his backpack down and unzipped it. "Today, my friend, is your lucky day."

"How so? In case you haven't noticed, I'm sleeping rough in the woods."

He produced a black bin liner from his bag and laid in on the rock. "Here, take a dry seat."

Penny put her bag down and did exactly that. She got her spare jumper out of the bag, took off her puffer jacket, rummaged on the extra layer, and put her coat back over the top.

Alex produced a bag of food. It was all junk, but food, nevertheless. It seemed shopping wasn't his forte.

"It really is my lucky day!" she jokingly exaggerated.

"It gets better yet, me old mate." He pulled out a thick blanket and dropped it over her legs.

She smiled warmly, even though he couldn't see it in the darkness, and thanked him. They sat chatting, sharing the blanket, and eating cheese puffs for a while.

"Shame we can't see the stars," Alex noted. "They'd be amazing out here away from the city lights."

"Stupid English weather. It's always cloudy."

"Well, I'll make sure I bring you out here in the summer with some actual camping gear."

"That'd be wonderful."

Neither of them slept very well on the hard rock, but at least they were almost warm and had a chance to rest their aching legs.

Penny awoke with a start like she had snapped out of dream that she couldn't remember. It was still deeply dark. She noticed Alex wasn't in the blanket with her. He wouldn't just leave her alone in the woods, would he? At first, she started to panic a little, but then she heard scraping noises coming from not far away.

"Alex?"

He didn't answer.

"Alex, is that you?"

"Yeah. It's okay, I'm here."

"You scared the hell out of me!"

"Sorry. I would never just leave you here, though. You know that, right?"

"Well, yeah. Or I wouldn't be here, would I? What are you doing over there?"

"There's something under this rock. I've gotta dig it out."

"It's still dark. Wait 'til it gets light."

"It's always dark in the winter." He half laughed, but he was focused on the task at hand. He didn't even have the torch with him. It was like his vision didn't even matter. The Fleck guided him but mostly so did the calling. He scrabbled around in the dark, digging down below the rock as though he could see perfectly. His actions were not his own, willed along by another force, one outside himself, yet somehow, still within.

His cold hands felt something smooth and solid. A wave of excitement flowed through him, and he knew all at once that he had found what it was he was searching for. "There's something here," he announced excitedly. Now he was almost frantic as he scratched away at the soil and the rocks. A moment later he had a box in his hands.

"The torch. Grab it. It's in the pocket of my bag. Quick."

Penny rummaged around in the darkness and found it. She got to her feet. The excitement in his voice piqued her interest.

"Here." She took a few steps over and handed it to him.

The torch sparked into life, lighting up the forest, momentarily blinding the pair. When their eyes got used to the light, they saw a transparent box. Alex shone the light through it to reveal two strange pink stones inside.

"What the hell are they?" Penny asked.

"I don't know. I've never seen anything like it before in my life."

"Are they stones?"

"You ever seen, like, radioactive pink stones?"

"No... How did you know they were there?"

"I don't know, Penny. I just know for sure this is what I was looking for. You had enough sleep?"

"Erm, no. Hardly any, sleeping on a rock, mate."

"Tell me about it. Come on then, get ready. We've got to go."

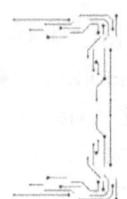

The Ambush Part II

For miles, the straight tunnel was quiet. They had seen no movement at all, but still the Mercenaries could little afford to let their guard drop even for a second. The silence was unnerving.

It was obvious, since the drones had found them, the child and the army must be aware of their presence. There was little chance they could have come so far completely unnoticed. They were on edge and nervous.

The quiet of that place built the tension evermore. The further they went, the surer they were something would attack them. The thought lurked, and it lingered, nagging away as it built steadily towards the edge of paranoia. Fate called them along into the places that even they feared to tread. They were wandering into the awaiting jaws of darkness, the haunted unknown.

That tunnel seemingly went on forever, frustratingly so. They couldn't see an end in sight. The weight quietly brought a cloud of depression. They wished they were somewhere else. Now they longed for the scene to change, if for nothing but the feeling that they were actually getting somewhere.

Here, the Elders followed Asu into such places that they wouldn't have followed another. None of them were certain that they were even going the right way. They had no evidence they were headed anywhere at all. So long they walked in that empty tunnel, it started to feel as if they would never reach the end, if indeed there was one.

There was no warning but a whooshing sound. The warriors moved, diving forward as deadly metal spikes flew from the walls. There was a gurgle and a thud, and Nessa slumped to the ground. Holes were pierced right through her body armour and, in turn, her flesh. The breach in her environment suit killed her in an instant.

There was no time for shock or grief. Triangular drones dropped from the ceiling and swarmed into the tunnels. The Elders, quick on the draw, opened fire. Drones above them exploded and crashed to the tunnel floor. More fired down upon the warriors, spitting deadly plasma, rapid firing from cannons on each tip of the triangle. The Elders fired again, activating their shields as they did. Plasma licked at the light barriers, but the Mercenaries were safe behind them. They switched the shields to range battle mode. They fired their weapons again, filling the tunnel with searing heat. Each, with incredible speed and skill, expertly sent drones sparking and crackling down. The extreme heat and vibration made the ceiling of the tunnel melt, and with a mighty rumble, it crumbled and fell.

"Move!" the Admiral yelled out.

They unleashed another wall of plasma, retracted their shields, and ran as the tunnel collapsed behind them. It trapped many of the drones, but others gave chase, quickly catching up to them. Try as they might, they could never outrun the robotic craft.

With weapons blazing, now the warriors took them down on the move. The drones buzzed overhead, spitting plasma towards them. The Elders ducked and dodged and ran with all that they had. They were slowed by their heavy environment suits, but still moved swiftly.

With nowhere to go, they stopped to make their stand. Again, they activated their shields, taking cover and opening fire at the same time. The drone's numbers began to dwindle. Many lay sparking and useless on the tunnel floor.

Again, the ceiling started to give way. They took out yet another row of drones and ran for their lives, holding their shields over their heads. Chunks of ice rained down and crashed onto the shields or onto the floor.

Then, with a deafening rumble, the tunnel behind them collapsed. Any remaining drones were now separated and few. They were quickly destroyed. The machines that would have easily bested a weaker group were little more than junk on the tunnel floor.

Now, in the quiet, came the pain. They reeled at the loss of another comrade in arms. Nessa, who had been with the Admiral for many years, was a fine soldier, a strong leader, and most importantly, a wonderful friend.

The Admiral was always hit hardest by the loss of his soldiers, but at this time, he was losing his friends. It broke his heart, though he would never show it. He was distraught knowing that he had brought them there to their doom. He snapped the thoughts from his mind. He accepted, as any warrior must, that death was simply a way of life. With heavy hearts, they left their fallen companion behind. The only burial for her would be beneath the icy boulders on the foreign planet so far from home.

There was no end in sight of this deadly tunnel, and the luxury of tension-building silence was firmly behind them. The path itself became a weapon. With every step, there were traps or drones. Spikes propelled from seemingly nowhere, sending them ducking behind their light barriers. The shields were activated constantly in the short-range battle mode to always be ready. There were sensor mines that took time and care to navigate safely. Sentry guns would fire without even so much as a clue that they were there. They couldn't know what would happen next, so they were relying only on instinct and reaction to keep them alive.

Each challenge was met and then overcome. Their skills and their hearts got them through. Never did they bow to fear or fall for the tricks on that, the most hazardous of pathways.

They ran, no longer afraid of alerting their foes; this was a question of survival. They had to get out of the tunnel before it took them, just as it had already taken Nessa. The only positive was, with such fierce resistance, now they knew for certain they were on the right path.

Their bootsteps echoed off the walls as they went. They hated to run. They would prefer to stand and fight, but when your enemy is the very walls around you, standing and fighting is not an option.

Their limbs ached and strained from the excursion. The mental exhaustion constantly drained them. Their bruises and strains urged them to stop, but finally, the four remaining warriors escaped that tunnel.

For the first time in a long time, they could pause, catch their breath, and gather their senses. Nessa and Farg were in the front of their minds, and there was great sadness in their hearts as they sat and rested. They needed to rekindle their strength. They sat in confusion. Despite the years of combat behind them, these weapons they had never seen. This left them uncertain and uneasy. The only thing they knew for sure was this harrowing journey would get tougher yet.

The Base

The darkness lingered to a misty morning but eventually made way for the light. Cold, tired, and wet from fog, Penny and Alex, blowing steam, made their way further through the woods. A low, pale sun did its best to lift the mist. The trees stretched upwards, jagged and haunting, dripping constantly. The chorus of birds sang the morning's tune. The wind rattled the branches above. All around was the sound of nature and their footsteps. They may have been in the elements, yet still the adventure drove them onwards. It would have been so easy to be grumpy, but after uncovering the stones, they were hopeful for what else their journey would bring.

Penny clutched the box in her hands, examining their prize within. She was fascinated by the strange pebbles, completely transfixed. They looked like nothing she'd ever seen, sending her imagination wild. Where had they come from? Did they have a purpose? Were they even of this world? What did it all mean? She was so lost in their mystery and beauty that at times she stumbled, not concentrating where she was treading.

A few steps ahead of her, Alex was distracted too, though for very different reasons. He was called along by The Fleck, drawn along a path to nothing. His mind was empty, he felt. He concentrated on the feeling, the instinct, the journey they must walk to a destination unknown. He grew excited. His pace increased. He could feel something on the horizon.

Penny rushed to keep up as the clouds rolled in, making it darker amongst the trees. After a while, Alex stopped and stared. His eyes fell upon a lone white decaying tree that stood out amongst the others. Just as it had when he was within his Mantis host, once again, it called to him. It felt familiar even though that memory had long since left his mind.

"Penny, look, that tree." He pointed towards it.

"So, it's a tree. What about it?"

"I think that's where we need to go."

"There's nothing there but other trees."

"Just come check it out. Trust me." He flashed her a smile.

"Sure. Why not? I don't know where the hell we're going anyway."

They headed towards the tree nervously, not knowing what to expect. Both of them felt as though the ground could open up and swallow them whole at any given moment.

Suddenly, the birds stopped singing, and everything around them was deathly silent, unnaturally so. The cold breezy weather made way for a thick and still atmosphere. It tingled upon their skin. They crept forward and then almost stopped. They were afraid; of what, they didn't know, but they felt it.

Flashes of light caught their eyes up in the clouds. Glowing orbs of different colours penetrated the gloom above. Now there was static electricity in the air.

"What is that?" Alex was astounded.

Penny stood in stunned silence. She had no response. She couldn't speak. She had no idea what it was.

Something burst through the clouds, a huge silver craft. It was round with tiers like a wedding cake. The lights flashed along the flanks, rotating. The hairs stood up all over their bodies. They were both frozen, staring on in complete awe.

The craft gently drifted across the sky. It was completely silent as it floated towards them. To their amazement, from behind it, a second craft emerged.

"Go! Come on, Penny. It's coming towards us."

Penny stood there staring. She was terrified.

"Penny. Come on!" He grabbed her coat.

She snapped out of her trance and ran with Alex. The only thought in her mind was that she was about to be abducted by aliens and experimented on. She had never been as afraid as she was at that moment. She followed Alex, slipping on the leaves, towards the white tree. The craft drifted towards them. It loomed overhead.

They ducked down low, trying to hide from view with their hearts thudding. Finally, they reached the white tree. They crouched behind it. The two craft above simply vanished into thin air. The trembling pair breathed a sigh of relief.

There was a green flash and a pop, and they were instantly transported to another place. They materialised in that same room where Alex and his host had been before.

Penny screamed and jumped at the sudden change in location.

"It's okay, mate," Alex said to try and calm her. The truth was he was every bit as afraid as she was.

"Where the hell are we? We're not onboard those spaceships, are we?"

"I don't think so. They vanished before we ended up here. I think they had gone."

"How do we get out of here?" She looked frantically around the room. It seemed they were trapped. There were no doors or windows or any furniture, only the pad they were standing upon. Penny was on the verge of freaking out completely. Had she been alone, she most certainly would have done.

Alex walked round the room, searching for a way out. The door opened from nowhere.

"I guess we go this way then. Stay quiet."

"Can't we just go back to the woods, Alex? Please, I'm scared."

"I am too, but I don't know how to get back to the woods. It'll be all right. Stay close, okay?" She didn't respond. There was fear written all over her face. This time he made sure they made eye contact and asked again. "Okay?"

Penny nodded.

"Come on," Alex whispered and put his finger to his lips to suggest they should remain quiet. He stepped forward and poked his head out into the bright corridor. He turned his head left, then right, and gladly found the corridor empty.

He beckoned Penny to follow him, and together they crept out into the hallway. They went along, stepping gently to stop the sound of their footsteps echoing off the walls. That place was another level of high-tech. It was like nothing either of them had ever seen before. UFOs above, strange technology... could this be an alien base?

That thought didn't help Penny with her fear at all. She was almost sure some brain-eating alien would just appear from nowhere at any moment. For now, the place looked empty, and for that fact, they were both very grateful.

They made their way down the long empty corridor. Eventually they came to a doorway that led to a huge chamber. Alex took the lead once more and carefully checked inside for any sign of life. The room was void of movement. Slowly, they went inside. There was a balcony overhead with stairs leading up to it. Then there was a platform at the far side with two glass tanks on stands upon it. Inside, there was a strange swirling mist.

Alex was drawn towards them. They called to him. It was an irresistible urge. He crossed the room with purpose, heading directly for the stage.

Penny followed along behind him. She hated every moment. As they neared, she could make out strange creatures squirming in the mist. She didn't know what they were. She didn't want to go anywhere near them. With every step she grew more afraid.

"Alex, I don't like this. Don't."

There was no stopping him. In no time they were at the very edge of the stage.

"Give me the box, would you?"

Reluctantly she handed it to him.

Alex opened it, taking one of the stones in his hand. The Fleck spoke to him, guiding him with images, not words. It pulled him towards the tanks.

"What are you doing? Alex, please. Don't go near those things. What are they?"

"It's okay." He stepped forward while his companion held her breath.

Penny felt like something bad was going to happen, like there was a looming shadow before her. She tried one last time to stop him. "Please, Alex, don't."

He shushed her rudely and continued making his way towards the nearest tank.

He stared longingly into it. Again, it called to him, silently whispering his name. He positioned himself beneath it. A transparent tube zoomed up from the floor and clicked into place around him.

"Alex. Alex!" Penny rushed over, banging on the tube, trying to free him from his prison. He hardly even noticed her.

The panel appeared, just as it had when he was within his alien host. Somehow, he knew what to do. He lifted the stone and gently put it in place.

"No. Alex. No!" Penny yelled to him, desperately trying to stop him, but it was too late.

The bottom of the tank opened wide, and the halithstord rushed wildly towards him.

Penny screamed, putting her hands to her mouth. Her eyes were wide from shock. She started frantically hammering on the glass tube, trying to break it, desperate to get Alex out of there. She screamed again, aghast with what she was witnessing. Blood and his screams filled the tube.

Alex roared and thrashed while the creature burrowed its way into his head.

Penny stopped banging on the tube. She froze, horrified. She was witnessing her friend's horrific death right in front of her, and there was nothing she could do to stop it. She was helpless. She screamed and wailed. She simply couldn't bear to watch any longer, so she clamped her eyes shut. She wished this moment wasn't really happening. She disassociated, like if she opened her eyes, she would be in another place.

Then the screaming stopped. Only then did Penny dare open her eyes, certain she would see a bloody corpse in the tube.

Alex stood and stared wildly with blood running down his face.

It was unnerving. Penny backed away.

He smirked at her, chilling and cold.

She turned and started to run.

The tube retracted, and now Alex was free.

"Wait, Penny," he called out. "You need one, too. It'll make you strong. The other one's for you."

She turned her head. "Get away from me!"

"But, Penny, it's the only way. It's why we came here. Embrace it."

She didn't answer. Her only thought was to get out of there and get back to the woods. She ran hard for the doorway. Alex leapt from the stage and swiftly bounded across the room. He was as quick as a flash. Swooping out an arm, he picked her up off the ground and held her there.

She squirmed and thumped at his face, desperate to get free. She kicked her legs. She scratched at him and writhed while he held her under one arm.

"Get the hell off me, you freak!" she screamed.

Alex smiled coldly. He rushed back towards the stage. Penny fought him, with every ounce of strength, with her entire being, but Alex was far too strong for her.

She screamed over and over, cursing at Alex as she did. Every second she fought to free herself from his iron grasp.

He leapt on the stage with a huge bound and threw her down beneath the second tank. She squirmed and moved and tried to run again. He reached out an arm and grabbed her.

"Even if you get me in there," she screamed, "I won't put the stone in. Let go."

To her surprise he did. Again, she started to run.

He took the stone in his hand, leapt up high, and clunked it onto the tank. A crack spread across the glass and some of the gas leaked out. He hit it again, and this time it smashed. Now the symbiote was free in the room.

The halithstord moved quickly, eager for its bond, slithering like a snake along the smooth floor. Penny looked back over her shoulder to see Alex still upon the stage. The halithstord sprang and leapt through the air. It hit her in the head like an iron bar, leaving her teetering on the very brink of consciousness, knocking her with a thud to the floor.

Snipers

The Elders rested for a while, but they could little afford to linger, so they continued their journey. It wasn't long before they met their next inevitable challenge. A stream of light came from above sending the Mercenaries diving to avoid the shot.

They quickly took cover behind their shields. Three clone soldiers holding sniper light rifles in anti-gravity boots zipped through the air. They moved like lightning. Their aim was deadly accurate. These clone soldiers, engineered to have hollow bones like a bird and lower muscle density than their fellow soldiers, were perfectly designed to hover for this purpose. They would have been quickly overcome in hand-to-hand combat, but for this task, they were perfection.

The Elders were pinned down for the moment as endless streaks of burning light rained down from above.

"Admiral, give me a distraction," Asu said. "We won't last long like this."

"Agreed, soldier. Nik, Jax, you know what to do."

Jax threw a flash-bang grenade. Two seconds later it exploded. A wave of bright light burst out, blinding the clones. Nik launched another. This time thick black smoke poured out, hiding the warriors within.

Asu burst from his hiding place, unloading towards their enemies. The snipers moved above him quickly, darting out of the way, narrowly avoiding the barrage.

The Admiral fired upwards with sidearms in either hand. The glowing plasma flew. The clones moved too quickly, even for him. As the plasma burst through the smoke, it glowed, giving the snipers a split second's warning. For beings such as these, that was warning enough.

It may not have killed them, but the plasma fire kept the clones distracted. Nik drew a blade, Jax drew hers, and in an instant, they hurled them through the air. These weapons were silent and dark and came at the last moment through the smoke. Nik's jabbed into the first sniper's chin, piercing its armour and sending it tumbling out of the air. A split second later, Jax's took the second one down, killing it instantly. Then only one remained.

As one, the warriors unloaded upon their opponent with devastating fury. The sniper tried to move but was rapidly overwhelmed, dead and falling, crashing to the ground with a dull thud.

Nik laughed. "They only sent three?"

"They can send as many as they want. We'll kill them all." Jax fist bumped her friend.

"Don't be too cocky," the Admiral said sternly. "There will many more to come. We'll be lucky to even get out of here."

Nik jabbed at Jax with her elbow. "Yeah, Jax."

They fought back giggles like naughty schoolgirls.

The Admiral shook his head. He couldn't stop himself from cracking a smile.

Complete

The searing pain stopped. Penny opened her eyes. A new power had stirred within her. She felt different and strong. She felt complete. She smirked. Standing up, she stared at Alex like she wanted to consume his very soul.

Alex swallowed hard. Guilt was eating him alive. He couldn't believe what he had done to his friend. He never wanted to hurt her. The Fleck, inside him, was warming him, pleased with him, conflicting him. It was even more pleased with itself. What needed to be done had been done.

"Penny?" His voice was nervous.

She stared wildly at him, rage like fire burning in her eyes.

"Penny? I'm... I'm sorry."

For a few seconds she said nothing, just continued the unnerving stare, blood trickling down her face with her fists clenched. She was coiled like a spring.

Alex took a step back, fearing a fight was about to begin. It would be a fight he deserved and one that even the symbiote inside him didn't want to have. They could feel the power flowing from her and buzzing around her. Alex was strong, but he could tell, Penny was something else altogether. She was different.

She leapt towards him, sending him skipping backwards.

Penny smiled. She knew her full potential had now been unlocked. Nobody that ever bonds with the halithstord regrets it, even if it was forced upon them.

"If you ever touch me again, I will kill you," she growled.

Alex was afraid. He cowered in her shadow. "I understand. I'm sorry."

Her mind swirled a little, caught between wanting to rip Alex apart and knowing it was the right thing for her. Now she was who she should have always been. She had been afraid and confused, but those emotions were gone. Anything could happen now, and she would welcome it.

The symbiote inside warmed her, it fed her, it loved her, and she loved it back. She doted on it. She was grateful for what it had done for her and what it had given her. The feeling grew by the second as she and the beautiful symbiote became one. It was the deepest love that she had ever known. Now she was special. She wielded great power, the like of which she'd never dreamed. Penny was superhuman, but little did she know, she would need to be.

She sensed and twitched. She could feel a dark presence lurking somewhere nearby. "Get ready," she said. The halithstord knew a fight was coming.

Alex prepared himself. The symbiote inside him urged him along, yearning for both blood and the challenge.

A large shadowy figure entered the doorway, slinking as it went. It zigzagged across the room, eating up the space between them quickly. Alex braced himself. He wasn't about to run from the clash; he would stand and fight. Garard the Reptilian, the guardian of the base, flew through the air, surprising Alex, kicking him in the head. He hit the floor, hard.

The Reptilian turned and faced Penny, drooling. Shock and fear were written across her face when she laid her eyes upon this monstrous beast. She couldn't help but take a few steps back.

From the floor, Alex spun his body round braced on one hand. He outstretched his legs, sweeping Garard's away. It was the Reptilian's turn to hit the floor. Alex didn't give the fearsome creature a chance to return to its feet. He flung himself on top of it, punching its face over and over. Then they started wrestling chest to chest.

The creature below him thrashed wildly, then sunk its teeth into Alex's shoulder. He roared out and pulled himself away, leaving a chunk of flesh in Garard's mouth. It moved quickly, putting its feet on Alex's hips, bucking its body, kicking him away. Alex stumbled backwards. Garard got back to its feet. It stood tall and stared him down with blood dripping from its chin. Alex clenched his fists and ran right for the creature.

There was a mighty clash in the centre of the room. Alex swung his fists while Garard bobbed and weaved, leaving the blows grazing its scaley skin but never quite landing. It jumped forward, grabbing Alex as it did, throwing him to the ground. He hit his head hard on the solid floor. The Reptilian jumped on top of him wrapping its long fingers round his throat. It opened its mouth, revealing sharp teeth. Drips of saliva fell onto Alex's face as he lay there helpless. The Reptilian roared, opening its mouth as wide as it could, and lunged.

Garard grabbed the sides of its head as smoke left the holes that were its ears. It screamed. It rolled over and let out a deafening roar. A second later, the Reptilian slumped down dead.

Alex scrabbled out from underneath the creature and turned his head to see Penny standing there. Her eyes had a strange glow. That cold smirk had returned to her face.

"W... What happened?"

"That creature was weak. Now it's dead!" Penny growled like a predator over a kill in a voice that he didn't recognise. Her face unnerved him to the soul.

"Thank you," he said nervously.

With a slight shake of her head, like a light had gone out, her eyes returned to normal. "What was that thing?" She sounded like herself again.

"I don't know. An alien, or a monster?"

"It looks like a lizard."

"It looks like a dead lizard. What did you do to it?"

"I really don't know. It was so strange. I kinda thought about it and felt this energy build up inside me, and then somehow, I felt it build up inside of that thing. Then it died." She shrugged.

"What?!"

"That's all I did. I swear." She seemed flustered as she recollected the feeling. "What is this thing inside me?"

"I don't really know. I like it, though. It makes me strong."

"You're not that strong," she joked pointing at his shoulder.

"Oh, that. Yeah, weird. I can hardly feel it, but it should hurt, right?"

"That should hurt a lot, mate. I bet lizard man has gross germs. We need to get that cleaned up."

"Oh, I didn't think about that. What if it's venomous? I could die!"

"Don't be so dramatic, ya clown. It's just a little boo boo," she mocked him. "We need to find some water for it or something and dress it. Is there any left in your bag?"

"Yeah, a little."

"Come on then. I'll fix you up, wounded soldier."

She set to work, doing the best she could with what she had.

He sat there stone-faced, even though it should have been agonising. "Hey, I'm sorry. I shouldn't have done what I did. I *had* to do it. I don't know why. I didn't have a choice. I didn't hurt you, did I?"

"No. I know, as stupid as it sounds, I *should* be super mad at you, but I know you did the right thing. That lizard thing would have killed us both if you hadn't."

"Please, just don't fry my brain," he joked.

"No guarantees there, pal. You better watch your step."

The Elevator

The Elders kept going, knowing the whole time that they would soon be challenged in battle again. Their presence had long been known by their enemies. They were poised for a fight, one that would undoubtably be upon them quickly.

They walked through bright white rooms, then corridors between. Each was empty and silent. Their path took them through a narrower corridor. There, they were nervous. They were vulnerable with no cover and nowhere to run. Should there be an ambush or more of the types of traps that had already claimed Nessa's life, they would be sitting ducks.

The narrow hallways opened out into a larger square room. The warriors stopped as Asu carefully checked within. It seemed empty. He beckoned the others to follow and stepped into the centre of the room. Their muscles were twitching in anticipation, their eyes always searching for any sign of their enemies.

With a whir and a jerk, the entire floor below them started to rise like an elevator. They readied themselves. There was little doubt that this was a trap and soon they would be fighting for their lives.

The Admiral looked up. This big wide shaft seemed to go up forever. Now the Elders readied themselves for the unknown. They silently prepared for a battle that was surely to come. The floor rose slowly for a few minutes, then clanked and stopped.

They were surrounded by walls which retracted quickly into the floor, exposing them on all sides. Five clone soldiers rushed in, blades drawn from all around them.

A fearsome battle to the death began. Jax, with her light sword in her hand, reacted, stopping her attacker's blow. Nik quickly backed her up with her whip and light shield. The clones were as fast as a blur. It was all they could do to avoid the incoming flurry of strikes, never mind landing blows of their own. These clone soldiers were a huge problem for the warriors.

The Admiral was engaged against two foes on the other side of the room. He was only hanging on.

Asu leapt forward, swinging his blade low. The clone soldier standing before him jumped over it and struck back. Asu blocked it expertly, parrying the blow and kicking his foe in the chest. It stumbled backwards and dug its feet in then lunged back at him. Again, Asu blocked the attack.

His attacker jumped a summersault right over his head then jabbed its weapon downwards. The strike bounced off the Spy's blade as he rolled over on the floor and thrust his weapon skyward. As the clone landed, it came down on the sword. It was dead in an instant.

Asu was back to his feet in the blink of an eye as a second soldier rushed at him. He arched his back and narrowly avoided the incoming blade, swooping a mere inch from his face. He sprang back upright, launching a dizzying overhand left. It crashed into his foe with a sickening thud. The clone soldier went stiff and then limp as it fell. Asu leapt high and jabbed his weapon down into the stricken creature, spilling its life on the floor.

Now Asu came to his comrade's aid. He jumped into the thick of the battle. With the power of both he and the Admiral, another clone was quickly taken down. Now only one of the deadly soldiers remained.

Jax and Nik went wild; they weren't about to let Asu steal their kill. Nik whipped the clone, removing its eye and a chunk from its head. A second later, with a second spark, its head fell from its body. They stood panting, offering each other a fist bump.

Again, the elevator clunked into action and started to rise.

"There will be many more," the Admiral warned. "We'll need to concentrate our fire on the clones as they enter. We can't let them get that close again. Be prepared."

The elevator stopped. This time, from the walls, two doors opened. Instinctively, the Admiral and Jax fired on the door behind them. The others, the one in front. Three clone soldiers fell coming through the doors, but five got in.

The warriors were struggling against this mighty enemy. They hung on, desperately fighting, trying to survive. While the Elders had to double up on them to take one clone down, Asu was another story. Fuelled by his symbiote, his genetically engineered body, and his experience, he made short work of the unthinking clones. He didn't use his guns any longer, he used his blade. Bodies, limbs, and heads were starting to pile up on the elevator's floor. The blood made it slippery.

On the journey upwards, the elevator stopped three times. Each time they were rushed by their enemies. Every time they would have almost certainly been killed if it were not for Asu. The Elders were exhausted. They were overwhelmed by hopelessness. The reality of the situation was dawning upon them. Though they were mighty warriors, they simply weren't powerful enough to overcome these soldiers in great numbers, and they knew it.

The elevator made its final stop. A single door opened, but this time they were not rushed by the soldiers.

Carefully, Asu poked his head round the door. There were four towers at the end of an open room. That was when, from the tall structures, a barrage of weapon fire came at the doorway. The Elders hugged the walls tight to avoid the volley. There must have been hundreds of soldiers. The deafening explosions boomed out, sparking and spitting. They could feel the heat and see their deaths. They were pinned down. It wouldn't be long until the clones would rush them, and they would surely be lost.

For an unnerving second, suddenly there was silence. There was a strange energy, like something else had entered the room. There were faint whispers, seemingly from another plain that tinkled in the background. They couldn't quite make out the words, but they were there. All the Elders heard them. They felt a presence.

From below their feet, something came into existence. It was a shadowy haze, deep black. It made no noise. It had no smell or warmth or coldness. It was a wisp. It snaked around the warriors' legs and then through the door, out into the room, growing and expanding all the time.

The silence was broken, and the weapon fire began again. The Elders pressed themselves against the walls, trapped. Then again, everything was silent. They were still afraid to move for a few moments more. Then Asu drew a breath and poked his head around the doorway. This time there was no plasma fire; it was silent. The clone soldiers were gone.

In Range

"We're nearing the system now, sir," the voice came through the comms.

The journey had been long, but at last, Jas, Varget, and more importantly, the core were nearing their destination.

Jas sent a message that would take hours to reach the Admiral. "We'll be within range by the time this reaches you. My next message will be when the drop is complete. Take care out there, Derk."

Now he turned to his companion, Varget. "We'll be meeting them on the far side of the planet's moon. There's a cloaking dome and a port pad, too. We'll need to escort the package to the buyer's base from there.

"The rest of the fleet will be stationed out here on the edge of the solar system. We'll go in with the landing team in the cargo shuttle. The fighters can flank us in case something happens. We'll take a neutral formation. We don't want to appear hostile."

"The leader is the Admiral's friend, though, is he not?" Varget asked. "We have nothing to fear from him."

"I've been doing this job for a while. I've never personally had dealings with these buyers before. We can't be too careful. Things feel odd."

"This should be an easy drop, Jas. A couple of hours and we'll be out of there."

"I hope so, my friend. Things have been weird. There's an uneasiness in the galaxy. I can feel it."

"Don't start getting all woo woo. You know it makes me paranoid."

"You need to think less and feel more. There's energy out there. It communicates with the cosmos. We are all part of the same body."

"Oh, here he goes," Varget teased him, but really, he absorbed his wisdom.

"The universe is a body, like yours or mine. The mind is consciousness. The flesh, dark matter, the black holes at the centre of the galaxies are the organs, the stars are like the veins. The planets and moons are the capillaries and nerve endings, and we are the microbes that live within the body. We are all a part of the same organism. You can learn to speak to it."

"Interesting, but now you *are* making me paranoid. Anyway, we're getting slightly off topic here. We have a job to do. I'm sure everything will run smoothly. If not, we'll just crack some skulls."

"If we end up cracking skulls, this task has gone horribly wrong. We must be careful. The planet's inhabitants are hostile. They are a violent, unadvanced, and ignorant species. We must use stealth. We can't afford to alert them to our presence."

They gave the orders to the crew on the ship and suited up then made their way down to the shuttle bay.

Leaving the fleet behind, hidden far from the star's warmth, the landing crew of twelve soldiers, Jas, and Varget along with the core headed towards their meeting place. The six-fighter craft flanked the shuttle for protection, yet so far from the fleet, alone, they couldn't help but feel vulnerable. Events had been so weird lately they could little afford to rule out any possibility. They could only hope that the drop would go smoothly, and they'd quickly meet with the rest of the craft on the far reaches of the solar system. Then, together, head back to the mercenary fleet at the rendezvous, hidden out in deep space.

Complete Part II

"What the hell happened here?" the Admiral asked. "Has anybody got any ideas?"

"We do," Nik said. "We've seen this before."

"You have?"

"It's like smoke, but it lives and breathes. It wraps around you, consumes you, and takes you somewhere else, or maybe nowhere at all. I don't understand it, but we have both experienced it." She indicated her friend who, as always, was at her side. "Daze could control it. Like there was something else inside her."

"That can't be true."

"I've seen this before, too," Asu said. "When I was back with The Sect. It's how I ended up on this ice planet. It is a wisp. There are ways to control it and some beings that can, like your friend."

"Who would even know we are here, much less do this to help us?"

"One thing I've learned on my travels is," Asu said, "there are many things that remain unexplained. This universe is complex."

"That it is, Asu. That I do know. Maybe someone is watching over us." The Admiral said the words but didn't really believe them. He was simply filled with gratitude. He didn't understand how or why, but it seemed they would survive for at least a little longer. "Let's go. Be ready. They could be hiding anywhere."

They moved on, trying to concentrate on the mission, but the question of why or how this had happened was always at the forefront of their minds. How could it not be? For some reason that they didn't understand, a miracle had been bestowed upon them. The only certain thing about these mysteries was that the Elders would take full advantage of it.

They crept through the room, weapons at the ready, always. They checked the towers. There was nobody. Hundreds of clone soldiers had simply vanished into thin air. The only evidence of their existence was the weapons that lay strewn on the floor. They had been dropped in place, like their owners had just disappeared. The sheer number of rifles and blades laying abandoned everywhere only told of the magnitude of what had occurred. It was a haunted scene, leaving an uneasy feeling. They could only be glad that whatever these strange forces were and whoever controlled them seemed for now to be on their side.

They gladly left the unnerving empty towers behind. They went out through corridors and different rooms, checking every corner, but finding no sign of life anywhere.

"This way. We are close." Asu sped up, almost to a run.

"Slow down, Asu!" the Admiral ordered but in vain. "We could run straight into an ambush."

"The way is clear, sir," he replied. "We have no time to lose."

"And how would you know that, soldier?"

"You'll have to trust me. I just know. I feel it."

"Wow, you sound like someone else we know," Jax pointed out. "Always following blindly because 'just trust me.' She's dead now, Asu. Just saying."

"Let's make no assumptions, Asu," the Admiral told him. "We mustn't be foolish. We must be prepared."

Asu was impatient, longing and itching to follow that pull, but he fought back against it. He listened to his companions and slowed his pace. They went on for a while, then within him the pull grew stronger. With that, the Spy knew that they were close to their destination.

"This door. We need to open it."

"Jax," the Admiral said, "can you hack it?"

"I can hack anything. It'll take a while, though."

"Get to work, soldier."

It took quite some time for Jax to open the door, which gave them an unexpected opportunity to rest and take on some fuel. They carried liquid nutrition in their suits, which they took on board through drinking straws to sustain their waning energy.

Finally, the door opened. The warriors readied their minds and their weapons and went carefully inside.

The room was the size of an aircraft hangar with dingy light. Their eyes searched the room for enemies. There were countless glass tubes hanging down from the ceiling, obscuring the view ahead.

"Get down!" Asu yelled urgently. Something within him had warned him of imminent danger.

Then weapon fire started, hurtling towards them as they ran and ducked for cover.

"How many, Asu?" the Admiral asked.

"Hard to say, sir. I know what to do. Follow me." The Spy ducked low and ran, using the glass tubes to keep them from the enemy's view. The others followed him closely.

The plasma fire ripped the fragile tubes apart, leaving jagged glass raining down on them and covering the floor.

Asu stopped as he reached a ladder that led up to a gangway. He ushered the others up and quickly followed behind. They rushed across the gangway, returning fire where they could, keeping their heads low when they could not.

From the metal pathway below, they stepped onto a transparent panel. Asu rolled a handful of micro grenades out ahead of him and activated his light shield. The rest of the group didn't hesitate to follow his lead.

There was silence, then a deafening explosion. The shockwave licked the shields, but the Elders were far enough away that they were safe from the blast. Below them, a jagged crack spread quickly across the transparent surface. One second later, there was a mighty crash, and the floor shattered beneath them. The Elders fell, plummeting through a strange mist, then hit the floor with a thud. In an instant, from within the thick mist, there was movement all around them.

"Quickly, remove your helmets," Asu urged. "Or they'll destroy the environment suits. This atmosphere will sustain you."

They helped each other, frantically removing them.

The symbiotes within the mist left the already bonded Asu alone but quickly found their three targets. They squirmed over each other to be the first to reach them. Each warrior screamed and writhed as the winning halithstord buried itself into their heads. Then with a pop, the bond between entities was complete. They replaced their helmets. They leapt and pulled themselves out of the halithstord nest and back onto the gangway.

Each mighty warrior was warmed. They smiled coldly and revelled in their newfound power. They stood silent for a moment, doing nothing but feeling their expanding strength. Each felt a glow in their veins, a new energy bubbling inside. They had found what was always missing within them. It was now a part of them. At long last, they were complete. Now, as one, their fearsome war cries, the warning to all who would dare oppose them, echoed out across the room.

They sprang into action like wild animals, tearing across the gangway straight towards their enemies. Clone soldiers were spread throughout the room. Guards, that just a moment before, would have easily defeated them, but now the Elders were more than a match for their foes. There were many enemies, but quickly they fell by the warriors' hand. They were ripped apart with plasma fire from a distance, or they were cut down, eyeball to eyeball. The Mercenaries stood panting, leaving around them nothing but death.

Now their bond was made, the first part of the mission was over. The warriors could head to their destination. They could march on and seek the one they had come for—the child.

"Fade out, little souls, or pop like overcharged lightbulbs. They spark their fury, spitting their flames like dragons. They are the monsters, lurking around their corner. Scream wildly for help, but it goes unheeded, unheard. It's extinguished like a candle in a cold, cruel breeze. The moments have come and gone, and now they must return to the obscurity of nothingness. They fall through the labyrinth of life, scurrying like rats up a drainpipe. That drainpipe will end in the bitterest disappointment.

"So, what if they disappear when they were here but a moment? Even the whispers of their existence will echo and then fade. They think they matter, that they are good and set souls free, but they are led into to a trap. They carry them forward into destruction. Though at times brave and surging with fury, now darkness will dominate the day, and nothing will greet the night.

"You cannot win. Your fate is sealed."

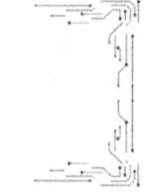

Blood Lust

The alarm started blaring within the empty underground complex.

"What is that?" Penny asked.

"I dunno, but this won't be good," Alex replied.

"Shh. There's a shadow in my mind. I see it. I can feel it. It's coming, closing in on us."

"Huh?"

"It's there. Something's coming. Something bad."

The symbiotes started churning inside them, excited and electrified. They filled them with adrenaline, calling for the battle.

"Hide. Maybe we can get out unnoticed," Alex said.

They ducked low beneath the stage as three figures entered the room. They were Reptilians like the other one, but these seemed to be armed.

"They thought someone would be here. They came for something. They must have come for the other lizard dude. They'll find its body," Penny whispered.

"How do you know that?"

"I don't know how I know. I just do."

"Stay low," he whispered.

"No!" Penny stood up, roaring as she did. Her symbiote did not want to hide; it wanted to fight. It wanted blood. The Reptilians turned and saw her. They fired upon her while she sprinted, with her head down, and rolled. The plasma crashed into the floor, narrowly missing her. She ducked behind the stage.

Alex now came out from his hiding place and tore after Penny. He kept his head low, but he was grazed by the plasma. He joined Penny and crouched, panting.

"After three, yeah," she said.

"What?"

"One, two, three. Go!"

Penny burst out from behind the cover and rushed towards the Reptilians. Alex blindly followed her. Their newfound speed and agility drove them as they ate up the distance quickly. It was like nature, like their bodies had always been able to move that way. Compared to them, the Reptilians were clumsy and slow. They reached them in seconds, unhurt, and launched themselves through the air.

Penny hit the first two simultaneously, and they fell like bowling pins. Alex landed on top of the other, with his knees crashing into its chest, crushing its body armour. He reached down and, in one flowing movement, removed the blade from his foe's leg sheath and forced it through its chest. Never before had he killed, but here and now, he did it without thought or remorse. Inside, as he looked down at his slaughtered prey, his humanity screamed, but his symbiote silently smiled with satisfaction.

The remaining two Reptilians got back to their feet, with the nearest rushing at Penny. It fired its weapon. She moved. She grabbed its gun in both hands and rolled backwards, jabbing her foot in her attacker's midsection and flipping it over her head. It flew over and landed with a thud on its back. Penny, still with the weapon in hand, jumped up. She fired down upon the stricken alien, killing it instantly. She spun around and shot again, dropping the other.

The pair stood victorious above their fallen enemies and basked in their own glory. The symbiotes inside them glowed with momentary satisfaction.

They removed the weapons from their fallen enemies and took them for themselves. Now they both had a rifle, a sidearm, and a blade. If there were more of those things coming, they would be ready.

"What do you think they want?" Alex asked.

"I dunno. Who cares? Let's go."

"Sir, Garard is here, but it is dead," the Reptilian hissed the strange language over the communication system.

"What? How did this happen?" the Reptilian Commander replied.

"There are trespassers here."

"The place was supposed to be empty."

"It was, sir. It is not. We've already sustained losses."

"Kill them! Then you must carry out Garard's part in the plan. It falls upon you."

"I'll do my best, sir."

"Your best is not good enough. Complete the task or the punishment will be severe!"

The Reptilian swallowed at its leader's words. "You and you." It gestured to two of its soldiers. "Go. Finish them." It pointed towards the doorway.

The two reptilian creatures burst through the doorway. They were quickly dispatched by the savage glowing weaponry of Penny and Alex.

"There could be loads of them," she said. "We need to be careful."

Alex peered around the doorway only to see a barrage of plasma come hurtling towards him. He moved so fast with his heightened reactions, like the world was in slow motion. He jumped back and ducked behind the wall. The plasma glowed bright as it licked the doorway right where he had been standing.

"Penny, stay back."

Penny stood calmly by the wall, awaiting the flurry to end. "We can't stay here. They'll come to us, and we'll have nowhere to go. We need to move."

They awaited a break in the plasma explosions that quickly came. Then they heard footsteps.

"You take the left. I'll go right. Go now!" Penny moved like lightning with the words, spinning out from the doorway, unleashing her weapon, sending Reptilians sprawling. Alex came rushing out a second later joining his friend in the corridor firing.

They were ripping through scaley flesh, taking down the aliens, leaving their foes laying limp and lifeless on the floor.

Though they had never even seen weapons such as these, they used them by instinct to deadly effect. The symbiote inside showed them the way. It needed to. It yearned to kill.

They couldn't know how many of the Reptilian soldiers there were in the base, but they had to move, Alex insisted. Once again, a destination called to him.

They didn't know where they were going, and they were sure to be pursued the whole way by their enemies, but they went all the same. Penny followed Alex closely.

They were not running from combat; that, the symbiote welcomed. They were running for a destination. Their hearts raced with exhilaration, and power and strength surged within them. The killing made them feel alive. They felt unstoppable.

Through the seemingly endless base they went. Each area looked almost identical to the last. It would have been so easy to get lost in that complex, but Alex was drawn along by that mysterious pull. Maybe his eyes and mind could be fooled, but this instinct could not.

The Buyer

Slowly, the shuttlecraft with the core onboard landed at the arranged meeting place upon the moon. The buyer and his crew were already there, eagerly awaiting the precious cargo.

In their environment suits, Jas and Varget stepped off the shuttle along with the landing crew.

The twenty awaiting Tall Whites towered high over the Mercenaries. The leader welcomed them warmly.

"Is the core onboard?" it asked anxiously. "I would like to inspect it." Though the language was foreign to them, it was translated through the comms system.

"It's here. Please, follow me," Jas replied politely.

They went back across the moon's surface and up the ramp into the shuttle. The Tall Whites stood around the core, seemingly very pleased with the purchase they would make. "We must take it to the port pad. We'll port down to our base from there."

They put the core carefully upon an antigravitational trolly and moved the precious cargo.

"Sir, we have incoming. It looks like a Reptilian fleet coming in fast from the outer solar system." The startled voice from the fleet out by the Ort Cloud came over the Mercenary's comms system.

Jas's disappointment was almost palpable. This was exactly what he had feared could happen. "How many? Can you intercept them?" he asked.

"Two motherships and some fighters. We're on our way to intercept now. You only have six hours before they reach you."

"Do your best, son. We'll get out of here now." He turned to the Tall Whites. "It's a set up. Reptilians are on their way. Our fleet will try to intercept. We have to get off this moon, quickly. How far is the port pad?"

"The Reptilians have betrayed us! They've broken the treaty. The Mantises will make them pay. The pad is not far. We'll port down to the Mantises' base. We cannot lead them straight to our own. Our defences are poor, but the Mantises will help us repel the traitors."

Now they couldn't afford to be as careful with their precious and explosive cargo. They pushed it along as quickly as they could, across the rugged and uneven surface. The process was painfully slow.

Then plasma fire lit the darkness. Deadly shots jagged towards the group. Jas saw a squad of Reptilian soldiers firing upon them from near the port pad. Garard was supposed to lead this ambush, but thankfully for the Mercenaries and the Tall Whites, it had already met its demise.

The landing crew took cover and returned fire, as did the two Elders. The Tall Whites were slower to react, but they finally joined the battle.

"Get the core to cover," Jas yelled out, knowing they'd all be dead if it exploded.

The Tall Whites struggled with it but moved it out of the line of fire.

"Mercenaries, on me," Jas ordered. Half the squad stood and fired, keeping the Reptilians pinned down. The others burst from their cover and made up some of the space between them and their attackers. Now the more advanced group covered the others as they pushed up.

"Tall Whites, bring the core closer. Behind this cover." He gave a hand signal. "Fire!"

The Mercenaries unleashed, leaving the Reptilian soldiers stuck huddling behind their cover. The group of Tall Whites brought the core up on its trolley.

"Mercenaries!" Jas cried. "Push forward."

They made up more and more ground using the same technique. Two of the landing crew had been lost, but they had taken down many more of the Reptilians. They inched up, getting ever closer.

Once again, Jas, with Varget by his side, took cover for a moment.

"We couldn't intercept them, sir." The sound Jas had been dreading came over the comms. "They got through. We took out most of the fighters, but the motherships got through. We've taken heavy loses. I'm sorry, but they'll be there soon."

"Follow them in. We'll need the backup, son."

"Aye, sir."

They fought on, taking ground all the time. The Mercenaries were far better warriors than the inexperienced Reptilians. Finally, Jas and Varget took their enemy's last position and, with it, their lives. Blades slashed through armour and flesh leaving a bloody trail in their wake. The Reptilians may have been taken easily, but they had cost them time they couldn't afford. Worst of all, they had cost them lives. They rushed towards the port pad, desperate to get the core to the Mantises protection.

Finally, they reached their target with not a moment to spare. There was a green flash and a pop, and the Mercenaries, the Tall Whites, and the core appeared instantly in the Mantises' complex below the ground.

Jas immediately took charge. "You four, take the core away from here. Find a place to hide it. You three, find the Mantises, and tell them what's happening. The rest of you, cover the port pad. They'll follow us through, I guarantee it. We'll hold them off as long as we can."

The Tall Whites rushed away to carry out their orders. Some with the core, others in search of the Mantises. The remaining Tall Whites and the Mercenaries, led by the Elders, took up positions and readied for the coming battle.

Weapon fire boomed in the base, surprising the Tall Whites that were transporting the core. Reptilian soldiers stood in front of them.

"Stop. Hold your fire," the senior Reptilian soldier addressed his charges, holding up its hand. "The core will blow if it's hit. Use your blades, your teeth, or your claws to claim our prize. Many of our kind have fallen here. Let their deaths not be in vain."

The creature finished the words when a blade suddenly appeared poking out its chest. The reptile was pierced right through its body from behind. The sword was retracted quickly, and the soldier fell limp. The other three Reptilians fought back yet were quickly and expertly defeated. Now Penny and Alex stood there, staring at the bizarre creatures before them.

"What the hell... are... those things?" Penny was astounded. If she had thought that the Reptilians were strange, then the Tall Whites were something else altogether. They glowed and shimmered, as if they were illuminated from within. They were tall and slender and quite beautiful. Penny and Alex were in awe, but they were not afraid.

"I have no idea," Alex finally replied after standing silent for a moment.

"Put your weapons down," Penny whispered. "We'll show them we aren't a threat. This thing must be what the lizard men are after."

They both sheathed their blades and put their hands out with their palms facing the aliens.

The Tall Whites spoke, but all the humans could hear was a series of tweets and chirps, bird-like and incomprehensible.

"I... I don't understand." Penny shrugged her shoulders.

It chirped at them again.

"We are humans. We mean peace," she said the words slowly and deliberately.

This time the Tall White spoke into the comms. "Leader, there are humans here. They stopped a Reptilian ambush. They saved the core. We cannot communicate with them, but they are good fighters."

"Okay, we'll bring them in."

The Tall Whites scuttled away. They could linger no longer. The core was far too important.

The imposing figure of Varget appeared and beckoned Penny and Alex to follow him. Gladly, he wasn't as shocking a sight as the other aliens had been. Huge, with a strange skin tone and a beard with a deep blue tinge, maybe, but he looked close to human from what they could make out beneath his helmet. They didn't question; they followed him.

They joined Jas, the Mercenaries, and the remaining Tall Whites. They were in position near the pad, ready to guard it.

"Get a couple of those communicators, son," Jas said.

The soldier fixed them to Penny and Alex.

"Can you hear me?" Jas asked.

"Yes, I can! This thing is amazing!" Penny said.

"Okay," he lingered on the word, slightly confused by her excitement. "Understand me, if you try anything, you will be dead in an instant. What are you doing here?"

"Let me speak, Alex. I like using this translator thingy." Penny was still a little excited. "We're gonna help you. We're on your side. We killed the weird lizard people."

Jas was confused. They were not the words of a warrior, yet somehow, he felt mighty power exuding from them. At times, he could see things that most could not. He felt a glow emanating from them, like they were there to help, or maybe even that their destinies were entwined.

"Where are the Mantises?"

"The what?"

"Insectoids. To you, maybe, aliens."

"We've only seen the lizard monsters and these tall angel things. No insects, so they're not here. We've been all round the building. Wait, do they have six legs?"

Jas shook his head and rolled his eyes. "Just come with me. We need to protect the core."

"Wait," Alex said. "There is a safe room in the big chamber. We should hide it there."

"Right, son. That's perfect. You two," he addressed the two humans with him, "I'll get the Tall Whites to wait for you. Take them to the safe room and get back here as quickly as you can. Once the invasion starts, it'll be too late."

Alex and Penny ran through the base the way they'd come, back towards the main chamber with the stage. As promised, the Tall Whites met them there with the antigravity platform.

"Follow." Alex ushered the aliens now that they could understand him with his translator.

Silently, a conversation began inside him. *"Hey, Fleck, how will I know the code? I need your help here."*

"We have the code. Never fear. The Fleck notices all. The Fleck remembers all."

He rushed to where the panel to enter the safe room came up from the floor and typed in the code that The Fleck showed him silently. As it did before, the door opened.

They rushed the core within, then Alex closed the door. The Tall Whites remained behind. They would be the guardians of the core, the last line of defence.

Penny and Alex rushed through the base, back to Jas and Varget.

"Okay, the core's safe," Alex said.

"The core is far from safe, son. They will be able to read the radiation traces straight to it. We must defend it. Get behind cover. We don't have long. This is gonna get wild."

"Good. I like wild!" No longer was this her excited schoolgirl tone; Penny's voice was a primal growl. The symbiote inside her bristled, eagerly awaiting its bloody feast.

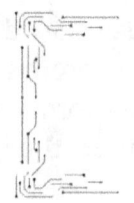

Drones

Eventually the Elder's journey led them back onto the icy planet's surface. The howling wind and snow didn't slow them anymore. Their halithstords inside fed them, gave them power, healed them, and gave them strength. They were stronger and faster than they had ever dreamed they could be. They skipped across the icy tundra for hours. It was flat and snow covered. Led by Asu, finally, they could see mountains in the distance.

Those mountains called to the Spy, almost beckoning him towards them, pulling him in, seducing his will. He followed, thoughtless and hypnotised, drawn by a force he didn't understand.

In the pale starlight, the planet was gloomy even during the daytime, but still Asu caught a flash of light in his sharp vision. It was something metallic in the sky.

"Drones!" he shouted to warn the others.

They spread out, readied their weapons, and waited, poised for the incoming battle. Their symbiotes twitched, eagerly awaiting their moment that was soon to arrive.

Glowing green orbs shot out of the small, silver, disk-shaped craft. The Elders scattered as they exploded all around them. They moved from danger and returned fire. With almost every shot, one of their attackers hit the ground, useless. The Elders with their newfound power were even more accurate than ever and even fiercer. Many craft had exploded and sparked and crashed to the ground, but there were still more coming in fast.

Green orbs crashed into the ice, sending glassy, jagged chunks skywards and crashing down, rumbling the ground. The warriors were as quick as a flash, but the explosions were ripping the smooth surface to pieces. The weapons went off all around them and total carnage ensued. Flashes of light reflected off the snow and ice that rained down constantly from above. The smoke was thick in the atmosphere as the very ground beneath them shook. Huge fissures opened in an instant, and cracks spread across the frozen tundra. Like a shadow, more of the drones loomed above them in formation. Seconds later, once again, the sky was on fire.

"We need to move!" the Admiral yelled.

The streams of plasma fire lit up the sky as now the warriors took out the drones on the run. They needed to find cover somewhere. Out in the open like this, despite their power and shields, they were little more than sitting ducks. They tore across the landscape, unleashing fury with their weapons as they went.

The ice burst open in front of them, and now tubular drones took to the sky, each spitting rapid fire plasma. The robotic craft were buzzing everywhere overhead. Explosions boomed around them, and plasma rained down as they ran, straining, towards the mountains. The drones had no chance against these skilled and now enhanced warriors, but there were so many, they could only just avoid the incoming chaos.

They jumped and zigzagged and floated across the surface as fast as they could. Every second, each of the fearsome warriors took out more and more of the machines. Any lesser beings would have been overcome quickly, but these mighty warriors would find a way to win this battle.

The drones had thinned out, and the ice all around was blackened and scattered with fallen machines. They finally had hope they would reach the relative safety of the mountains. Their lungs were burning, and their muscles were straining inside their suits as they got ever closer to their destination.

Then, in the poor light, the warriors saw a wall, but this wasn't a constructed wall; this was a wall of clone soldiers.

"Turn back, people!" the Admiral cried. "We need to use the craters in the ice as cover. There's hundreds of them."

The warriors stopped and turned.

"Only hundreds? Is that all? This'll be easy," Nik joked.

"Whoever kills the least has to buy the drinks," Jax said.

"If we survive this, *I'll* gladly buy all the drinks," the Admiral responded.

"Deal!"

They ran back the way they came, still fighting against the remaining drones as they went. Finally, they reached the scars of the heaviest part of the battle where huge chunks were taken out of the ice. They each jumped into one of the bigger craters, ducking down. Quickly, they popped up and took out the last of the drones. Then there was silence that would not remain for long. The Elders felt a rumble. This time it was not of an explosion but hundreds of feet tearing across the landscape towards them.

"Dirk, it was a double cross," Jas's voice came over the comms. "The Tall Whites have the core, but the Reptilians have ambushed us. We've got limited numbers here to fend them off. We're up against it, but we'll give them hell." There was a slight pause. "It's been an honour to serve under you but even more of an honour that you are my friend. Thank you. Good luck, Dirk."

The broken signal had taken many hours to reach them. A response was, at this point, almost a waste of time.

"Great, more for me to worry about," the Admiral said.

He sent a message back. "Fight them well, my friend. Give them everything you have, and I'll be seeing you soon. The honour is all mine."

He turned his attention to the problem before him—an army of powerful clone soldiers baring down on their position.

The Attack

Penny and Alex joined the soldiers in building barricades and created some cover with anything they could find around the base. They acquired several antigravity trolleys like the one on which the core was carried. Solid, heavy, and metallic, these made for perfect cover. They set them up not far from the pad. They crouched ready with just their heads and weapons exposed.

Together, their humanity trembled, afraid of the battle that approached. They were still only Penny and Alex in part, and that part of them feared both pain and death. They thought of the things they enjoyed in the world. The nice things they didn't want to let go. They were just dreams or memories, there in that strange place, fighting for and against alien beings, for a cause they did not understand.

Luckily for them, the symbiotes inside them had very different ideas. They did not long for happiness, or good times. They longed only for war. They twitched impatiently for the carnage to begin. They would not have to wait long.

Up ahead, the uneasy silence was broken by weapon fire. With that, they knew that soon the lizard-like army would stream into the corridor. The foolish Reptilians would be running right into their awaiting predatory jaws. Penny and Alex prepared themselves, offering each other a reassuring glance.

A grenade hit the floor with a thud and rolled towards them. Although this was like no grenade they'd ever seen, they both knew what it was. They ran and dove as the blast rang out and echoed around the entire complex. The heat grazed their bodies while they rolled over face down and covered their heads. They waited for the blast to burn out before they returned to their feet and again took cover.

The Reptilians streamed round the corner. Penny and Alex opened fire before their enemies did. They took the first line of them down before the second wave returned fire. They ducked to avoid the onslaught. They waited for a break in the explosions. Only then did they pop up their heads, firing their weapons. Scaley bodies were scorched with the plasma. They came, they saw a flash, then they died right there.

Penny's mind began to whir as more and more of their enemies came. They had clearly broken the line in front, and now the two of them were the first line of defence on that side of the port pad. All the time they were getting closer and closer. Their weapons got ever nearer to their target.

She had lost all fear. She was present but distant at the same time. Her body instinctively raged through their oncoming foes. Her mind, on the other hand, searched hard for connections in another realm.

Somehow it wasn't distracting for her. It was her nature. She followed the mystic connections between entities. She snuck inside her enemy's mind. She confused them with images and distracted them with illusions. Then, while lost in a world behind their eyes, the Reptilians were helpless.

The enemy soldiers were running in circles from imaginary foes or screaming as flames licked them. They were diving on the floor and kicking their legs.

The incoming fire from the humans quickly laid waste to those of them that were nearby.

"What happened to them?" Alex yelled.

"Don't worry. Just go." Penny could already feel the exertion of holding the connections. She feared she would not be able to hang on for long. They needed to make the most of their advantage while they had it.

Penny came out from her cover, blasting any creatures she saw moving. She marched forward. Alex took the other side of the corridor, unleashing fury on the confused aliens. In no time, that hallway appeared void of Reptilian life. Dead bodies lay strewn all over. Fallen and blackened corpses with horrific scorch marks and the stench of cooked flesh lingered in the air.

The pair shuddered to their very souls at the grim scene created by their own hand. They carefully stepped between the bodies. For a moment, humanity ate away at them both. To kill so remorselessly left them arguing with themselves, yet still they felt pleasure. They felt powerful, maybe even invincible.

An injured Reptilian, barely hanging on to life, reached up a hand and grabbed for Penny's leg as she passed. She saw the movement from the corner of her eye. Jumping out of the way, she drew her blade and thrust it through the fallen creature in an instant. It died right there, gurgling.

Still, weapon fire echoed off the walls coming from the other side of the port pad. The fight was not over yet. In fact, it had just begun.

"We'll be at destination soon, sir." The voice from the Mercenary ship came over the comms. "I have a visual on the motherships, but we're staying out of range."

"Damn! That was not what I wanted to hear." That meant they were now massively outnumbered and outgunned. Jas thought quickly. "Do you think you can take down the motherships in a surprise attack, Commander?"

"They know we're here. We'd have no chance."

"Can you get past them and retreat to the planet?"

"I'm going for it, sir."

"Wait, what are you doing?... Commander?... Commander?" There was no answer.

There hadn't been a single moment that Jas and Varget had stopped fighting since the onslaught began.

Varget's gun barrel spun in a blur as deadly rapid-fire plasma spat out. It scorched their foes or carved them in half where they stood.

Jas had his staff, which fired light harpoons from either end. Alternatively, it could become a double ended plasma blade. He wielded it expertly, ripping through flesh and body armour with ease. They were the first line of defence on their side of the port pad. They took down all they could, the ones that stood and fought, but some escaped and headed towards the core.

The first wave of Reptilians had ported in from their own base, but now even more were at the pad on the moon. They were the bigger second wave. The Reptilians came in droves. Each shuttle landed for the occupants to disembark and pour onto the moon's surface, twenty at a time. The shuttles took back to the air to make another run.

They gathered and then swarmed into the complex. They were armed and prepared to fight fiercely. So long had they been out in the far reaches of the solar system, training, awaiting their moment. With their prize, the core, their moment would come quicker than expected. The terraforming would be completed, almost overnight, and then they could defeat the humans, and the planet would be theirs. At last, once again, they could walk on a planet's surface.

The Tall Whites protected the corridor. The one that their brethren with the core had gone down a matter of hours before. The core was now securely locked in the safe room in the main chamber. That was the path the Reptilians needed to follow, but to get on that path, they would have to get through the Tall Whites. There were eighteen of them taking cover behind doorways in the long corridor. This gave them an advantage. The Tall Whites, however, after years of failed genetic experimentation, were weak. Despite their huge size and expanded lifetimes, they were frail. In hand-to-hand combat, they would be quickly overcome.

Their strange glowing weapons, however, were effective from their advantageous position. Bolts jagged out like spears of light, leaving gaping holes in their targets, cauterizing their wounds, leaving a bloodless yet mortal injury. The bodies were piling up, but the Tall Whites were being overwhelmed by sheer numbers.

Two of their Tall White soldiers were lost, and the Reptilians rushed forward and took their positions. Now their advantage was lost.

Penny and Alex headed up the corridor towards the Tall Whites. They heard their shrieks over the comms. They cried for help. It was clear that before long they would be overrun. That would leave no defences between the Reptilians and the core. It would not take them long to find and capture it. They rushed to the Tall Whites' aid, spraying the narrow corridor with deadly plasma fire as their enemies came into view.

In the crowd of Reptilians, many died from the surprise attack, others retreated. Penny and Alex swarmed forward, covered by the remaining Tall Whites. They quickly quelled the resistance and retook the two positions in the doorways. There, behind the cover, they had evened up the odds.

As Reptilians came, they fell. The ruthless humans raged, tearing through flesh and bone and loving it. Still, they were conflicted, like one battle raged without and another raged within. To inflict such pain and misery was against their very nature, but they eagerly inflicted it just the same.

They pushed forward—Penny, Alex, and the Tall White soldiers—destroying all in their path, clearing the long hallways of anything that moved.

"We're in attack formation now, sir," the commander's voice came over the comms.

"No, you fool! Abort. They'll tear you apart. Do you hear me? Abort!"

The cannons on either side of the Mercenary's craft fired, lighting up space. They crashed into the side of the nearest Reptilian mothership. Part of the craft was blown off, sucking

Reptilian passengers out into the vacuum of space. They were dead instantly.

The mothership returned fire. The Mercenaries veered and began to race towards the moon. The weapon fire ripped huge chunks from their hull. The Reptilian cannons boomed out again, smashing into the craft, crippling it. Slowly, it fell apart and all onboard were lost.

The Orders

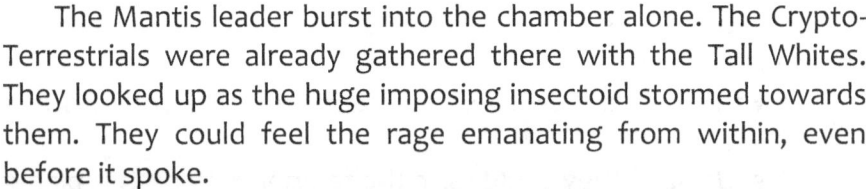

The Mantis leader burst into the chamber alone. The Crypto-Terrestrials were already gathered there with the Tall Whites. They looked up as the huge imposing insectoid stormed towards them. They could feel the rage emanating from within, even before it spoke.

Its tone was angry. "The Reptilians have broken the treaty! They are storming our base as we speak."

"Why haven't you stopped them?" the Crypto-terrestrial leader asked.

"That is not the question. How did they know we wouldn't be there? We didn't run from the battle. We had other business."

"Cut off their port pad. You never should have given them access like the rest of us."

"It was part of the treaty, and you are well aware of that."

"I knew they could not be trusted. Why can't you, the all-powerful Mantises, stop them? You are the overseer of the treaty after all. You bear responsibility for this."

"We bear responsibility only for the punishments to come, not the war. Our craft are on the other side of the galaxy. We will never return in time. The Reptilians knew this."

"Send your Grays to fight for you then, cowards!"

"They are observers, not soldiers. They will be useless in this battle. This is not our war! Our mission is peace in the galaxy, this you know. *You* must stop them. You are the custodians of Earth. The humans will become embroiled in an inter-planetary war that they cannot compete in. They are not ready."

"What do we care for the plight of humans?"

"The Reptilians are after something. They would not risk the treaty if their goal wasn't a big one. The humans are the least of your worries."

"What are we supposed to do?"

"As the custodians of this planet, you must gather your forces and stop them before it's too late. We don't know why they bring war at this time, yet still, they do. We are aware of their terraforming efforts, but it will be an age before the planet is ready. There is little point taking it now. What do you know? Speak now."

"The core," the Tall White's leader chirped. "They've come for the... our core."

Now the Mantis grew even more enraged. "Are you aware of what it could do?"

"Yes. Using it, they could raise the temperature on this planet in almost an instant." The regret in its voice could be heard. "The planet's surface will quickly become uninhabitable for the mammals and the birds. The ocean's temperatures will rise until the sea life is all but gone. Then it will be a desert with just the insects, the flies, and them. All the diversity will be gone. That is the thing that brought us here in the first place. We came to gather samples to reseed our dying planet. We have been fools."

"Why would you bring such a power here, knowing what you know?"

The Tall White paused. Though they are beings of less emotion than humans, its words came with a bitter edge. A wave of pain flowed within the creature. "To go home."

"The reason now matters not. You must stop them. The humans cannot know. The battle must be fought inside our base or on the lunar surface beneath the cloaking dome. The Reptilians, they gather on the far side of the moon. They are porting into our base from there."

"How many of them are there?" the Crypto-Terrestrial leader asked.

"We detected two motherships. There will be thousands of them."

"Our numbers are low. We cannot fight an army of such size. We cannot risk being annihilated. Our Earth presence will be extinct."

"Then make sure you win. At this moment, battle rages in the base. We can sense it."

"The Mercenaries!" the Tall White squawked excitedly. "The space pirates from whom we purchased the core. They are very powerful. They will make useful allies."

"Mercenaries will do anything for the highest bidder. You cannot rely on their aid."

Beyond the Cabal's knowledge, most of the Mercenary's fleet was not with their party, and most of those that were had already met their demise. The Tall Whites' hope was misled.

"Go now. You mustn't linger any longer. Gather your forces. Stop the Reptilians before it's too late. Use the port pads to get in unseen by the humans. You cannot afford to lose the core, no matter the cost."

First Wave

Back on the ice planet, an enormous battle was about to begin. It was the clones lined up in in rows, a huge army, versus the Elders with their skills, experience, and mighty strength. For these warriors, there was one goal—to break through enemy lines and make it to the mountains. There was no chance, despite their power, that the Elders could defeat an entire army. They just needed to cut a path through them. But first, there was a more immediate problem at hand. They needed to repel the first wave of clones and make a dent in the insurmountable numbers of soldiers they faced.

The very ice beneath them rumbled as the army grew closer. The fearsome wall of weaponry and flesh bared down upon them like a rogue wave on the ocean. The comrades in arms looking on were outnumbered hundreds to one. They would need every bit of their skill, every ounce of strength, and all of their experience to even survive, let alone complete their mission.

The Elders held steady in their cover in the ice holes as the clones swarmed towards them.

Jax looked through the digital scope of her sidearm. "They'll be in range soon, Admiral."

"Okay, soldiers, we need to take as many out as we can before they get anywhere near us. Shout when they get in range, Jax. Everyone lock and load. And good luck people."

The warriors with symbiotes inside were yearning for the blood of their enemies. Those enemies loomed and would so quickly be upon them.

"Nik, come with me," Jax beckoned her friend. She handed her a small bomb and took a second one in her hand. "We gotta be quick, okay? We need to get out of there before the clones come within range. You know what to do, right?"

"Yep, reading your mind again, like always. Let's do it!"

They jumped out from the crater and scurried across the ice.

"No, stop! What are you doing? You're crazy!" the Admiral yelled into the comms.

"We just might be, but don't worry. We know what we're doing."

"Okay, Nik, set it a hundred metres over there." Jax pointed the way then sprinted in the opposite direction. They planted the bombs firmly in the ice and then ran back towards their cover. They dove back into the hole in the ice. Jax fiddled with her wrist control panel, setting the bombs to blow when she pressed a button.

They ducked down in the ice holes, peering over the edge, watching the incoming soldiers.

"They're in range... Now!" Jax informed the group.

"Fire!" the Admiral screamed.

Each of the Elders and the Spy unleashed a savage volley of weapon fire towards their foes. They were deadly and accurate. With almost every shot, a clone fell, or at times, several. The soldiers jagged and zigzagged to avoid the incoming fire, but the Elders seemed to be able to predict their every move. It was almost as though they were psychic. They aimed not at the place the clones were, but where they would be.

"Get ready, Jax!" Nik yelled to her distracted friend as the soldiers tore past the bombs planted in the ice.

Jax readied her finger upon the control panel button.

"Hold on," Nik said. "Just a little longer... Now!"

An explosion flashed and boomed, sending out a huge shockwave, tearing apart the clones that were nearby. Jagged cracks spread across the ice like forks of lightning. Beneath the weight of the countless soldiers, the surface collapsed into a sheer glistening cavern. A huge number of clones fell out of sight. Others stopped at the edge, desperately skidding on the ice, teetering on the very brink of doom.

A huge cheer went up amongst the Elders. They watched on, laughing at how brilliantly the ingenious trap had worked.

Nik and Jax smirked at each other and fist bumped. Then they returned their attention to the countless soldiers that had made it past the trap and were now tearing towards them.

The clones that were behind the enormous fissure were forced to break left or right to avoid the deadly obstacle.

The Admiral and Asu concentrated their fire on either side of the cavernous opening in the ice. The clones were forced to gather and bottleneck in those two areas. They were easier targets for the amazing marksmen, and of that they took full advantage.

There were still a number of clones that had avoided the explosion and the falling ice. They had made it beyond the crevasse and were eating up the distance between them quickly. They fired upon the Elders as they ran, thundering across the icy surface.

Nik and Jax drew their weapons as the light sword sparked into life and glowed like fire. Nik's whip was on her hand attachment, where it was meant to be. They waited patiently, staying low, coiled like springs until the clones were almost on top of them. They gave each other a nod. With that, they sprang from their hiding place. Instantly, clone heads left clone bodies, and limbs were left pumping blood, unattached on the ice.

They charged towards their enemies, screaming like wild women. They dropped them one after the other, leaving the ice littered with bodies. The soldiers did their best to fight back. One pointed its rifle towards Nik. Before it could even pull the trigger, her arm cannon boomed. The clone's head fell from its body and crashed, rolling onto the ice. There was no time to admire her handiwork. She spun on the spot and, in one motion, flung her whip out with all her might. There was a blinding flash followed by a deafening crack, and another foe fell lifeless.

One of the soldiers had Nik in its sights. Jax caught it in her peripheral vision. She finished the two clones that stood in front of her with their blades drawn, first hacking their blades in half followed swiftly by their bodies.

She roared and ran, she jumped and swooped, her sword carving instantly through the clone's arm. It no longer had Nik in its sights, and quickly, it was no longer alive.

"Hey, thanks, you!" She flashed a smile of gratitude towards her friend.

"I gotcha, girl!" Jax waved to acknowledge her gesture.

The warriors continued their fatal assault until all the nearby clones were dead or dying on the ice. Only then did they head back for their cover. They joined the others and began firing upon the still onrushing crowd. They were now streaming from either side of them.

"Move!" the Admiral shouted out. "Push up."

There were more craters in the ice from the firefight that was still raging. The Elders scrambled from their cover. "Nik, Jax, you take the ones on the left. Asu, we'll take the ones on the right."

Unleashing plasma fire as they went, they took cover. Hordes of clones ran past the huge canyon in the ice, bunching up as they rounded the corners. They fired towards the Elders, leaving sparks exploding all around their icy cover. The Elders poked up their heads and fired back, taking them down in rows. The clones, however, just kept coming. Despite how many of their enemies they took down, the realisation dawned upon them that they would not be able to stop so many before they reached their position. Hundreds lay stricken or dead on the ice, but it was only a matter of time before they made it past the Elders' fire and reached their hiding places.

Overrun

Jas, Varget, and the remaining Mercenaries had defended the port pad well. The Reptilian numbers had started to dwindle.

Further inside the base, Penny, Alex, and the Tall Whites defended the corridor bravely, leaving bodies piled high on the floor. Now they had a much bigger problem—two motherships full of Reptilians were coming for the core. They, the defenders of the base's numbers, were far too thin for them to stand any chance against the incoming army.

For a while the Reptilians stopped porting into the base. Jas and Varget wasted no time in taking out the stragglers at the cost of another two of the Mercenary soldiers. They fell back and joined the others.

"To reach this corridor," Jas spoke to the soldiers, "they'll have to bottleneck at the end. They cannot get the core without coming through here, and to do that, they'll have to get through us. Here, we'll have an advantage. We can hold them up, but they will break through eventually. There could be thousands of them."

"We must retreat!" One of the Tall Whites squawked the words like a bird that was being attacked by a cat.

"If we retreat, they'll find the core quickly. Nobody is going anywhere. Is that understood? We die fighting, coward, never running." Jas was firm.

The Tall White turned and ran away from the group. The Tall White's commander ordered it to return to its position.

"Let it go," Jas growled. "We have no use for cowards." His words were bitter with disdain. This ancient and mighty warrior lived by the warrior's code, and there was nothing he despised more than cowards. The Tall White would die anyway. It could not escape the base.

An hour passed and the base was now silent. The scars of the battle that had raged were all around them. Charred bodies and blackened doorways told the harrowing tale. The echoes of explosions had fallen quiet, but the anticipation grew. The soldiers were all too aware that this was just the calm before the coming storm.

Penny and Alex impatiently hated the silence. They yearned for battle, yet they feared it at the same time. The symbiotes within were churning and baying for blood. They prepared for battle, but it would be easier to fight, to be present, than to think about the uncertainty of a future that would soon unfold.

Penny was silent and staring, but she saw visions behind her eyes. She drifted away. Within her mind there was an electric fuzz. It gradually cleared, then she saw true visions of another place. She saw the Reptilians gathering and preparing on the far side of the moon. They landed in a constant stream of small shuttlecraft. She saw a flash of the future, and with that, she knew when their enemies would come. The mystical vision showed her the Reptilians' plan.

"They're gathering by a teleporter thingy, up on the moon," Penny said. "There's loads of them there. They'll be coming as an enormous group. We've got about an hour or so before, well..."

"What?" Alex was astounded. "How could you possibly know that?"

"I don't know why or how, but I saw them. A vision. Not my imagination but the future."

"I knew it!" Jas's voice came over the comms having heard her words. "I can sense a great power in you. Both of you have it, but especially you." He pointed at Penny from across the corridor.

"Me?"

"Yes, you. I can only hope for the sake of us all that I'm right." Then he addressed the rest of the soldiers. "Believe the words she says. Prepare for battle. A shadow is coming, and soon it will be upon us."

The soldiers felt the Reptilians rumbling through the base long before they came into sight. They readied themselves for the imminent attack. Moments passed, then the onslaught began. Their scaley foes appeared in droves. They bottlenecked at the end of the corridor. Only a certain number were able to get through at a time. They squeezed tight together, squashing against the walls, slowing them. They met nothing but plasma fire and death. Now the Reptilians were forced to drag their fallen brethren out of the corridor just to be able to get inside. Again, the weapons exploded and all that moved, quickly did not. When the corridor was void of life, the gunfire stopped.

"Something else is coming," Penny announced as another vision entered her mind. "Sliver disks."

"Drones!" Jas warned.

"Oh, my..." She never finished the sentence.

"What is it, Penny?" Alex asked.

"There's hundreds of them!"

"Take down as many as you can, and get ready to move. We won't be able to stay here," Jas gave his orders.

The drones silently zipped down the corridors and into the bottleneck. The warriors opened fire again. Many of the drones exploded in sparks and crashed to the floor, but there were so many, they started to break through. The disks swooped in, dropping micro grenades all down the corridor.

"Go. Now!" Jas yelled it and the entire group left their cover and ran as fast as they could.

They ducked into doorways or around corners as the huge explosions rang out and a mighty fireball rolled up the corridor. Most of them now were incinerated in an instant. One Tall White, one Mercenary, Varget, Jas, Penny, and Alex narrowly avoided the deadly explosion. They unleashed fury and cleared the corridor. The last Tall White was taken down. For a second there was silence.

Then Penny yelled out, "There's silver balls!"

"Rollers!" Jas said. "Let's go. We need to get off the ground."

They ran while Varget and the remaining Mercenary took up the rear, blasting everything that came into sight behind them.

"There's a chamber with a balcony above. Follow me." Penny started to run towards the main chamber with the stage.

The Mercenary now fell, leaving only four. Varget backed down the corridor, never relenting, but this made him slow. Jas grabbed his friend by the shoulder to guide him and hurry him along.

Finally, they made it to the larger chamber. They rushed up the stairs and took quickly to the balcony above. Jas released Varget's shoulder and told him to run. He fired one more volley and turned. Now unhindered, the rollers zoomed towards him. They spun around as they went, flinging deadly spikes from within. They zipped through the air silently and passed through the retreating warrior. They pierced his body armour, his flesh, and in turn, his organs. With his environment suit breached, he fell with a crash to the ground, dead in an instant.

Jas screamed out at the death of his friend as pain burned in his heart. There was no time to mourn him. He knew he must honour him by winning the battle, although currently, it seemed impossible. The balcony jutted out from the wall and was lined with solid rock. It provided good cover. They ducked low.

The flying drones rushed towards them, fired, then circled round for another run. The warriors fired back, sending many crashing down to the floor. The rocky platform took the brunt of the blasts, keeping them safe, at least for now. The rollers lined the ground in their hundreds below. Before long, they separated, moving aside for an enormous swarm of roaring Reptilians that burst into the chamber.

The three remaining warriors looked down upon the sea of flesh in wide-eyed, shocked silence for a few seconds.

"Penny, take the stairway left," Jas said. "Alex, you take the right. I'll take the middle."

"We've got no chance against them!" Alex screamed.

"Then we die right here. Give them hell!"

Breaking the Line

The clones rushed, baring down on the Elders from both sides. They were getting close. Nik and Jax took turns throwing micro grenades amongst them, ripping apart their flesh with mighty explosions. Another huge chuck of ice cracked and tumbled into the crevasse, taking countless clones with it.

"We're coming to you," the Admiral yelled into the comms. He beckoned Asu to follow. They ran towards Nik and Jax's cover. Together they zigzagged across the ice to avoid the incoming fire before diving headfirst into the crater. Plasma thudded into the ice around them.

"Hey, fancy seeing you here," Nik joked.

"Okay, you ready? Let's take 'em the old-fashioned way." The Admiral smirked.

Jax drew her sword with a cold smile upon her lips. "I prefer the old-fashioned way."

Asu pulled his blade while Nik readied her whip, and the Admiral reached, grabbing two swords from the sheaths on his back. For a second, they waited, poised, then as one, they leapt from the crater. Immediately the Mercenaries set to work carving up the flesh of their enemies. They moved as quickly as a blur.

The clones came rushing at them, each falling to the Elders' weaponry and skills. Hacking their way through the crowd, they scattered their foes, leaving them dead on the ice. These enemies showed no fear of death; at times it seemed they welcomed it. While each of the clones were deadly and powerful, they were zombie-like in their attacks. With subdued fear and pain and without a cause to fight for, they would make mistakes that against most foes wouldn't have mattered.

The Elders, on the other hand, took full advantage of even the slightest misstep. Many fell to the mighty and experienced warriors. They were fuelled with the deadly bloodlust of the symbiotes within them. Flowing like water, each movement was perfectly connected to the next, like words in a sentence. The Elders deflected attacks and finished their foes before they could blink. They removed heads and limbs from bodies as they went, leaving behind a trail of destruction in their wake. A pathway of blood showed from where they had come. Ahead, still, there were scores of their foes.

The clones behind them were forced to stop shooting at the Elders as they would only hit members of their own army if they did. The warriors were surrounded but were cutting a path through the masses. Their enemies mindlessly surrounded them like a shield, swarming like bees. Viciously they carved their way through the wave of flesh that constantly crashed against them. Soon after the Mercenaries passed the edge of the crevasse, they looked up to see a huge wall of clones. There was no choice but to keep fighting. They had to break through if they were to have any chance of reaching the mountains.

"Shields, people. We're gonna need them." The Admiral said it loud and clear while sheathing one of his swords. The warriors obliged.

The Elders pushed further on, fighting every second. They were like a bubble, ripping through a sea of clone soldiers. Fit and powerful the Elders may have been, fuelled by the halithstord perhaps, but now they were starting to tire. Their destination was still out of reach. There was no end in sight.

Suddenly ahead, the clones spread out. The warriors ran for the gap. Finally, there was a chance to make some ground. Drones swooped in low over their heads.

They sheathed their blades and drew their sidearms. Drones were falling from the sky.

"Grenades. Now!" the Admiral yelled.

The warriors threw handfuls of micro grenades in all directions. They ducked behind their shields as they exploded. The shock waves forced them backwards and left a vast ring of blackened ice and charred clone remains around them. Finally, they had broken the line. With still many clones chasing them, they ran, muscles straining, their chests heaving in and out, straight for the mountains.

Weapon fire once again lit up the surface of the ice planet. The warriors zigzagged and jumped in all directions to avoid the plasma coming from behind. It scorched their body armour. The heat of the explosions reached desperately for their souls. Drones swooped over them, dropping their deadly payload in the Elders' path. They banked right or left to avoid the carnage, springing, rolling, or using their shields to evade the blasts.

The Elders kept their heads low, tearing across the smooth landscape. Ahead, there was a structure that brought them hope. Jagged cliffs of ice jutted up proudly from the surface. If they could make it there, they could take cover and catch their breath.

Drones flew over again while the clones still chased down their prey. The Admiral fired his sidearm, sending a drone into a wild spin. It jagged backwards and crashed then exploded. The metal shrapnel flew amongst the crowd of clone soldiers. It left maimed creatures, torn in half, sprawled across the ice. The Elders used their sidearms to take down the silver disks. They could outrun the clones with their head start, but the drones were quite another matter.

They took down the threats from above, thinning their numbers. Still, the army thundered after them. With their limbs burning and shaking from the exertion, finally they reached the cliff. They ran behind it and waited. At last, they could breathe, but it would not be long before the clones arrived. They crouched low, panting, preparing for the next phase of the battle. Still, they took out the remaining drones as they rounded the cliff.

"Jax, set another bomb by the base of the cliff," the Admiral said.

"It's my last one."

"Hopefully we can take a few down before they reach us. Nik, Asu, cover her as she sets it. Go."

Jax set out on her toes, rushing around the cliff. Through the ground, she could already feel the boots of the clone soldiers coming. She reached a point where the bomb would be hidden as the clones rounded the cliff base. She jabbed it down into the ice and then set it. She turned and ran back towards the others.

As she neared her companions, the first shots came. There were clones firing from behind and her comrades fired back from in front of her. She gestured frantically, and Asu and Nik turned and ran with her as she passed. Another three seconds went by, and Jax pushed the button on her wrist unit. For a spilt second, time stood still, then the huge explosion tore through the ice, sending clone soldiers flying. The cliff shook and groaned with the vibration.

The warriors looked up, wide-eyed, as a jagged crack split the cliff. There was a mighty rumble, and the huge overhanging icy wall slipped off the side. It came down like a guillotine blade and thundered outwards like a wave. They ran with everything they had, straining with the effort. Huge chunks of ice crashed down, smashing into the planet's surface. The Elders narrowly avoided the largest chunks that jagged into the ground, smashing huge craters as it did.

It was no use. No matter how they tried, they couldn't outrun it. They were being consumed by the freezing landslide. They were knocked off their feet as the ice tsunami passed, then bulldozed over the top of them. They curled into balls and covered their heads with their arms. That was all they could do. The ice beneath them gave a fearful creak, a crack, and the ground exploded open. A deep and dark crevasse appeared, swallowing the ground, the cliff, and the helpless warriors whole.

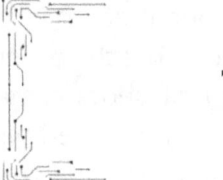

The Cavalry

The fierce battle raged in the Mantises' base inside the mountain. The three remaining warriors—Penny, Alex, and Jas—took out any Reptilians that were foolish enough to try and take the stairs. They sent them tumbling back downwards. They fought bravely with their entire souls, with every hope and dream, with their love of the special people in their lives; nevertheless, they would soon be overrun.

The first of the Crypto-Terrestrials and Tall Whites materialised on the port pad. The Reptilians gathered nearby were caught completely by surprise. The pad couldn't be locked on more than one location at any one time, so for now, it was on the Crypto-Terrestrial's mountainous fortress. That was the Mantises' only role in the battle—overriding the location. That meant, for a time, no more of the Reptilian's on the moon could port into the base.

More of the new coalition army came into the port chamber and quickly set about the Reptilians nearby. They cleared the chamber and stormed out into the hallway. There was no room to fire weapons in there, so this was blade against blade. The Tall Whites and Crypto-Terrestrials pushed forward as the Reptilians retreated to rifle range. They lined the narrow corridors of the base. The explosions echoed off the walls and shook the base as a fierce firefight began.

The three warriors up on the balcony were becoming exhausted. It was all they could do to hold back the onslaught that had lasted for what seemed an age.

"We can't stop them all!" Alex yelled at the top of his lungs. He was starting to panic. He wasn't ready to die. More of the leathery-skinned assailants rushed the stairs below him adding to his distress.

"Keep fighting, Alex. Don't give up. I'm with you," Penny reassured him.

Just hearing her voice reminded him what he was fighting for. He was fighting for the good souls. He roared and stood up, spraying every inch of the stairs. He ducked back down, panting, as return fire zipped past his head.

The Reptilians edged forward towards the stairs. Plasma slammed into the rocks around the warriors, keeping them pinned down. They tried to fight back, but soon they would be overrun, then there would be only death for them.

There was a bright flash and then a mighty boom as an explosion ripped through the chamber. The Reptilians were scattered and torn to pieces.

The lizard-like soldiers that were on the stairs turned to see what had happened.

"What the hell?" Penny peered over her cover and smiled.

The Tall Whites and Crypto-Terrestrial soldiers burst into the room. Penny had never seen the elongated-headed beings before, but she welcomed them all the same. They were making short work of the Reptilians.

This gave the warriors another wave of energy. The hopeless had suddenly become hopeful. They took down the enemies on the stairs, half of which were distracted by the battle behind them. They went together, blasting their way through the crowds, working their way back down.

Moments later the room was filled with death. Many bodies were Reptilian, with some Tall Whites and Crypto-Terrestrials scattered amongst them, but the one that hurt most was the body of Jas's fallen brother in arms, Varget.

"The base is clear for the moment, but there will many more coming," the Tall Whites commander warned the soldiers under its command.

"Commander," Jas approached, "there are two motherships up there. They come with many drones and rollers. I fear the next wave will be even bigger than this one."

The Commander bowed to him. "Thank you, soldier." And then to Penny and Alex. "Thank you for buying us time. You fought bravely."

"Thank us after this is over," Jas growled.

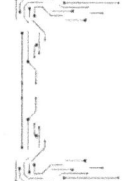
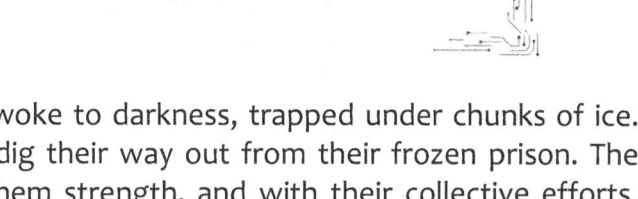

The Hollow Planet

The Elders awoke to darkness, trapped under chunks of ice. They started to dig their way out from their frozen prison. The symbiote gave them strength, and with their collective efforts, they freed each other. Each of them was bruised and winded, but they were still alive.

For a moment, in silence, they all thanked their lucky stars. They could have easily been killed in the fall. Maybe fate was smiling on them after all. More frozen boulders fell on them through the gaping hole above. They covered their heads for the second time.

There was movement. Nik's whip cracked in quick succession, ripping down the clone soldiers that had fallen in with them and survived. Jax set to work on two more. There were several clones down there, but they were scattered and injured in many cases. The Elders made short work of them.

They got their bearings and scanned their surroundings. Their flashlights glowing on the ends of their rifles was the only light. They were in a wide-open chamber beneath the planet's surface. In the sheer walls, there were icy tubes like an ant's nest. No wonder the ground was so unstable; it seemed a good deal of the planet was hollow.

"Maybe we can get to the mountain through these tunnels," Nik suggested.

The Admiral pointed upwards. "Well, there's no way we're climbing out of here. I don't think we have any other choice."

"Admiral, I think I can find the way," Asu said.

"You've led us this far, Asu. Take point. We've got your back. Stay alert. Anything could happen down here." The Admiral had no idea how true those words were.

Nik and Jax knew what the group could face. They remembered the hive the last time they had tangled with the child. They remembered the uncertainty that followed them through the tunnels while searching for their goal. They saw flashbacks of the bioweapons that had awaited them at every turn, and mostly they felt the fear. The sisters in arms were on edge, and the others could sense it.

"After you, kind sir." Jax dramatically gestured forward to try and lighten the mood a little.

"Thanks." Asu laughed.

They crept forward, not speaking, taking time to recover, moving slowly and deliberately. The ice above them constantly creaked, like it was straining to stay together. They couldn't trust the structure. It was clearly unstable and could cave in on them.

From above, drones zoomed down and followed them into the cavern, lighting the darkness with exploding balls of plasma. The warriors rolled out of the way of the blasts and opened fire. Now in the darkness, these machines were much harder to target. The disks zipped left and right overhead. The Elders' weaponry flashed over and over, but there was a whole swarm of them. With no choice remaining, they had to run.

Ducking their heads, they almost glided on the icy ground and quickly disappeared into one of the narrow tunnels in the wall. There, they waited. The drones swooped in for the attack, zooming into the tube. The Elders unloaded upon the bottlenecked craft. The icy walls rattled with the explosions. Quickly, the drones were little more than scrap metal.

Only once they were sure it was clear did they carefully make their way up the tunnel. The warriors headed towards the mountain. They could only hope that Asu knew where he was going. The twisted labyrinth of tubes could take them anywhere.

Always listening for signs of being followed or enemies up ahead, they crept through the tunnels. They hoped that they could get to the mountain, unhindered and undetected.

The Elders went for hours, all the time their anticipation building. It was quiet, unnervingly so. The warriors were comfortable in battle. They would march bravely into any danger that lay ahead, but the unknown drove them silently crazy. To be called into action was their comfort, to be in battle was their home, but walking through silent darkness was almost more than they could bear. The symbiotes within them were impatient. They yearned for battle and for blood. They fizzed within, bubbling up excitedly. Still, anxiety lingered.

Ahead of the group, Asu followed the calling within, drawing him along. It showed him the way. The Fleck that always lurked in his being never spoke in words. Its words were useless here and now, so it spoke in images. Always he felt his connection to The Fleck. He trusted it. He loved it. It was the one constant through his wild adventure.

He silently thought ahead, and he thought of the past, but mostly he thought of the battles to come. If this journey was destined to end in death, it was his duty to make sure they won. This was more important than his own life could ever be. It was a life he didn't even have anymore.

He was imprisoned in that shell of a body, in that place, neither of which were the things he wished for. He had been alone with his thoughts inside The Sect for so long, he no longer even remembered who he was before. Now he was just this—an experiment, a monster, a freak. His flesh shell was faceless and nameless, just like the others. He was a mindless killing machine of limited intelligence. It was Asu's soul that made him different from the others, still he feared he was just the same as them.

His senses twitched, like The Fleck warned him of danger ahead. He stopped, signalling with a hand for the others to do the same. They stood silently, their lights crisscrossing on the ice, searching every inch of the tunnel. The walls glistened almost magically as the lights hovered over the surfaces. The warrior's eyes were darting everywhere, ready. The symbiotes bristled within, hoping for blood and death. Then with a mighty clunk, a metal door slammed shut, closing off the tunnel ahead. Asu, who was the closest, ran towards it and examined it closely.

"We cannot get through this door," he warned.

"We can," Jax said. "It'll just take me a while. I guess we'll be stuck here for a bit."

"How long will it take?" the Admiral asked.

"Hard to say. I'll know more after I've had a closer look." She crouched down near the door and started to fiddle with her wrist unit.

"So, maybe I should do a little song and dance number, just to pass the time," Nik joked, lightening the mood in an instant. She did a few exaggerated, dramatic dance moves.

"Oh, please, don't," Jax said. "I remember what happened last time."

"Yeah, that sucked. They didn't have to start throwing stuff at me."

"Well, the best time for a 'song and dance number' isn't in the middle of a battle. They were trying to kill you."

"Yeah, that's why the right time is now."

Asu and the Admiral were chuckling away as the conversation unfolded.

Nik looked up. Something caught her eye. From the smirk and cheeky twinkle in her eye, suddenly her face was serious. She was alert and poised as her whip sparked into life. "What the hell is that thing?"

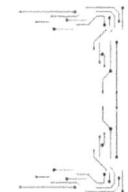

Holding the Base

"Now we've taken the base, we should be able to protect it," Jas said to an absorbent Penny and Alex. "I've got to talk to the Commander. I'll help set it up. We don't have much time.

"I have to go. Stay out of the hallways, you two, okay?"

"Can we just stick with you?" Penny asked. "You know what you're doing, and we do make a good team."

He smiled. "Sure, kid. You two are useful. Just don't get me killed, all right?"

They followed Jas over to the Tall Whites' commander. "How many soldiers have you got?"

"A couple of hundred."

"That could be enough, but we need to be smart. You see where you have soldiers lining the hallways? Get them in the doorways and the ends of the corridors. Put the biggest defence in the front line, by the port chamber."

The Tall White leader was glad for the advice; after all, it had never led the troops in battle. Yes, they'd trained, but this was a scenario they never truly expected. Things had been at peace for so long, none of them remembered the before times, the times of war. None of them had fought, even amongst themselves.

Jas took the Commander round the base, setting up the troops, instructing them in what to do. Penny made sure she was never out of ear shot. As was her way, she wanted to know what was going on.

Jas put each squad in place. He showed them where to retreat if they were overrun. It wasn't long before they were well organised and ready. Jas was nervous, however. With this inexperienced army, in the chaos and savagery of war, the outcome was uncertain. He had seen countless warriors in his many years of existence. In his wisdom, he knew during the battle some of the soldiers would thrive in the carnage, others would crumble. There was no telling which, until the moment of truth.

On the moon, the Reptilian forces had gathered in their hundreds and still more came. Their army was impatient, salivating at what was to come. Their time was here at last. Preparing for this moment had been the focus of the entire species for so long. It dominated their waking thoughts and even their dreams.

They had been blessed with enormous luck to have a core brought to them to speed up their fate. To them, they only cared about the result, not the method. They hated humanity. To begin, they watched and learned, but then they started to despise. They stared bitterly, green-eyed with envy. The humans—this inferior, ignorant, greedy, hateful, and parasitic species—had everything that the Reptilians wanted. They would take it for themselves. Now was time to storm the base.

It took them time to lock the port pad back onto their location, but finally, they were ready. They lined up in rows, with their weapons and their armour, prepared to port into the Mantises' base.

Time passed in silence. The uneasy nerves rattled around the soldiers. The fear of what was to come was thick in the air. Hands shook on rifles as they waited. Every second ticked by painfully slowly. The anticipation built of the moment they never wanted to arrive, but they didn't want to wait for. Jas walked the lines, offering words of wisdom. His presence called them to follow him into battle, and they would.

Then the port pad buzzed into life. The soldiers readied themselves. A pad full of rollers materialised and exploded the very instant they appeared. Metal darts ripped through the chamber, taking down the unsuspecting soldiers on the front line. With a second buzz, the Reptilians appeared and now were free to gather in the chamber.

The coalition soldiers were shocked by what had happened. So many of their army had fallen in one instant. To them, that did not bode well for the rest of the battle.

The warriors prepared themselves as the murmurs amongst them died down. The Reptilians surged forward behind a wall of plasma. The defenders of the base returned fire. Their moment of truth had arrived.

"Come," Jas beckoned to Penny and Alex. "We can help here."

They sprinted through the base until they reached a T-junction in the corridor just back from the port chamber. There, pressed against the walls, they waited.

"When the soldiers up ahead retreat, we'll push forward. The ones behind us will push up, too, and back us up. We need to take back that port chamber. Got it?"

"Got it," Penny said.

"Yep," was Alex's response.

Now he went on the comms. "Commander, order Squad 2 to push forward when I give the word."

The Commander gave the order.

Upon hearing the cry over the comms system of "Fall back!" Jas, Penny, and Alex readied themselves.

A scattering of soldiers flew past them.

Jas threw a handful of micro-grenades into the crowd of chasing Reptilians. The explosion made short work of the frontline, but they were only the beginning. They opened fire as the next row came into view.

"Squad 2, forward now!" Jas yelled.

The coalition soldiers came and joined them.

Now they sprayed the tunnel with plasma, ripping through enemy armour and flesh. Jas, Penny, and Alex pressed on as the coalition soldiers covered them from behind. Jas ducked into a doorway on the left, Penny and Alex, one on the right. The soldiers behind them unleashed again, taking down more of the Reptilians.

Jas, Penny, and Alex moved up again, lighting up the hallway with plasma fire and rushing to the cover of the next doorway. Behind them, Squad 2 took cover in the doorways that Jas, Penny, and Alex had left behind.

They repeated the action over and over, and inch by inch, they took back the corridor leading to the port chamber. Luckily, they had sustained minimal losses under Jas's masterful command. They gathered at the entrance of the port chamber. This would be their defensive position.

"Now, listen up," Jas addressed the soldiers. "If they push you back again, retreat and rejoin the squad behind you. Then go forward again, just like we did before. Be watchful for drones or rollers. We must hold this corridor. Understood?"

There was a resounding, "Yes, sir."

"Come, let's go. We must meet with the Commander."

Penny and Alex followed Jas as he rushed through the base and back to the main chamber that just hours before they were defending for their lives.

"The port chamber is covered, Commander, but you'll need to get your soldiers ready to back them up. If the Reptilians get loose in the base, we'll be quickly overrun. This is our only chance.

"We'll set our final stand in this chamber. Defend it heavily. If they make it this far, though, I fear we will already be done."

"Understood."

The Orb

There in front of them in the ice tunnel, swinging from side to side, was a strange orb. It was covered by strands of dim light. They were hair-like strings, snaked like spaghetti all around its form.

"Jax, how's that door coming along?" Nik asked.

"A while yet, you'll just have to—"

Her words were cut off by Nik's whip flung violently towards the orb. It struck it and sparked but bounced off its hard shell. With a buzz, the strands went from the dull light to burning fiercely white in an instant. It zigzagged, jerkily, fiery and menacing, buzzing with great power emanating from within.

"I think I made it mad," Nik half-quipped.

It stopped and spun around fast on the spot. The centre of the orb glowed red, and then like a flash, it zoomed into life. It zipped like a bullet through the tunnel, sending the Elders scattering to avoid a damaging impact.

Asu rolled over and fired a shot. It crashed harmlessly into the wall. He never missed, but this thing was quicker than even the shot.

They were all on their feet, poised for battle. The warriors drew their blades. The orb looped round, speeding up all the time and violently jagging left and right, turning right angles in an instant.

It smashed into the Admiral, denting his helmet and sending him down. It zoomed at Asu, but he leapt over it, flipping his body and landing cat-like on his feet.

Nik flung her whip out and struck it again. The orb stopped.

"I think I made it really mad!"

It shot out the wiry strands straight towards her. They zipped onto her armour, sparking. While she was safe from the blow, there was a surging pain like lightning through her body. She was flung across the tunnel. She teetered on the very brink of consciousness for few seconds. The symbiote inside her fed her strength. It called her back from the darkness and once again into the battle. She staggered to her feet.

The orb shot toward Jax. She ducked her head just in time, and the glowing ball clanged into the door behind her and bounced off. It left a huge dent in the metal.

Asu helped the Admiral up, and they prepared for the next attack. They desperately had to find weakness in this foe somehow. In that tunnel, there was nowhere for them to run.

Nik struck the orb again with her sparking whip. "How do you like it, huh?" Now *she* was mad. The strike didn't damage it, but it did make it pause in the air just for a split second. "I have an idea!" she announced. "Jax, come stand by me."

Jax sprinted across the tunnel, sword in hand, ducking the orb again as she went. She knew exactly what Nik was planning to do. Their bond ran so deep they were almost telepathic.

"Admiral, Asu," she ducked to avoid the orb, "drive it towards me, if you can."

They drew their sidearms and fired behind and around the orb, sheep-dogging it with their plasma. It rushed for Nik. She waited, only a split second, just to get her timing right. Out went her sparking weapon. It slapped into the orb, and for that one split second, again it stopped.

A split second was all Jax needed. She jumped and brought her sword down in fluent motion as she landed. It hit the orb, gouging a savage gash in its shield. It hit the floor. Quickly, it rose up again and zoomed away like a wounded animal. Now it was scrambled. It wasn't as fast or as in control of its movement as it was before it met with Jax's sword. Its balance had been affected by the blow, even though it had proved not to be a fatal one.

Asu opened fire as the orb circled around. His shots now warmed the outer coating of the damaged sphere.

The Admiral swooped the blade in his hand to hit the moving, glowing ball. The strands around it flicked out and entangled his weapon, sending jolts down his body and ripping it from his grip.

The Admiral stood dazed, his mind was cloudy, and his vision was blurred. The orb rushed in to finish him.

Asu fired desperately to force it to change direction. They were masterful shots that flew between his stricken comrade and his would-be killer. The orb turned and came at Asu. It went over his head as his shots heated its edges. Plasma tore into the ceiling.

There was a frightful creak. Jagged cracks forked out in the icy structure above them.

"Run! Now!" Asu screamed. He grabbed the Admiral and dragged him while the others ran towards the door.

The ceiling gave way, and boulders of ice came crashing down. They desperately dove forward as chunks of the roof rumbled to the floor. Before long, the tunnel was blocked. For a second, they breathed a sigh of relief. It would not last long.

Out of nowhere, Jax was hit with a shock that jolted her whole body. The orb was in there with the warriors.

There was hardly any room for the orb to move. It was trapped between the door and the fallen roof. It spun on the spot for a second or two, like it was trying to decide what to do, then flashed right towards Asu's head. He lifted his hands, cupping them, and caught the orb in mid-flight like a basketball. His whole body jolted. He fell convulsing to the floor. The smoke started to pour out of his hands, but still he refused to let go. He fought the pain with every ounce of his strength and hung on desperately. Every part of his body was in burning, writhing agony. The Spy's eyes rolled back in his head. The orb glowed its brightest yet.

There was no time or room for error, but Jax reacted. She sliced through the centre of the orb, splitting it in half. In an instant, the glow went out. With any miscalculation she would have removed a limb or taken Asu's very life, but with her skills, she did neither. The two halves fell from his hands and thudded onto his chest.

Around the Spy, the world fell silent. A grey mist descended upon him. It was as though time had stopped and he'd drifted forever. His breath was ever weakening, his heart teetering on the brink. No longer could it summon the energy to pump the blood around his body. His thoughts faded and he slipped into a misty dream, but this dream was the realest he'd ever known. With his last shred of consciousness, he felt his heart stop. He floated free from his body, and his last breath was drawn.

Through a haze he fell, and out into nothingness. Then the visions came. They were visions of time long gone. He was a child again. He went back to a place long since forgotten. A time when he knew who he was. He felt no fear of that place, *living* in that foreign body was the real fear. Now he could just be who he was, never pretending to be someone else again. At long last, from a life of torture, he was free.

The Fleck, however, wasn't ready to let Asu go just yet. The symbiote that needed him to live squirmed, trying to heal its host from within.

The Fleck spoke. *"No, Asu, now is not your time. There are still things that must be done. We cannot fail now."*

"Let me go," he replied.

"You can't go, Asu. The Fleck needs you. We must do what must be done. Come back, Asu... come back."

"I have nothing left to give."

"You have it all to give. You hurt because you don't know who you are. Fight on, Asu. Come back. That is who you are. There are other tasks to complete. Come back, Asu... "

"Come back, Asu." The Admiral knelt by his side. Locked inside the environment suit, there was nothing they could do for him. All hope was fading.

To the surprise of the group, Asu gasped a breath and opened his eyes.

"Welcome back, my friend." The Admiral gently put a hand on his chest and smiled down at him.

Asu realised then, maybe he had a reason to live after all—he now had at least one friend. He couldn't muster the will to speak even though he wanted to, but he smiled. He lay staring up, trying to make sense of the moment. His head was heavy, his eyes couldn't focus, but somehow, he was alive.

"You're one tough dude, Asu." The Admiral looked down upon him and then up. "Right, Jax, get working on that door. You either hack that thing, or we'll die in here. Old Asu here, he's already tried that one, so we'll have no more of it."

"On it, sir."

"We have little food or water remaining. Ration it. This may take a while."

A New Enemy

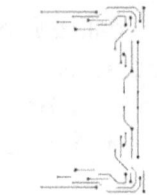

"I bring news of the battle, sir," the Reptilian hissed in its strange language. "I hate to break such news, but we're getting annihilated down there. Our loses are massive, theirs are few."

The two formidable beings stood watching on as their Reptilian soldiers climbed onto the port pad, only to meet their death. Jas's plan was working perfectly.

"Stop them. We mustn't lose any more troops. This core is becoming more expensive than it's worth."

With that, the commander gave the order, and the Reptilian soldiers on the moon's surface remained in place. They were alert and lively. The fear of the oncoming battle and the excitement for their cause stirred them into a frenzy. Hissed conversations broke out amongst them. They clutched at their weapons, twitching and ready.

Out on the edges of the solar system a huge craft appeared. The long journey through interstellar space was over. On board there were countless clone soldiers. They sat in regimented rows, never growing anxious or running out of patience for the journey. They were only created to fight. Soon they would be in the chaos of the battle that they craved, each with a symbiote yearning for blood squirming within. They were headed for war. The clone soldiers had come with only one purpose—to kill. The child's fearsome army was on its way, and their destination was the moon.

Jas heard the gunfire die down up ahead and eventually stop. A huge cheer rolled through the base. The soldiers guarding the port chamber were jubilant. "The fools think this is victory. The Reptilians have only retreated. They plot something."

"But what?" Alex asked.

Penny drifted for a moment. "There's still lots of them."

Jas addressed the troops. "Save your celebrations. They will come again. That was only a taste of what's in store. Those of you guarding the chamber, rotate with Squad 7. Take a rest. Well done, soldiers. Now, stay ready."

Alex thought for a few seconds. "I suppose they had to back off eventually."

"Well, they were getting pummelled, so I guess they'd have to try something new," Penny said.

He looked up at the ceiling. "I wonder what's happening up there. On the moon. It's amazing, Penny, isn't it?"

"It's mind blowing... When you stop and think about it."

"I wonder how many types of aliens there are. Probably millions, I should imagine."

"Yeah, there's loads of kinds, I'll bet."

"To think, they've been here the whole time, and we've been oblivious."

"Stop. It does my head in when I think too much about it. It's too crazy to make sense, but then, it makes perfect sense as well."

They were quiet and thoughtful for a minute as they pondered the realities of a cosmos that they had only just become aware of. They could only hope they would live long enough to find out more.

The clone soldier's ship crept ever closer. Many hours had passed. Now every Reptilian soldier was on the moon. The motherships had long since left and were headed back to the outer reaches of the solar system. They scanned the incoming clone ship.

"Sir, a craft of unknown origin."

"Ah, our back up has arrived. ETA?"

"Within the hour, sir."

"Very good."

The huge spacecraft came into the army's view. Shuttlecraft started to leave the flanks of the ship, each filled with clone soldiers. They made their way to the surface of the moon.

Penny was silent, lost in a haze. She stared forward blankly, not seeing what was in front of her but something altogether different. She was disconnected from those around her for a moment, but connections to others clicked into place. She saw not what was in her mind but visions from outside of her. Flashes, like photos of things in the cosmos, mysterious yet inviting.

Penny felt as though she floated free from the flesh-like prison that was her body. Colourful lights streaked by as she drifted out into the universe. She heard Liam's voice, whispering, but never loud enough to hear. She strained in the nothingness to hear his words. She reached out for him and longed for his warmth. Her beloved friend was always just out of reach.

She wanted to cry. She lingered there, in that place. A lost place, yet one that felt to her like home. Dwelling in this cosmic playground, beyond space or time, beyond even life and death.

Visions flooded into her mind. No longer were there thoughts of her friend. He had long since drifted silently away. Now they were visions of what was to come in a place nearby. She saw the near future. She saw the clone army gathering above. She saw death. Then she snapped out of her haze, wide-eyed.

"There's an army gathering above. I... I saw them. They all looked identical. There were hundreds!" Penny blurted out the words.

"Identical? You're sure?" Jas asked with urgency.

"Yes, exactly the same, all of them."

"I have seen them before. An army of clones. We only just escaped with our lives last time and there were not many of them. This many, in this place? I'm not sure we can hold them off.

They are powerful and hard to kill. With this inexperienced army, I don't know what our odds are."

"What will we do then?" Penny asked.

"Defend the base or die here. There is no other choice. I must warn the Commander. Let's go. The coalition will need us now more than ever."

The clones gathered on the moon in rows, pushing the Reptilians aside to get into position. There were protests amongst the lizard-like soldiers, but the clones didn't even acknowledge them. They stood in regimented rows, mostly infantry, but with snipers hovering above them. When there were enough of them standing ready, the child silently gave the order, and the fearsome clone army began to storm the base. The first wave packed themselves onto the port pad, and with a flash and a pop, they vanished and materialised inside the base.

The soldiers of the coalition opened fire when they entered. They may have had success against the Reptilians this way, but these clones were something else altogether. A shot that would have finished their previous scaley foe bounced off the identical warriors. They darted around so quickly it was hard to hit their targets. They were wild and ferocious. Unlike the coalition's army, these super soldiers had no fear, not of pain or of death. They piled into the port chamber and rushed forward.

"Concentrate your fire on one at a time," Jas addressed the soldiers of Squad 7 who were the first line of defence as panic was setting in.

They took down many of the first wave, but some started to break through the line. The clones drew their blades and stormed down the corridors, slashing limbs from bodies and removing heads. They ripped through armour, flesh, and bone, leaving carnage and death in their wake.

"Fire!" Jas yelled as the first of the clones came into sight. Penny and Alex roared, firing upon them, dropping them one after the other. "Give it everything you've got! We need to hold the line."

The Ring of Fire

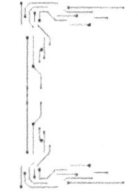

"Are you done yet?" Nik asked. Three seconds later she repeated it, just as she had, seemingly, a hundred times. She stood next to her friend, arms folded, tapping her foot in the most distracting way possible. "Come on. I'm bored."

"Pressure!" Jax laughed. "You're so annoying when you want to be."

"Thank you very much." She did their signature dramatic bow.

"Well, no thanks to you, I think I've got it!" Jax fiddled with her wrist unit.

"Yeah, yeah, you said that last time." Nik rolled her eyes.

"Well, yeah, but this time I really *have* got it."

"I hope so. I'm so bored, I'm starting to get dangerous."

"You're always dangerous."

"Of course, but I'm next level dangerous now. I'm bordering on going completely insane."

"Look, let me concentrate, would you?"

Nik gave her wide-eyed sarcastic look while she pretended to zip her mouth up.

Finally, with a hiss, the door opened. The Admiral and Nik cheered.

"Asu, we have to go. Can you walk?" The Admiral reached down a hand to help him up. He had done nothing but recover since his ordeal. This was the first time he tried to move. He grunted as he pulled himself up, taking his weapon in his hand once again.

"What are the odds there'll be more crazy traps like this one?" Nik asked. From their previous experience, they knew they had to expect absolutely anything.

Asu spoke. "There won't be. This I can tell. The mountains are not far. We were never supposed to find this tunnel. We were never supposed to fall through the ice. Resistance will be fierce, but not here. When we're at the mountain."

"Well, you've led us this far, my friend." The Admiral patted him on the back. "Let's go before that door shuts again."

"Yeah," Jax cut in, "fighting battles to the death against countless clone super soldiers is one thing, but being stuck with her..." She pointed at Nik. "When she's bored, now *that* is dangerous."

"Well, I still owe you a song and dance number, remember, so it won't be all bad."

Laughter rolled for a moment, but they knew they had to be quiet. Despite what Asu had told them, they still needed to be on guard. They didn't understand the methods he used, so they would be foolish to trust them completely.

They went carefully through icy tunnels. They crisscrossed and rarely seemed to be going in the same direction. It would have been easy to feel hopeless and lost, but Asu constantly reassured them they were on the right track. He ignored his pain and followed the pull, silently guided by The Fleck.

Just as Asu had promised, they met no other resistance, and at long last, ice made way for rock. They had finally made it to the mountain.

Cautiously, they pressed on in silent contemplation. Around them was the buzz of psychic energy, though they could not feel it with their electromagnetic protection. Now would be the time where strange visions would flash into their minds, crippling their senses from within, but this was a burden from which they were free.

After a while they came to an unnatural chamber. It was cut cleanly and reinforced, not the seemingly random rock formations that had been round them before.

Here, they were nervous. Their bodies were tired. The damage from the battles they had already fought was a constant reminder that they were still alive, but now they knew, the hardest battles were yet to come. So long they'd searched for their destination; always it had been in the future, but now it was the present.

The tension filled them; it was palpable in the air. Jokes and conversation were long since over. There was only an unwavering focus on the daunting task at hand.

They carefully entered the chamber, weapons trained.

"Stay by the walls," the Admiral whispered. "It's the only place there's any cover at all. We're sitting ducks in here. Nik, Jax, take the wall on the far side, we'll take this one and meet you at the end. Watch those overhead ledges." He pointed to them on either side of the room.

They nodded and separated. They approached the walls and crouched for a moment.

"No sign of any hostiles, sir," Jax said through the comms.

"We've got nothing either. Get moving."

Tight against the walls, heads low, ready for anything, they scurried around the chamber. They headed for the doorway on the far side of the room. They weren't far away, but if these warriors had hoped they would get out of the chamber unhindered, they were wrong.

The walls glowed fiery blue. There was a flash, and an electric buzz burst into life.

The Elders ran away from the glowing walls, out into centre of the chamber. Sparks spat outwards angrily, reaching for the warriors and burning brightly. With a mighty fizz, like a wave, the fiery mass rolled down the walls and onto the floor. There it flamed, stretching skywards, creating a white-hot wall around the warriors.

"Asu, what is this?" the Admiral asked.

"This thing is alive, sir."

They stood staring. They didn't even know what it was, let alone how to defeat it. It surrounded them, flickering menacingly. The fiery waves reached up, morphing and changing by the instant. Then the ring of fire contracted quickly, burning up the space between them, wanting to swallow the warriors.

For normal beings, that would have been their last instant, but the Elders leapt high over the flames. The fire creature swooped out forking limbs, grabbing for them as it passed beneath. It licked at their body armour and warmed their flesh below.

The flaming wall's glowing tendrils whipped out from within the fire. They stretched for the Elders who ducked and rolled to avoid the painful strikes. They opened fire, aiming low by the base, but the flame-like mass absorbed the plasma. Greedily, it sucked the weapon fire within, feeding off it.

They switched tactics, unleashing a volley at the top this time. Now the plasma passed harmlessly through. Against this foe, their rifles were completely useless.

The glowing mass swooped out tentacles of flame, winding outwards from its base. The warriors used every ounce of speed and skill to avoid them, still occasionally they were struck. It burned agonisingly, like hot coals being pressed into their flesh, even through their armour. They screamed and reeled, yet somehow, the symbiotes inside forced them to ignore the pain, to keep fighting.

They drew blades. Nik cracked her whip. It had no effect on their enemy. They rushed at the creature, but the heat stopped them in their tracks.

The Elders were starting to fear the worst. Their weapons were useless. The flaming wall attacked them every second, never relenting. It was all they could do to not be completely consumed by its fury.

"Follow!" Asu yelled. "I have an idea."

They ran past the glowing beast as it tried its utmost to stop them. It flung fizzing branches of hot flame towards the warriors. They leapt over them or ducked beneath, desperately trying to avoid them, sparing themselves the pain. They streaked by it and ran back the way they had come. The creature gave chase.

Through the darkness of the caves, the Elders ran with the creature constantly on their heels. It desperately chased them, longing to consume them. At times they could feel the heat on their backs, which spurred them on and pushed them harder, beyond even the boundaries they thought were possible.

The flaming mass was fast. It could morph in such a way that obstacles didn't slow it down, unlike the Elders. It gained on them again. They pushed themselves harder, running as fast as they could, legs straining, lungs burning, tearing through the darkness.

"Asu," the Admiral panted, "where are we going? We can't outrun this thing for much longer."

"We're nearly there. Keep going."

The wall of flame rolled like a tsunami through the caves, lighting the dark as it went. It was a constant reminder of the danger close behind them. Finally, they burst out of the cave, and the rocky ground made way, once again, for ice. They headed down the tunnel. The flaming creature followed.

Now the warriors caught onto Asu's plan. Finally, he stopped. The others followed his lead. They turned around. The creature rushed towards them but before it could consume them, the intense heat melted the ice below it. The flaming mass disappeared through the floor. It plummeted through frozen layers as it went, hopelessly flailing. They watched as it dropped silently and disappeared into the darkness of the ice planet's interior.

"I have pushed them. The insignificant pawns are in place. Their time is done. Their days are numbered. Soon they will fall, and control will be mine. This galaxy teeters on the very brink of destruction. The planets will float like carbon through space, black and lifeless. The star's light will burn out to nothing. They will be denied their kind's usual spectacular death. One day they will burn, glowing fiery, and their light will exude and the next, become black and lifeless. The souls of billions will be lost, one by one. The good and the bad. The light of life will no longer shine.

They should give up, surrender, curl into a ball and cower. They do not understand this cosmos. They do not understand what they are. These, the lower beings, are doomed, as are you!"

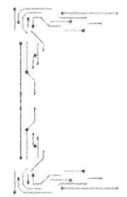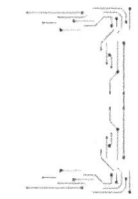

Making a Stand

Alex waited in anxious silence. His mind was churning. The emotions ran through his body. So many feelings, most foreign to him, some all too familiar, but all would become his weakness if he allowed it. The reality faced him down. The fear surged at the uncertainty, at the doubt. He saw no way out. His hands started to tremble. To stand and fight for survival was one thing, to fight for nothing but death was quite another.

The battle raged in the chamber ahead; it was all he could hear. Not the explosions as much as the screams of pain. That was what he faced. It wouldn't be long before the clone soldiers breached the line again, and that would become his end. His bravery was abandoning him.

"Coward! Now is not the time to cower. Now you must fight. You must be strong. This is your time. This is what we have waited for," The Fleck hissed like a viper, angrily, coldly. It read his intentions and his emotions, and it knew. It could feel his fear.

Alex fought, yes. He fought hard, but he dreamed of running. Now he was longing to run, a mere single step from doing so. The battle ahead felt hopeless, even though they had held them off for hours now. All the time reinforcements were needed just to quell the clones. They lost soldier after soldier, each replaced by the hopeless next. They knew that they marched to their death and so did Alex. He could see no other outcome.

"It is up to us to stop them. Do you not understand? There is no one coming to save you. Fight like a savage. Send them to their death!"

The symbiote had been quiet, hiding within, but now The Fleck probed and manipulated it. The symbiote squirmed, feeding Alex strength, feeding him courage. The courage that he would surely need.

He psyched himself up, readying for what was ahead. The symbiote fed his emotions but only those that were of use in battle. The Fleck warmed him. It was pleased.

He told himself over and over that he was a killer, a hero, that he would survive the fight. If indeed he would not, he'd take as many of these things with him as he could.

Plasma flashed from the corridor ahead followed by an explosion that rattled the walls of the complex. Five clone soldiers rushed into view. They'd fought their way through the soldiers that protected the port chamber.

Alex, Penny, and Jas opened fire, taking down the first soldier quickly, followed by the second. Alex roared as he drew his blade and carelessly charged towards their foes.

Jas tried to stop him. He tried to call him back, but it was too late.

Roaring, Alex flew towards the clones. They clashed, blade against blade. He thrust his sword right through the first and withdrew it quickly. It fell to the ground, spilling blood, mortally wounded. He spun around, avoiding an incoming blow and swooped out his blade, instantly removing the second one's head.

He jumped as a shot came from behind him, followed by a thud. He turned around. Jas was stood there, his weapon smoking, shaking his head. Alex looked down. A clone soldier lay dead by his feet. "Thanks. That was close," he said.

"You damn fool!" Jas was furious. "You may have a death wish, kid, but the rest of us, we need you. Stay in formation. We need to work together."

"Sorry... I'm sorry." Alex had disappointment etched all over his face.

"You remind me of another kid I knew. His name was Sollen..."

Memories that had been lost flashed with the mentioning of that name, leaving Alex shocked. Could it be possible that Jas knew?

"He's dead now, kid. You get it?"

"Yeah. I'm sorry. I guess I got a bit scared and went a bit mental or something."

"We're all scared, my friend. The warrior does feel fear; we just learn to control it, to use it as a weapon. It can break us, make us crumble. That is when we fall. It can drive us, fuel us, push us on in our fight. The warrior's purpose in times such as these is not to kill; it is simply to survive. If we are to die, we will die nobly, as is the warrior's way. Not needlessly with ego or emotion."

It made sense to Alex even if the words he uttered did not. "Okay, cheers, yeah, right, got it." He took himself back beside Penny. She offered him a comforting hand upon his forearm and a smile as he passed. It wasn't much, but somehow, it helped.

Now was the time for him to learn from his mistakes, to become a master of himself. He had been fighting for many years, but it seemed he still had much to learn. Here, by the fear that threatened to take him and the mighty warrior beside him, he was humbled.

The gunfire ahead died down and stopped.

"Get ready," Jas growled.

The frontline was completely overrun.

"Fire!"

The clones ran into a hail of plasma. Smoking corpses were scattered upon the floor. They didn't care. Still they came, now unhindered, in great numbers.

"Push forward!" Jas yelled. "Retake that chamber!"

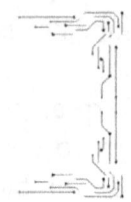

Betrayal

"What are you doing?" the Reptilian leader demanded to know. He hissed at the clone soldiers. Were these things incapable of understanding, unable to speak, or just plain ignorant?

The army forced the Reptilians out of the way and looked at them like they were nothing. This fearsome fighting force worked for them yet treated them with complete distain. They were supposed to do the leader's bidding. It had paid a handsome price for their services, and here they were, mindlessly doing whatever they pleased.

The Leader was angry. It hated to be ignored. The truth was the creature's ego was bruised, and for Reptilian-kind, the ego is fragile. Maybe in them being a homeless species, they felt inferior to others. They merely scrounged a living like worthless vermin, and for it, they hated hard.

Again, this time shouting its displeasure, it confronted the clones. The leader was wasting its breath. The words fell upon deaf ears. The army couldn't speak, nor could they understand the Reptilian's language. Yelling at them, apart from giving the reptile a way to vent its displeasure, was completely pointless.

These clones in this army of nightmares took orders from no one but the child, and the child had no interest in the Reptilian's plight. They had a very different goal. They wanted the core for themselves. With this powerful technology, they could fulfil their plans. They wanted it all—the galaxy, the blood, the fear, and the death. Finally, they would reign supreme.

The Leader, spitting and raging, screamed at the clones one more time, but through the soldier's ears, the only being that heard them was the child. They could hear everything being said and see every sight through hundreds of pairs of ears and eyes. They mostly heard the creature's hissing. They heard the whining and the demands that would never be met. The child grew irritated. The Reptilians were like flies that wouldn't stop buzzing around. The scaley beings were of no use to them, and now they were hindering them. Like the coldest of warlords, silently the child ordered the attack.

All at once, as one, the hundreds of clone soldiers opened fire. The Reptilians were caught by surprise. The betrayal was swift and calculated. Death was all around them. The scaley soldiers fell to the might of the clones. They cared not for the treasure the Reptilians offered, the privileges they promised, or the mercy for which they begged. They robotically carried out the child's orders.

Many of the reptiles fought back, unloading their weapons, but in vain. The clones were quick and skilled, accurate and strong. They were ruthless, they were fearless, and they were merciless.

Most of the Reptilians ran. They fled across the tricky surface as quickly as they could with no more success than the ones that fought. The clones mowed them down. Those that fought back died bravely. Those that fled died like cowards, but they died all the same.

A betrayal of such magnitude threatened to steal the entire species from the universe. They would be little more than a memory in a cosmos that is so quick to forget. Scant numbers lingered on the motherships now out on the edge of the solar system. They were all that remained.

The Reptilians' greed had cost them everything. If only they'd waited and not given in to their impatience, maybe their kind would have thrived. Now they would hide like rats, rejected by the humans, the alliance, The Cabal, and now rejected by the clones. Today was supposed to be the day that once again they could breed and spread, but instead all they found was death. Now they were a species on the very brink of extinction.

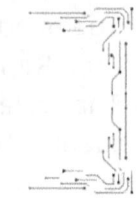

Blinded

The Elders returned to the chamber where the fire creature had been. This time, gladly, they passed safely through. They headed out into a narrower corridor.

Asu felt great tension growing inside him. He could feel the call of destiny. He could see images beyond his mind, and now, he felt the draw of the one for whom they had come. They were close.

They reached another chamber, this one slightly smaller. There were similar overhead ledges as before. Those ledges were there for a reason. They needed to get out of there, and quickly. They ran through the room, pushing to reach the other side. Then what they feared would happen, did. Clone soldiers lined the balconies above and started firing down upon the warriors.

The Elders scattered left and right, using their shields to deflect the blows. They were grazed by the onslaught, but somehow, they remained unhurt. Now they zigzagged, running for all they were worth, desperate to reach the other end of the chamber and the doorway that invited them towards it.

Their shields, skill, and reflexes, enhanced by the symbiotes, kept them safe. Had it not been for them, they would never have made it out of there. They were scorched, but they made it through the chamber and into another corridor. There, they stopped for a moment and caught their breath.

"There's sure to be more," the Admiral said. "Before we reach our—" He was cut off by the sound of footsteps coming from all around them.

Jax and Nik spun around instinctively to protect the rear. The Admiral and Asu kept their eyes and their weapons fixed firmly ahead. They crouched behind their shields and waited.

Clone soldiers swarmed into view from the front and behind. The Elders unleashed deadly fury upon their enemies. The soldiers went from sprinting at full speed to dead on the floor in flashes. Micro grenades ripped flesh from bone, leaving charred remains distributed on the floor.

At the rear, Nik and Jax drew their favourite weapons—the whip and the light sword. They tore into their foes. They deflected their blows and incoming fire with their shields then ripped them down, stealing them from life, or leaving them maimed and dying.

Before long, the area behind them was clear of soldiers, so Jax and Nik joined the Admiral and Asu. There were far more clones coming from that direction.

They stayed behind the shields, protecting them from the incoming fire. They took every opportunity they could to take out the clones. The instant they had a clear shot, it was taken, and their targets fell. The warriors inched forward, dropping their foes as they went. The bodies were starting to pile up, but there was no sign of them stopping.

They launched more grenades. All of them did at the same time. An enormous fireball ripped through the crowd of clones, leaving a scene of devastation and death. They opened fire, raging bloody fury, killing everything that moved. They pushed forward, more quickly now.

The clones started to retreat as their numbers thinned out. The Elders, however, would not let them escape. They would show them no mercy.

Leaving bodies lining the corridor and bloody carnage in their wake, they pressed on. They went through another door and into a dark cave. The atmosphere changed in an instant. The air inside was thick and moist and there was a lingering mist.

Jax and Nik immediately became nervous. This was like the harrowing underworld of the hive. There they had faced unrecognisable foes in strange forms with strange weaponry. They had warned their companions over and over about what they could face, but still the reality was harsher than they could have imagined.

"This is bad," Nik warned.

"Just keep going," the Admiral responded.

There was movement above. A huge, dark form on the ceiling.

Long, shadowy tentacles zoomed out, flying towards them. They moved like lightning, avoiding the reaching arms. There was a flash of silver and a creature above them darted across the ceiling. It had a long thin body and huge eyes. The four squid-like limbs reached out from its head.

The arms whipped out again, now sparking electric blue. The warriors did all they could to avoid them. Jax drew her sword and slashed at the incoming limb. Sparks flew, but it bounced off harmlessly.

Nik flung her whip ceilingward, right towards the creature's eye as it stared down upon her. It cracked in the air just short of its target. The strange beast was out of range.

The Admiral opened fire. Asu joined him, but their shots bounced off the creature's rubbery flanks.

"What is this thing?" Asu asked.

"They're biological weapons," Jax responded. "It has a weakness. We just need to find it."

The creature flashed across the ceiling again, reaching desperately down for the warriors. They parried, blocked, or ducked the incoming blows. The tentacles came in waves, flicking out quickly. They defended themselves but were struck on occasion. Surges of electricity jolted through their bodies for seconds. The shock would have felled lesser beings, but with the protection of their body armour and the halithstord, the Elders were far tougher than most.

"Jax, gimme a boost." Nik looked up at the huge eye that reflected what little light there was in that wretched place.

Jax stooped, bending her back and putting her hands on her knees to brace herself. Nik rushed towards her. She planted a foot on Jax's back and pushed. She flew skyward, and at the height of her jump, out went her whip. It hit the creature's eye with an enormous crack.

A tentacle reflexively flung out at her while she was still airborne. It knocked her down, crashing onto the ground. Winded, she groaned and looked up. The huge eye that glimmered before was blackened. The creature was now half blind.

Jax rushed over and helped her friend back to her feet. "You know you're gonna have to do that again, right?" She giggled. "Come on, up you get."

"Yeah, gimme a second." She hardly finished the words before she had to move. Tentacles flew with fury all around the chamber. The half-blind creature was distressed and frantic.

The warriors were purely on the defensive. Blocking, parrying, and avoiding the incoming barrage was all they could do.

"Right, Jax, let's do this!" Again, Nik ran towards her friend, twirling her whip around her head like a helicopter. She placed her foot on her friend's back and flew upwards, flinging out her weapon. She struck the creature's good eye, instantly destroying it. Gladly, she landed back on her feet this time.

Inside a cloak of total darkness, the creature shot down from the ceiling like a swirling mass. It flicked its tentacles in all directions, rolling around and squirming.

Now that the creature was helpless, there was little point in killing it. That would be risky. So, the Elders took flight, slipping right past the writhing mass to the far wall of the cave. There was a narrow opening leading out. The Admiral stopped, bracing his shield, deflecting any of the random incoming blows. The others rushed past him and vanished into the opening. Only once his companions were safely through did he follow them. They ran, panting, through the darkness, leaving the stricken creature blinded and helpless in the chamber.

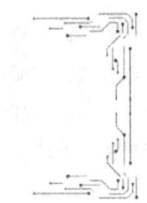

Hanging On

"Retreat! Fall back. We're overrun!" Jas yelled. Chaos reigned supreme in the Mantises base. Despite their best efforts, the soldiers had not been able to retake the port chamber. They had sustained terrible loses. Their fallen comrades lined the hallways of the complex. There was no more backup. They were pushed further and further back. The defenders of the base were worn thin.

They periodically tried to make a stand in the easiest places to defend, but the clones ripped through them and swarmed further and further into the base. Death was everywhere. Reptilians, Tall Whites, Crypto-Terrestrials, and clone bodies littered the hallways.

Not for a second had Jas, Penny, or Alex been able to stop fighting or catch breath. The swarms of clones came, in seemingly endless numbers, and cut through the soldiers that tried to stop them. They backed away again until they were inside the main chamber. This was the place where they would make their final stand.

All that remained of coalition soldiers were the most powerful or the luckiest. Now they shook with fear in the chamber, jumping at the explosions, like beings who know death is certain and coming for them.

Cover was set up in the chamber and the entrance was blocked. The last of the sentry guns guarded that room. They cut down their enemies, but quickly, even they would be overrun. Then the clone soldiers would break through the barricades and be free in the chamber. It was surely only a matter of time.

Every Reptilian on the surface of the moon now lay dead. This had not been a battle; this was a massacre. The clones piled the bodies high, out of their way. These lost souls that the clones threw around like they were sacks of potatoes had thought the clones would come to their aid; little did they know that they would become their conquerors.

The remaining forces were now free to gather and port down at will, unhindered by the needs of the Reptilian leader. There were countless faceless soldiers waiting above, ready to enter the battle. That was all they longed for, all they wanted, their only purpose. The plight of their enemies within the base was surely hopeless.

It was with heavy hearts the defenders of the base heard the sentry guns fall silent. The clones, like a swarm of bees, started frantically working at the barricades.

"They come," Jas addressed the soldiers. "Before long, they'll be inside. This could be our final stand, but we must fight them with everything we have. They want to take this place and then the core. If they succeed, the galaxy will be at tremendous risk.

"You fight not for this place, here and now, but for the future. The future that will not be your own but that of your loved ones, that of your species. We must not bow to fear and tyranny. We must not cower in the face of death. We must meet our destiny head on.

"We must stand now and fight. Open fire the second they make it through. Get ready, soldiers. Let's give them hell!"

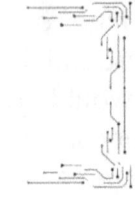

The Pit

The Elders continued, anticipation growing with the passing moments. Not only did they have to worry about clone soldiers and the child, but also biological weapons that could be awaiting them anywhere at any time. These hallways, unlike the cave, were brightly lit, which brought them slight comfort. The biological weapons dwelled in darkness and mist, so here in the light, with a little luck, they would be safe.

They could sense that they were marching towards their destiny, but Asu felt it the most. He saw their enemy, the child, in his mind's eye. He felt a longing, a great need to reach them. He wished he could just teleport right there to save the time travelling. There was excitement and anxiety in a strange mix inside him. He tried to focus, to be present, but endlessly, his mind wandered. It drifted from the here and now to a misty future that may or may not come to pass. He couldn't control his thoughts any longer. He fought with them. He needed to be aware of what he was doing and where he was going.

Asu continued to lead the way through the well-lit tunnels, deeper into the mountain. Gradually, the path became darker, putting all the warriors on edge. The smooth manufactured walls made way for what looked like a natural cave. The lights on their rifles cut through the darkness to start with, but the further they went, the mistier the cave became.

Nik met Jax's gaze with hers. They looked wide-eyed at each other, knowing what was coming, yet completely unsure at the same time. This was as close to afraid as these two fearsome sisters in arms ever were. Their environment suits at least meant they could breathe in the mist and wouldn't pass out as they had last time. They wished they could turn back. They were tired and didn't want to fight any more, but here and now, that was little more than a useless thought.

The mist began to linger again until they were completely shrouded in a gloom. The air grew thick, not only with the fog but also with tension. It was clear some creature or trap would be in there somewhere, hunting them. That thought didn't leave them, even for a second.

Though they were as brave as any beings could be, expecting the unexpected was wearing them down. Still, they would never give in to the urge to turn around. Failure was not an option. They would secretly rather take their chances against the army of clone warriors out on the tundra than what they could face inside the mist. At least out there, they'd know who they faced, what they could do, and more importantly, how to kill them. Here, in this place, it could be anything.

The mission called them on, deeper into the darkness. Their flashlights couldn't cut through the mist any longer. It surrounded them, smothered them, and swallowed them whole. Now almost completely blinded, they inched along. They dared not speak or even breathe too hard. There was palpable fear amongst them. They felt like eyes watched them from everywhere. They didn't know what would happen, but they were certain that it would happen soon. Fate had grown impatient waiting in the wings, and now it was coming for them.

Something dropped from the ceiling, hitting Asu on the boot. He shone his light down to his feet. There was a shell like an egg, cracked and oozing a clear substance on the floor. Then, one at a time, more dropped down in their dozens, covering the floor.

They continued onwards, but getting a grip with their boots was hard. The slimy substance was slippery. Then, with a mighty rumble, the floor dropped down in front, creating a ramp. It jerked as it locked in place.

The warriors slid and fell on the slime covered rocks. Frantically they tried to stop themselves. They scratched at the floor and walls as they slid down the slope. A dark hole was ahead of them. It greedily wanted them, bellowing mist from its depths, waiting to consume them.

The Elders accepted that they were going to fall. They couldn't stop themselves no matter how hard they tried. They were on this ride wherever it would lead. One at a time, they zipped off the ramp, sailing through the mist, and fell into nothing.

With a crash, they hit the rocks at the bottom of the pit as the disturbed mist above them swirled. Without time to even gather their senses, there was movement all around them. Small ant-sized creatures, green and scuttling, scurried from their hiding places, swarming all over the warriors. They secreted an acidic substance, leaving their armour smoking and degrading. They jumped to their feet, frantically brushing the creatures off them. Gladly, their gloves protected their hands. They stomped the creatures under boot.

A swarm of buzzing, flying bugs came from nowhere. They zoomed around the warrior's heads. A noise like elastic snapping came from the creatures, sending a dart hurtling from their abdomen. The Elders moved like lightning, trying to duck the projectiles, but there were far too many to avoid them all. The sharp missiles became lodged in their body armour. Had the darts been long enough to totally penetrate their environment suits, they would have been dead in an instant. Thankfully for the warriors, they were not. Their armour smoked from the acid as more darts jagged into their suits. Taking such punishment, they would not last long.

Light shields were quickly deployed and protected them from most of the darts. The swarm of flying bugs was huge, so still on occasion their weaponry got through. The Elders gathered against the wall huddled behind their shields; this gave them at least some protection.

The warriors' sidearms went off through the gaps in their light barriers, illuminating the pit. The creatures were too small to hit deliberately, no matter how good their aim was. They blasted randomly upwards. The flying bugs were vaporised as the white-hot plasma passed through them.

Now there was movement on the walls. Summersaulting bioweapons came spinning through the air. They moved like a blur, launching star-shaped projectiles from their six limbs. They landed, hanging from the sheer wall for a split second, then jumped again. They were quick, leaving the Elders struggling to avoid the attacks. They blocked the stars with their shields, or avoided them, leaving them embedded deep in the rocks.

Weapons went off around the pit as the warriors desperately fought off the attacks coming from all angles. Though the creatures were killed in great numbers, it seemed there were always more.

With a rumble, a huge four-legged animal came charging at them like a rhino.

"Brace me!" the Admiral shouted as he turned his shield towards the roaring monster.

The Elders retracted their shields and huddled behind him. They pushed like they were in a rugby scrum. There was a mighty crash as the huge, straight horn in the centre of its head thudded into the shield, knocking the warriors everywhere. It circled around for another charge.

The Elders fired upon the beast to little effect. They needed to act and act quickly.

"Jax, do you have any fire grenades?" the Admiral asked as the battles raged all around him.

"I have one, but in here, it'll cook us."

"These bioweapons will cook us. Everyone against the walls and behind your shields. Jax, do it!"

"Really? Okay, then. Dude's crazy." She threw the grenade. It bounced as the enormous charging creature was now just a few steps away.

She joined the others covering them all sides with their shields. They waited. There was an explosion, and a fireball engulfed the pit. The raging fire expanded in an instant, rolling up the walls. The creatures, with no body armour, had no chance. The Elders were toasted. Their body armour was blackened, but somehow, they were still alive. Ashy corpses lay all round as the smoke cleared.

"Told you we'd need our shields," the Admiral joked as he examined the smoke drifting from his armour.

"Man, I wanna be medium rare, not well done!" Nik complained.

"Well, at least you're smoking hot," Jax retorted.

They laughed, half at the jokes and half in relief.

The Elders, smoking and blackened, jarred and exhausted with no time to dwell had to find a way to escape the pit.

The charging creature must have found a way inside somehow. It was hard to see in the mist, but eventually they found a pathway cut into the rocks. They headed through, grateful for having escaped that place with their lives. The mist started to thin, and for a moment, the limping warriors breathed a sigh of relief.

They were a mess, in pain, fatigued, mentally exhausted, and still, their toughest test was yet to come. They stumbled along towards what would, one way or another, be the end of this journey.

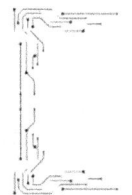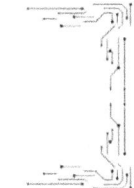

The Last Line

The barricade finally gave way with an enormous explosion. The clones surged inside the chamber. The wide-eyed coalition soldiers unleashed fury. Their enemies charged blindly into a hail of plasma fire. Many fell, but they never would quit, not until the last one of them was dead. They finally broke the line and took the first life inside the room. The coalition fought back and took their comrade's killer down quickly, but for every one that died, many more came.

The fear flowing through the soldiers was in the air. They fought bravely, for each other and to live, but in their heavy hearts, they knew they would lose. All around was death, chaos, blood, and screams of pain.

Like a wave against a rock, the clones crashed against the defences, stumbling over their fallen comrades as they went. Thoughtlessly and without fear, they rushed eagerly into the wall of fire. Occasionally one would break through and cause carnage and destruction.

They stole the lives of the base's defenders, with blade or fire or fist. Each time one of the coalition soldiers fell, there was one less rifle to hold the clones back. The situation was snowballing fast. Tearing through flesh, stealing souls, wild and furious, the clones kept coming, inching further and further into the chamber.

"Get back up to the balcony," Jas told Penny and Alex. "That will be the last place they take. We will make sure we fall last and take as many with us as we can.

"Commander, on us." Jas beckoned to the Tall White Commander to follow.

They wasted no time. Keeping their heads down, they scurried from their cover and back up the stairs onto the balcony above. Jas, Penny, Alex, and the Commander took the centre of the balcony. The coalition soldiers lined up on either side of them, and below, they took up positions on the stairs.

The roaring crowd of clone soldiers streamed in. To their blades, more of the base's defenders fell. Death was everywhere. The few that still hung on were sure to be dead soon, and their fight would be lost.

From their position, Penny, Alex, and Jas fired from above, trying to protect the remaining Tall Whites and Crypto-Terrestrials. They ripped down dozens of their foes, but there were just too many to hold them back. On the balcony, they were desperate, and down below even more so. It was clear that all remained for them was death.

Finding the Child Part II

The Elders limped along until they reached a brightly lit chamber.

Asu slowly poked his head through the entrance. "It's clear."

They stepped carefully inside, training their weapons on every corner as they went. The smooth white walls were tall. There was a heavy buzz in the air, and it was one that Nik and Jax recognised only too well. Thankfully, this time their electro-magnetic headwear stopped the crazy visions they had last time. Despite their protection, they could still sense the energy all around them. They were sure that before long they would be face to face with their foe.

They stepped forward bravely, ready with their weapons poised. There was a woosh and a clunk, and the door they had entered through closed behind them.

"Guess we can't run then," Nik whispered.

A menacing figure was standing in the room. A fearsome warrior, tall and imposing, muscular and powerful.

Jax and Nik gasped as one.

"Daze?"

Their friend didn't speak. She stared through them, like she wished nothing but death upon them.

"Daze, it's us," Nik urged.

Daze roared her fearsome war cry and ran at them, drawing her blades from the sleeves of her suit. She leapt through the air.

Jax drew her blade, blocking Daze's attempt to behead her. Nik flung out her whip, cracking into the attacker's body, knocking her off her feet.

"Actually, on second thought, I don't think that's Daze. She seems a bit off," Nik joked.

"Either that or she hasn't had enough sleep," Jax responded.

"She's a clone!"

The Elders readied themselves as Daze flipped back to her feet, flinging darts from her sleeves as she did. They moved and rolled and were back up in an instant. A second later, the room was lit up by plasma fire. The Daze clone moved like lightning, launching her projectiles and avoiding the incoming fire. The warriors activated their shields to deflect the missiles flying towards them. Just as their friend had in life, this Daze clone certainly had her speed and accuracy, but there was something missing in her, and it was glaring.

Physically she was the same, but mentally she was a blank. She could never have Daze's experiences, wisdom, or passion. Her actions were controlled by the child who was hidden like a coward somewhere. As much as Jax and Nik may have wished it was their friend, the soulless creature before them had only her face; it could never have her spirit or soul.

The Daze clone was so fast she expertly avoided their fire, moving like a blur. She constantly held the Elders back with darts from her sleeves. These darts would pierce their armour, unlike the creatures in the pit. If the suit breached, the ice planet had nothing like a breathable atmosphere. One mistake and it would be over. Before their wounds would even kill them, the air would.

The symbiotes boiled fiercely within the warriors, more than they had before. Through its will, the parts of themselves joined together and became one. The warrior within, their love and power, and the halithstord worked in perfect unison.

They went to another plain—they reached ascension. It was as though time itself slowed down. They drew energy from all around them, pushing them along, making them more. They harvested the very cosmos for power that they never knew they had. They fought back with vigour. This clone was not even close to the woman that Daze was.

The warriors swarmed towards her, avoiding the deadly darts as they went. Daze drew her blades and jumped at Jax. Nik's whip exploded into her, bringing her down with a crash. She stopped and flung her whip again as the clone tried to stand. It sent her rolling over.

"This bitch is mine!" Jax leapt through the air, landing on top of her stricken foe, jabbing her sword right through her chest. She crouched on top of the clone, staring wild in its eyes. It looked up desperately. Jax stood up, ripping her blade from the body with a roar. The clone's head fell back. It was dead.

A wave of energy that rippled the air came from nowhere, filling the room. The warriors were knocked down like they'd been hit with an explosion. They rolled over and struggled to their feet. There was a scream, high-pitched and child-like. A figure stood there. A silhouette in the light that glowed around their frame. The child stepped forward, smirking coldly.

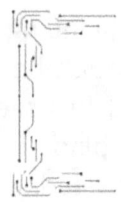
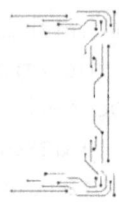

Fight to the Death

The lines of coalition soldiers were starting to run thin in the Mantises' base inside the mountain. The carnage, the fear, and death were all around. Explosions rocked the base, and the sounds of screams and blades clashing echoed from the thick walls of the chamber. They fought like wild animals, mostly eyeball to eyeball, spilling blood and stealing souls. It was being against being, entity against entity, and life versus death. Bodies below were everywhere.

Jas, Penny, and Alex tried with all they could to protect the helpless soldiers. They fired from above, deadly and accurate, but their enemies were too powerful and too many. The clones broke lines of defence and then greedily moved onto the next, leaving bloody chaos in their wake. Each time, the resistance was fierce and desperate, but the wall of faceless soldiers would not be stopped. The coalition soldiers fought on, they had no other option, trapped in the place that would become their resting place. Any breath they took could prove to be their last.

The clones fought their way to the stairs leading up to the balcony. Jas, Penny, and Alex went wild holding them back, desperately trying to spare the coalition soldiers below them. They had to hang on for as long as they could. The soldiers lining the staircases, despite their best efforts, fell one by one, and the clones started to climb the stairs.

A shot flashed and the commander slumped down onto the floor. There was a smoking hole in its head. It was dead before it hit the ground. The other soldiers, upon witnessing their leader's demise, gave up any hope at that moment. Their spirits were broken and soon so would be their bodies.

Blades clashed on the staircase, and blood was shed while bodies fell. Now only three remained—Jas, Penny, and Alex. They fought with wild fury, although they were exhausted. They had no choice; there was nothing else they could do. Now they hung on, teetering on the brink. It seemed death and failure were knocking on the door.

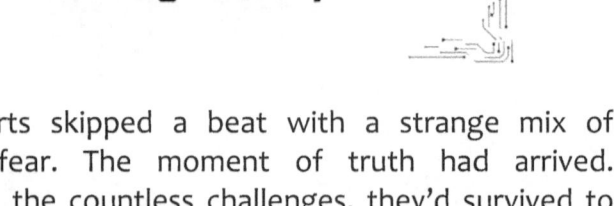

Meeting Destiny

Collective hearts skipped a beat with a strange mix of excitement and fear. The moment of truth had arrived. Somehow, despite the countless challenges, they'd survived to reach their goal. Destiny stood before the warriors, menacingly, in the form of a child.

This being, though small in stature, exuded great power from their core. The Elders could feel the buzz of energy all around them. This child's capabilities far exceeded their own, so they couldn't afford to give up the advantage. They attacked immediately. Plasma fire flew but was blocked by an invisible force. It was like the child had a bubble around them. The rifles were useless.

A second wave flowed out from the child's mind, knocking them down. They were left reeling in pain and fuzzy headed from the blow. The child said nothing, just gave the slightest nod. There was the sound of a door opening and then footsteps. The warriors shook off their pain and got back to their feet. Five Daze clones walked towards them from the edges of the room. The Elders took a few steps back, readying their weapons as they did. The enormity of their task became all too real. In a lifetime of battles, this would be their greatest. The child watched on, smirking.

The Daze clones were every bit as deadly and quick as the one before had been. The Elders would struggle to defeat so many of them at once. Plasma exploded from their weapons while the clones zigzagged or ducked. They rolled or jumped, skilfully avoiding the oncoming fire. The darts flew from their foe's sleeves, leaving the warriors ducking behind their shields for cover.

Now they slung their rifles upon their backs and drew their blades. The clones came flying at them, randomly, from different directions. It was hard to keep up with the chaos around them.

Jax and Nik double teamed one of the clones. It seemed the best way to defeat them. Nik flung her whip out like lightning. The clone moved, ducking the blow. Now Jax swooped in for an attack to be blocked expertly by Daze's blades. Again, the whip went, this time striking its target. Jax swiped her sword low. Daze jumped over the blade, but it caught her foot, slicing right through it. She crashed down to the ground, pumping blood from the wound.

"This one's mine!" Nik shouted as her whip went flying out once more. With a crack and a spark, it removed the top of the clone's head.

The Admiral clashed his two blades against his attacker's. A wild fight took place. The clone's speed and skill were matched only by his. The clone came in again and again, in fierce clashes, while the Admiral blocked her lightning-fast strikes. She came at him one more time, behind a handful of darts. He ducked low and spun, swooping his blades, helicoptering round like a blur. The Daze clone ran right past him. Her legs fell off her body and she hit the ground. He finished her with a clinical swipe.

The two remaining clones were on Asu, and he was locked in defensive mode. It was all he could do to survive, let alone land attacks of his own. His shield was the only barrier between life and death. The Admiral, Jax, and Nik rushed to his aid, firing their sidearms to scatter the clones. The four of them together, now with the advantage, rushed forward.

Asu rolled, jumped, and grabbed the nearest clone. Her blades flashed past his head. He threw her against the wall like a rag doll. He drew his blade in an instant and jabbed it right through her chest. She coughed and spluttered, and blood bubbled from her mouth. The clone slumped down dead.

Another wave went through the air, knocking down the warriors and the remaining clone. The child gave another nod, and now five more Daze clones entered the room. The warriors were on their feet and engaged in battle before they could breathe.

Asu moved swiftly, blade in hand. He rushed not for the clones but for the child. He jumped high, extending then swooping his sword through the air. He landed expertly on his feet.

The child stared ahead, the smirk still on their face. A ball of blue energy left their head and spread quickly across the room. Then they staggered and blinked and slumped forward and hit the floor.

The energy hit Asu and surrounded him. It exploded with a boom, sending him flying through the air. His armour split wide open, and he hit the ground with a crash. In an instant, the Spy was dead.

"Asu!" the Admiral yelled out desperately as he ducked under the darts that flew towards his head. "What? They're still fighting."

"The child...was it a clone?" Jax questioned. "Now we're screwed."

"What now, Admiral?" Nik asked as darts rattled off her shield.

"Now we fight. The real child must be around here somewhere."

They could have given up hope at that moment. Their hearts could have crumbled, but these warriors would never quit on themselves. When things were at the bleakest, the symbiotes inside fed them. Their blood flowed like fire in their veins. They looked at Asu's body, there on the floor, as a reminder of the sacrifices that had been made.

The Elders raged forward. They would take these enemies with their blades. They were angry, and the clones would feel their wrath. If they were to die here, then they would leave their mark.

The three of them fought side by side. The clones fought hard, but they could never defeat these warriors with their halithstord within. Unlike their enemies, they worked together for the benefit of all. They finally took down the Daze clones one at a time. They headed for a door at the opposite end of the room, and with heavy hearts, they left Asu's body behind.

They went into the next room where there were Daze clones in their dozens, like a production line of super soldiers. They were hanging up, much like the Spy had been when he had entered the clone's body. They were each perfect, unmoving, waiting for their turn to fight. That time would never come.

"Take 'em out before they wake up," the Admiral said. Not waiting for the others, he opened fire, killing the defenceless clones. The Elders couldn't afford to fight them in such numbers.

Explosions boomed from grenades and plasma, killing every last one of them. With each kill, it ate away at Jax's and Nik's soul a little. It was like they were destroying a part of their friend over and over again.

She was a friend who was dearly missed, and they would do anything to have her back by their side. Now she was an abomination, and she would have never wanted to become this. She would have hated for their enemy to use her body without permission for evil deeds. It was against her nature to fight cruel battles for the child's own ends. She would fight in perpetuity against greed, fear, and hate. Her closest friends would spare her that fate. It was the last thing they could do to honour her.

Leaving the stench of cooked flesh behind, they marched out of the room and into a corridor. It was filled with countless clone soldiers. The Elders fought their way through and started desperately searching for the child. Eventually they came to a locked door.

"The kid must be in here," the Admiral said. "Jax, can you open it?"

"You know I can." She stepped towards it. "I'll get right—"

Her words were cut off as the door opened on its own. Several grenades flew through the gap. The warriors ran back the way they'd come and hit the floor covering their heads. The fireball passed over them. Once the door was fully open, countless clone soldiers came streaming through. There were hundreds of them within.

"The room was the shuttle bay." Jax panicked. "The kid's not in there."

The warriors fought, but they knew, now they had no chance. All was lost. This battle was beyond them. All that remained for the Elders was death and failure.

Finding the Child Part III

Penny and Alex, with Jas at their side, desperately defended the balcony. Still the battle raged. They were holding on and only just. Swarms of clones came up the stairs from either side of them but met nothing but death as they reached the top. Countless enemies rushed at them only to tumble back down the stairs, having been taken from life. Then the flying snipers came, forcing them to keep their heads down even more.

"I'll take the snipers. You stick to the stairs." Jas set to work immediately with his weaponry, using all the skill he possessed.

The snipers were fast and changed in random directions, making them hard to hit. The deadly streams of light whistled past their heads, keeping them pinned down. Quickly they swarmed and overwhelmed them in the three-dimensional attack. The snipers were too elusive for the warrior as he desperately tried to take them down. The best he could do was keep them at bay. His panic was palpable. Penny and Alex felt it. The sinking feeling began, the one where they knew that all that awaited them was death.

The battle continued, but Penny felt strange. It was like something inside her was happening. She still frantically took down the clones, but she disassociated. Her body was on autopilot, but her mind wandered somewhere else, like she lived in two different realities. Things went blurry, yet somehow she knew that clarity was coming. It would have been easy to be afraid, but this was her path, her fate, her destiny, and it felt right. She didn't fight it, she accepted it. She let disbelief and fear slip away and accepted that this was where she was meant to be. It was where she was going, and she embraced it. The real world as her body knew it no longer remained.

Whispers entered her mind. She couldn't make out the words, but still they were familiar. Then they became clear, golden words that warmed her heart.

"*You must find them.*"

"*Liam! Is it you? Is this real?*" She was filled with the tenderness of love, backed with a longing for her friend whom she missed so much.

"*It's me, Tiger. You must go. Follow the connections.*"

"*What connections? Follow them where?*"

"*Use our energy. Follow the path to the child.*" This was a voice she didn't know, a female voice.

"*Huh? Who are you?*"

"*You know who I am. Search your heart.*"

It didn't feel real. She was confused, and afraid. This was beyond her understanding, then it clicked. "*Isha?!*"

She was shocked, but it also made perfect sense. *Of course* it was Isha. Everything *is* connected. She *could* use their energy.

She silently accepted the truth, one that she had known all along, just beyond her recollection. Her mind was a conduit for her consciousness, only a part of her, not everything, as she had always believed. She was not bound to that place or that body, but her spirit could wander. She was not tied to matter, space, or time. For the first time in her life, she was truly free.

"*Follow us, Penny,*" Liam softly said. "*It is the only hope that remains.*"

There was a flash and a scream; that was the last thing of the world she knew. Her senses now came along for the ride. She floated away as though she left her body to the fearsome will of the halithstord. It fought the battle in the here and now, and she drifted beyond that realm and into a new reality.

It was like the battle never even existed. Penny felt the entities connected to her. They were with her, guiding her, and making her more. Time drifted away, and she skipped through strange and marvellous pillars of light, backed by the darkness of infinity. Fear wanted to surge, but the beauty brought her peace.

Liam was with her, once again holding her hand, pulling her along to the place she belonged. Isha's presence calmed her and gave her strength. It was like she'd known her soul forever. She felt their love and with it came hope. The two beautiful entities pulled her along, not like a force dragging her, but like a seed afloat on the breeze, heading for its destiny. The time meant nothing. Her body was long forgotten. All there was, was the here and now and the wild journey that she warmly embraced.

She was filled with child-like wonder. The stars flashed by as she zoomed through the cosmos. The journey, wondrous and amazing, went on forever, or maybe it was an instant. Where she was, she couldn't know nor did she care. There was no urgency, no emotion, just presence in a place somewhere beyond the real. The glorious sights were backed by silence, yet not a silence that was uncomfortable; one that was the way it was meant to be.

Her journey seemed little more than a lingering moment. Finally, Penny stopped, and like it materialised around her, she was in a room, dark and foreboding. She couldn't see her surroundings, but she could feel the enclosed space. No longer did she drift freely in the cosmos. She was somewhere confined. For a moment she felt afraid and stranded in this prison-like box of darkness. Never had she felt so completely and utterly alone as she did then. She silently reached out for the connections, longing for the presence of her guides, anything to quell the loneliness.

Gentle warmth filled her, even though she had no body. It was the warmth of companionship and love. The two presences were there with her, or maybe inside her. She felt their energy once again, and it brought her comfort. She sensed and accepted their light, warmth, and the power they fed her. They were with her, to guide and protect her, and that was all she needed, there in the abject darkness.

Like a flash, something changed. A heavy presence entered the room, or maybe it entered her soul. She couldn't tell which, but she certainly feared it. This presence was evil. It exuded hatred and spite. It yearned for her death, and she could feel it.

Penny shuddered to the grain, but without a body, never had she felt such darkness.

This shadow echoed round her soul, wanting to consume her. It wanted to consume everything. It was there watching, waiting, dwelling, and snarling. Cold realisation clanged down around her, and for a moment she teetered on the brink of madness. This presence was the one she'd come to find—the child.

There in the darkness, a battle would begin, but this was no physical battle. This was one of consciousness.

Meeting Destiny Part II

The child attacked her, showing her pictures, for never would they use words. They wanted to confuse her, make her go insane, and take over her consciousness completely. Images from her life flashed before her. Deep secrets, like the child knew her fears and how to hurt her. To bring her pain brought them joy. It entertained them.

They showed her the time her mother was drunk and called her terrible names because she was having a "bad day." That cut her deeply now, just as it had cut her then and would forever more. It was the reason Penny was never close to her mother again. From then on, she kept her distance. The criticism came and the disappointment that Penny wasn't like her. The jealousy that she was closer to her dad. Those feelings washed over her again.

The image faded, but the attack was far from over. She wouldn't get a break from the pain. It showed her the creepy old man at the bus stop who had tried to follow her home when she was a young teen. She was forced to run and hide with no one around to rescue her. She felt her heart race and the abject terror as she scrambled over the fence and scrabbled into the bush. She sat there shaking, breathing, frightened he would hear her as the footsteps slowly went past. He stopped. She held her breath. *Please don't see me. Please don't hear.* She said the words in her mind again, just as she did then. The footsteps started once more.

The child toyed with her trauma, stacking it up back-to-back with no time to breathe, not a second of relief, no moment to process the pain. All at once Penny was no longer the mighty warrior with the halithstord. She was only a frightened little girl.

Then came the images of being bullied in school because she developed a little later than the other girls did, and she would rather read and study than wear makeup and listen to music. That feeling came again. The anxiety she felt every night before she went to sleep and every morning when she had to go face them.

She didn't want to go to school. They would be there. They were always there. It left her trapped, like there was no escape. She slipped back into the shyness and became introverted once more. She wanted to be invisible, to just stay out of the way, to blend into the shadows, but she had a spotlight on her. Those emotions came flooding back, sapping her confidence, draining her fortitude. They were the cruellest of images, ones that made her feel weak and hopeless.

Then came the worst of all. The one that would cut her to her core. The child somehow knew it. They wanted to break her, and this was intended to send her into the death spiral. It was meant to snap her soul in half. They showed her Liam. The child blamed her for his death, and in the vision, Liam blamed her as well. She needed no second invitation to blame herself. The sadness and depression, the hopelessness, the grief, the guilt, and the pain all flooded back in waves. It filled her soul.

Once again, she felt alone, but now she was close to emotionally broken. Inside she cried. She died a little, lost in this silent wilderness. Wrapped in her agony and her fear. The halithstord couldn't come to her aid in this, the most harrowing of places.

How could her enemy know such secrets? They were ones that Penny didn't even tell herself about. Internally, she gave up and curled into a ball, submissive and whimpering. She was totally dominated, scared, abandoned, and lost. She crumbled inside as her heart snapped in two.

The child bubbled with glee. This should have been more of a challenge. These humans were weaker than they thought. They lorded it over this pathetic being, basking in their power, revelling in their glory.

All was lost. She was at the mercy of this terrible foe. Then came the agony of defeat. The battle was over. The fight in her subsided. Then, as her consciousness would be lost to her body and death would quickly follow, a touch of warmth reached down. It picked her up from the bitterness of despair. It was the touch of friendship, the glow of purest love.

Liam held her hand again, yet not in body, and she could feel it. He had not abandoned her. He showed her the truth in images and the deepest emotions. She could see what had happened to him. He told her it was not her fault. He loved her hard, and she knew that he had spent the best days of his short life with her. He had never been happier than with this special soul right by his side. His friend who was there with him through everything, who allowed him to be. The greatest gift a friend can give is without expectation or reward, to let another just exist. Should he want to cry, be angry, or laugh and go crazy, he could. He showed her how she warmed his soul; even the thought of her existing brought him a hope that could never be explained.

He told her that he waited, out there in the cosmos, awaiting her soul so his could be complete again. Her energy would live on, and she had nothing to fear. It was beautiful, not frightening any longer. Her Earth form was only a part of her, and her own higher being was out there, waiting for her return. First, she had to learn the lessons and complete this soul journey. The biggest lesson of all would be defeating the child.

Penny swelled. She grew in strength and power. Her determination burned.

Then came Isha's turn. She, too, had things to show her. Not things that were so personal but ones that warmed her further just the same. Along came visions of light and wonder. It made her smile. It soothed her soul. It made her present. There were images of the beauty of life, nature, friendship, and love.

She showed her alien worlds and other beings, each filled with magic, each in their own unique ways. There was culture and music and sunshine and flowers. She showed her the little tales of heroism from all over the galaxy. The ones that kept her going when all else seemed lost. To look at war from afar is to see the most horrific thing, but to look up close, there were stories of bravery, and comradery, of sacrifice and love.

Then Isha guided her. She had confronted the child before. She had fed images into their guardians. She could create and control the wisp, so she coached her from within. She fed her unrelenting powers, ones the like of which she could never even dream. Isha took her to the connection, the one that led to her own higher being, and then it was time to fight back.

Penny followed her, and she felt complete. Like somehow, she had always longed for this moment or was born for it. If the child could search her deepest trauma, she could do the same.

Penny probed and searched for their darkness. To find it was easy. Everything they had was darkness. That was what they were. She was ruthless and as cruel as she had ever been, feeding visions into her enemy's mind. This child—loveless, friendless, and deeply disturbed—started to reel. Their only joy was to bring pain and misery. Like a mindless zombie of darkness consuming joy in a tsunami of hate, she showed them the bodies, death, broken families, floods of tears, and blood that lay in their wake. Then it was their twisted feelings, emotions ill-spent, used for cruelty and simply to take.

Penny projected their over-swollen ego. The child's misguided belief that they were better than any other being, even though they were less than. She showed them things that they had never known—laughter, love and joy, the beauty of life and friendship. They were just a cold, grey being, soulless and lifeless, so pathetic, scared, and alone in the cosmos.

Penny may have felt alone for a time out there. She had escaped, but the child, they were truly alone. There was nowhere to escape from that. That was what they were. Nobody was out there who would come to save or help them. No one would care if they lived. In fact, the entire galaxy would be joyous if they died. The child, powerful and menacing, this merchant of terror and destroyer of worlds, this all-consuming warlord that reigned through fear and cared only for the self was, in fact, nothing at all.

The child reeled beneath her might as Penny ripped a hole right through the very core of their existence. She dealt a blow so powerful it tore their soul in two. Their consciousness was broken as they whimpered like the lost child that they were. They drifted out of control.

Penny summoned energy from everywhere, like the entire cosmos fed her. She concentrated upon the child's being, focusing with all she had. Liam and Isha joined her, pouring more and more pressure upon them. Their foe's consciousness grew fuzzy, then ragged, then stretched.

The child screamed an empty scream, one of despair and terror, but there would be no relief. It was like all the energy in the cosmos worked against them. Before long, they were whimpering, curled in a ball as the reality broke them. Then in a mystical explosion, their energy cracked and blew apart. Mighty psychic shockwaves rushed through the cosmos like a tidal wave of energy. It travelled lightyears in seconds, expanding all the time. Like their molecules tore apart and rushed away from each other in different directions until they no longer were connected. There wouldn't be a single psychic being in the universe that didn't feel it as it passed them by.

Far away, in their hiding place, sneaking in the shadows, this merchant of hatred and destruction, the child, the one that had brought so much misery and fear, was separated from their body and dead.

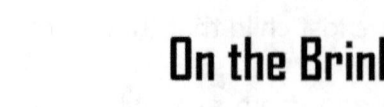

On the Brink

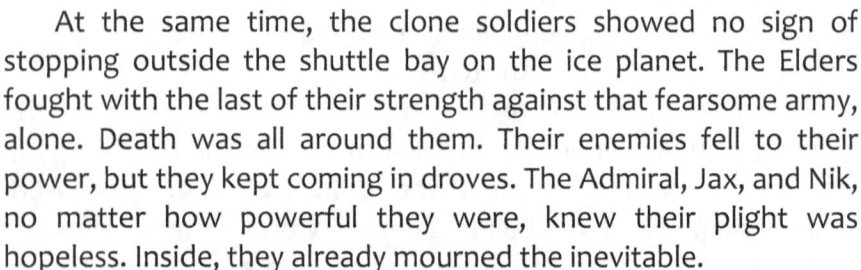

At the same time, the clone soldiers showed no sign of stopping outside the shuttle bay on the ice planet. The Elders fought with the last of their strength against that fearsome army, alone. Death was all around them. Their enemies fell to their power, but they kept coming in droves. The Admiral, Jax, and Nik, no matter how powerful they were, knew their plight was hopeless. Inside, they already mourned the inevitable.

For Jax and Nik, the harrowing ordeal they would face if one should see the other fall was too much to even contemplate. Each silently wished to be the first to go. They couldn't stand to watch their sister fall. They may not have been sisters of blood, but a sister in arms, struggle, war, love, and for life. Their bond went beyond blood. They could just lay down their arms and accept their fate, but each would fight for the life of the other until their last breath, until no fight remained.

The three warriors backed away down the corridor. An endless barrage of plasma crashed into their shields. They felt the heat, and the impact forced them back. They dug in to hold their position then pushed forward trying to steal any inch of ground.

The clones rushed through the wall of plasma, using their fallen comrades as shields. The Elders knew what to do—they threw their rifles to the ground and drew blades. With these weapons in their hands, they would die there. A crowd of faceless soldiers with knives or swords or bayonets charged, roaring towards them.

The clones circled in on them, towering over them. They stood, dwarfed in their vast shadows. Even using all their strength and skill, courage, and determination, it still wouldn't be enough. But these warriors would fight until their last breath, which would very soon inevitably be drawn.

Now exhausted, even the symbiote could feed them nothing more. Hope had escaped silently, like a shadow in the night. The mist descended upon them as death knocked on the door. Their time had come.

They prepared to lay down their lives when, like a miracle, the clones around them let go of their weapons. As if a puppet's strings had been dropped, their bodies hit the floor. They lay limp, unmoving, unbreathing. They were dead. Without the child, this mighty army was nothing more than empty shells.

The Elders cheered. They raised their hands aloft. They each dropped to their knees, panting, and then laid down on the floor. They looked up at the ceiling in relief, smiling wide. Quietly they thanked their luck. Someone, a hero, faceless and nameless to them, somewhere had defeated the child.

From the brink of death, never before had the Elders been so grateful for life.

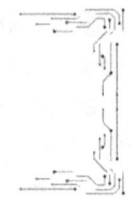

Awakenings Part IV

"It hurts."

"Shh, be at peace. The time arrives for all beings."

"Is it the end?"

"It's just the next step."

"Am I dying?"

"No, a transition to the next state of being. Your body will die, your energy will remain."

"I'm not afraid."

"You need not be."

"I can escape?"

"Your Earth journey is over. You take those lessons onwards."

"I only learned pain."

"Pain is a lesson in itself. You will feel pain no more. Don't fear, The Fleck will guide you."

Penny flashed out of her haze back into existence. Around her, the carnage of battle was over. The clones lay unmoving everywhere. In her mind she had been gone an age, but in existence she was only gone an instant. Immediately, she remembered the scream she had heard as she drifted away. She looked to her side and her heart sank in an instant.

"Alex... No!"

He lay pail and stricken, his life oozing onto the balcony. She took his hand. He felt her warmth, and his eyes opened a crack.

"I'll be good." He croaked the words with a weak smile.

"You saved me? The shot was meant for me?"

"Nah, don't be silly." He weakly laughed. "I expertly blocked it with my body."

"Jas," she looked up, "we have to get him out of here. Get him to the hospital."

"Penny…" Alex interrupted her and tugged on her hand. "I'm done. Leave me here."

She saw the look in his eyes, and she gave up hope for him. "I'm so sorry, Alex. I'm just so sorry." She wept. "If only I had been quicker."

"Don't worry, mate. I don't like this world anyway. This has been the best time of my life. My time with you."

"Don't go, Alex."

"Let me go," he croaked weakly. "I'm okay with it. I've made my peace. The Fleck will guide me."

"What?!"

He smiled but never said another word. He was gone.

Penny cried harder, with her head on his chest. Nobody would even care that he was gone but her, and that thought broke her heart. "Why couldn't I have been in time?" she wailed. "What have I done?"

Jas reached down and placed a hand on her back to offer some comfort. "You did everything. His was a sacrifice he was glad to make for you, his friend. He was a great warrior. We honour him by surviving this battle."

"What was this Fleck he talked of, Jas?"

"I don't know, my friend. Maybe a hallucination?"

"It—this Fleck has taken so much from me."

"I'm sorry, Penny. His existence was only pain, and now he is free. You gave him the happiest times of his life. Be grateful you knew him."

The words broke her heart, and as this ancient and noble warrior hugged her, she sobbed her heart out.

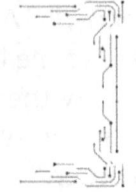

A Long Journey

The Elders climbed over the countless bodies slumped on the floor and could finally get inside the shuttle bay unhindered. Their eyes lit up as they saw the many untouched space craft.

"Here you go, Jax. You get the honour of choosing our carriage," the Admiral said.

"I like this one best." She pointed at the shiny craft. It looked like it had never been used. "That'll get us back to the fleet."

"But I like that one." Nik pointed to one opposite. "It has more cannons."

"It does. But I *still* like this one. It's faster."

"But you want me to be happy, don't you? I'll never shut up the whole way, I swear it."

"Look," the Admiral interjected. "Just make up your minds. I really wanna get off this snowball."

The pair looked at each other. "Rock paper scissors," they said in unison.

The Admiral rolled his eyes and chuckled a little.

"Ha! I win," Jax announced.

"No fair! Best of three?"

"No way. I won. You can't complain all the way, either."

Nik folded her arms and did an exaggerated huff. "S'pose."

The shuttle bay filled with laughter. Such laughter that had never been heard on that planet before.

They boarded the craft, took off, and slowly made their way off the planet and out into space. They thought of nothing but their fallen comrades. The senseless death of their brothers and sisters in arms. A deep sadness filled them as they watched the ice planet slowly vanish into the distance. Their friends would live on, but only in their hearts.

The Admiral sent out a message to Jas, which would take hours to arrive. He didn't even know that Jas had survived the battle and that they would be reunited.

Now ahead lay a long journey. The three warriors, beaten and bruised, exhausted and grieving, at last had a chance to rest on the way back to the Mercenary fleet.

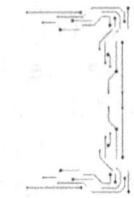

The Call

The phone rang three times as Penny dreaded an answer. The answer came anyway.

"Hello."

"Hey, Dad, it's me."

"Yeah, I know. Your name comes up on my phone when you call. Strange, that."

She laughed, though this just made what she would say even harder to get out. "I need to talk to you." Her voice quivered a little.

"Well, I guessed that, or you would have just texted me."

She laughed again but finished with a slight huff. "Can you be serious for once?"

"Yeah, sure, sorry. I was just tryna make you laugh."

"I know, Dad, but this is important."

"Okay, sorry. I'm listening, Pen Pen."

"I'm going travelling for a bit."

"What? What about uni?"

"I'm gonna leave for a while. I'll come and finish afterwards. It's nearly the end of the semester, and I have hardly been there recently anyway. I'll never catch up."

"But what about—"

She cut him off. "I know you'll be disappointed, but this is something I have to do."

"Well, why don't you come and see me before doing anything rash... Or I'll come to see you."

"No, Dad. I was gonna come and see you, but I've gotta go. Right now. There's a plane waiting for me." How she had wanted to say this face to face, but she could never explain the bruises and injuries from the battle. He would never believe the things she really had to say.

"How could you afford that?"

"I used my savings." She scrunched up her face awaiting a volley from him.

"What?! That was supposed to help you buy a house after you graduate."

"I know. I'm sorry. I used some to pay off the lease on my apartment, too."

"Well, I'm not impressed. It seems wasteful, but it is your money. So, you're going for a while then? Where?"

"Across Europe, then Asia, maybe Australia." A silent tear rolled down her cheek.

"Why now?"

"After Liam and everything, I've just realised some things are more important than college. For now, for the moment, I need to find myself and see the world while I'm still young."

"Oh, Pen Pen, you can't just leave me like this."

"I'm sorry, Dad, I have to. I'm not leaving you. This isn't about you. This is only about me. Please, try and understand."

"How long are you going for? When will you be back?"

"I don't know... I just don't know."

"How will you survive?"

"I'll work on my travels, backpacking. Loads of people my age do it. I'll be fine, Dad. Please don't worry. This will make me happy. This is what I want. I've taken all my stuff to a friend's place to look after for me. She lives near the campus."

He sighed down the phone. "Can I change your mind? Is there anything I can say?"

"No, you know I'm stubborn. My mind is made up. Please, could you tell Mum for me? I really can't face the grilling she'll give me."

"Sure, I'll tell her, if that's what you want. I really think you should tell her yourself."

"You know what she's like. She'll start thinking I've met a man or something."

"Wait, you haven't, have you?"

"No! Don't be stupid." Her tone was firm. The last thing she needed was her parents speculating about that.

"Well, I guess I can't stand in your way, can I? I wish you'd just come and say goodbye, though."

"I'm sorry. I can't. I hope you understand."

"I don't understand, no. But you are an adult, I have to accept your decision. It is your life. You must live it how you choose. You're not my little girl anymore." He paused. "Pen, I'll miss you."

"I'll miss you too, Dad. I'll think of you every day. And part of me will always be your little girl. That's what made me who I am."

"Call me if you need any money or you get kidnapped by pirates or something, would you?"

She could hear him sniffle a little with the joke.

"Don't be ridiculous. I'll be fine."

"I'm sure you will."

"Oh, I have a message for Sangeeta. Isha is out in the cosmos, awaiting their reunion. She should live her life to the fullest, and one day they will meet again. I just know it."

"Sure... What?" He'd never heard her speak like that before.

She never answered. She just said, "I love you, Dad."

"Wait, Pen..."

"I've gotta go. I love you. I'll call you when I can."

"I love you, sweetheart. Please do. Be careful, okay?"

"Of course, I will. Bye, Dad."

"Bye, love."

She cut off the call and burst into tears. She hated to leave him like this. She hated that she couldn't go and see him and have one last hug, but that was nothing more than a dream that would never come true.

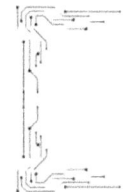

A New Treaty

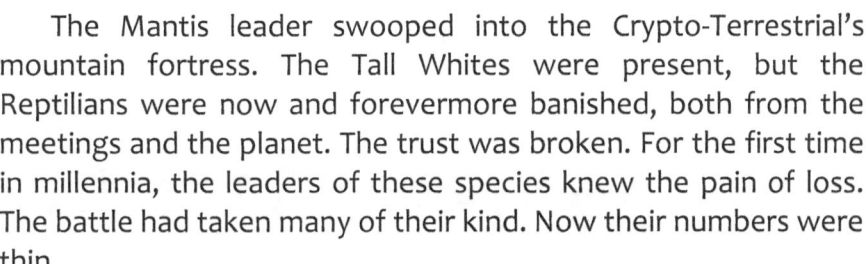

The Mantis leader swooped into the Crypto-Terrestrial's mountain fortress. The Tall Whites were present, but the Reptilians were now and forevermore banished, both from the meetings and the planet. The trust was broken. For the first time in millennia, the leaders of these species knew the pain of loss. The battle had taken many of their kind. Now their numbers were thin.

"We have lost our armies. We have lost many of our kind, and for what?" The Crypto-Terrestrial Leader was aggrieved. Their kind that had remained on the planet were now on the brink.

"You are the custodians of the planet. It was your duty," the Mantis replied.

"Now there is no defence for the planet but the humans. They are not ready."

"The Mantises will protect you."

"Oh? Yet you did not before. What is so different now?"

"The Tall Whites have the core. We will supply the parts they need, then they shall leave this place and stop meddling with the humans' evolution.

"This is a unique time to observe the species. They cannot keep contaminating our experiments. The Crypto-Terrestrials shall be replenished from the other world. In time, again, you will have an army. Until that time, you fall under our protection. Everything has changed."

"And what of the Reptilians?"

"They are banished forevermore. They grew greedy and impatient. Their weakness has destined them to float homeless through space. If ever again they come, we will be waiting for them."

"A new treaty must be signed, and we must rebuild. The few Mantises that are here will clean up our base and the moon and any space junk from the battles. The humans can never know what occurred here. Our work is far from done if we can ever dare to dream of peace amongst all beings in the galaxy."

A Long Journey Part II

With tears in her eyes, Penny stepped back under the white tree. There was a flash and a pop, and she was ported back into the Mantises' base. She rushed to the main chamber, observing the scars of battle all around. A few Mantises with their Gray minions worked feverishly, removing bodies from the base and incinerating them. Finally, in the main chamber she found Jas.

"I'm all set. I've dealt with my dad, and I'm ready to head off. What's next, Jas?"

"Are you okay, Penny?"

"Yeah... Yeah, I think so. Thanks for asking."

"You are welcome. Next is to rejoin the fleet and meet back up with the Elders. I've received word from the Admiral. Thankfully, he is alive and well. The Mantises have lent me a craft."

He picked up a huge bag and his weapon and nodded to the Grays nearby. They carried the two coffins onto the port pad. One of them for Varget, and the other one for Alex. At least these fallen warriors would be respected in the correct manner.

Jas stepped onto the pad.

Penny looked up at him and smiled.

"Are you coming, then?"

She smiled again, wider this time and jumped up onto the port pad. "Sure, but you know I have to get my clothes and stuff from my apartment or there'll be problems."

"I think the Grays can do that for you, my friend."

It seemed that the Elders and the rest of the Mercenaries had a new and most powerful member of their number.

"I curse you a million times. My spite for you burns more deeply than ever. My enemy reigns victorious. My enemy is superior. Superior maybe, but only for this moment. The good may win in this battle, but more wars will come.

"I yearn for more blood, for more carnage. It drives me when otherwise there would be nothing.

"In this galaxy, Light Space defeats Dark Space. The good Fleck proved stronger than the evil.

"They, the insignificant, must rebuild. Now a new balance exists, and a new dawn has begun.

We shall leave this place and move on to another galaxy. Upon arrival, this time I'll be the Light Space and you be the Dark Space.

"This game of life continues."

The End

Stars light the cosmos so if you enjoyed this book, you can show it some love by leaving a rating or review on Amazon or Goodreads today!

Up Next: The Dreamland Trilogy, Dreamland Part I: The Fabric of Dreams: For as long as he can remember, Eric has always had vivid dreams. When the lines start to blur between sleep and reality, he and his parents begin a desperate hunt for answers. But after he slips into a coma, Eric enters an amazing enchanted dimension where he's forced to fulfil an ancient destiny and defeat a nightmarish enemy.

Discovering he possesses incredible powers, Eric begins a punishing training schedule with an eccentric queen to ready himself for battle against his dangerous foe. Faced with aliens, dinosaurs, and vicious gargoyles, this young hero must master his gift quickly if he's to defend the realm from a terrible fate.

Can Eric destroy the coming doom and rescue a kingdom of magic?

Subscribe to Barry's newsletter for monthly updates, crazy polls, poetry, jokes, laughs and general shenanigans. That's Just the way I like it! - **http://eepurl.com/gkYk5P**

Check out Barry's blog The Diary of a Wizard: It's weird wacky wondrous wizardry weekly (almost) from the Enchanted Woods! Adventures and laughs abound and, all for FREE! - https://imaginationgeneration.fun/category/blog/diary-of-a-wizard

Other Works by Barry

Novels

The Entities Series

Entities Part I: Entities Connected
Entities Part II: Entities Divided

The Dreamland Trilogy

Part I: The Fabric of Dreams
Part II: The Masters of Light
Part III: The Veil of Shadow

The War of the Turnips

Short Reads

Home
Flesh and Blood
Savage Wild

Contact

Website
https://imaginationgeneration.fun

Twitter
https://twitter.com/BarrySBrunswick

Facebook
https://www.facebook.com/Barry.S.Brunswick

Goodreads
https://www.goodreads.com/author/show/16765230.Barry_S_Bru
nswick

Amazon
https://www.amazon.com/Barry-S-Brunswick/e/
B07PLBMLVL

Email
barry@imaginationgeneration.fun

Subscribe to Newsletter
http://eepurl.com/gkYk5P

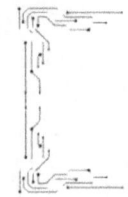

About the Author

'Once upon a time, there was a wizard and that wizard had a dream. His dream was to spark kid's imagination through the telling of amazing tales. So, with his pointy hat on his head and his long and slender fingers, he picked up a pen and began to write. The candle flickered as the pages turned one after the other, night after night.

He journeyed long and journeyed far. He went all the way to the mountains, through the forests and valleys. He travelled through the mists of time and through the wonders of space. He met dragons and ghosts and a myriad of magic creatures along the way. And, he did it all without ever leaving his chair.

As the images ran wild through his mind, his pen scratched away on the paper. Then one day, after many years and much toil, he had done it. He had created wondrous books to ignite kid's imagination and to help them to think and grow and dream.

And just in case you wondered, the wizard still journeys through story world and scribbles by candlelight to this day.'

Barry S. Brunswick